Mad, Bad, and Delightful to Know

A Biographical Novel

Gretta Curran Browne

$P/

Seanelle Publications Inc.

www.grettacurranbrowne.com

Dedicated with Love to my Son

SEAN BROWNE

Aurora fillii

When Sir Francis Bacon, a friend of the young Shakespeare, wrote the words *"aurora fillii"* meaning *"sons of the morning"* he was referring to those young men who go forward with hope, with heart, and strive for perfection; and if not able to succeed in changing the world for the good of all, they at least try and change their own lives and make it better and brighter, not only for themselves, but for their friends and family and all around them.

And I, too, see my own son, Sean, in the same light.

So, Sean, as you encouraged me to write about one of those most famous "sons of the morning", George Gordon Lord Byron, this one is for you.

GCB

PART ONE

'My old love of all loves'

~ ~ ~

"She was his first, and perhaps his only love."

Thomas Moore

"I can answer for the truth of poor Byron's never-dying attachment to Mary Chaworth, for I have frequently heard him romanticise for hours about her."

Beau Brummel

Chapter One

~ ~ ~

The dining room at Brooks's Club on St James Street was half empty, yet the laughter and noise from the gaming rooms increased as the night moved on.

In the dining room Byron was sitting with Beau Brummell at a secluded table by the green-damask wall, both sipping claret as Brummell confided that not only was he making love to Julia Johnstone; but also their friend Scrope Davies was now contemplating marriage to a young lady from Harrogate.

Brummell grinned. "I'll wager you a hundred guineas he will have changed his mind by next week."

"I'm more inclined to wager the same about you and Julia Johnstone."

An elderly duke paused at their table, and then stood to pass a few pleasantries, his eyes moving from one handsome face to the other, approving, admiring, until a more serious thought came into his mind.

"Now then, Lord Byron, what are we going to do about that bastard in Downing Street, the Prime Minister?"

"I don't know," Byron replied, unsurprised by the question. Brooks's Club was, after all, the unofficial headquarters of the Whig party.

"And the Prince of Wales, that damned turncoat, " the duke went on. "A Whig through and through until the day he became Regent, and then turned into a Tory as well as a two-faced liar!"

Brummell laughed his amused laugh, and the old duke turned to him. "Oh, of course, you know the prince very well, Mr Brummell, so tell me ..."

Brummell leaned back negligently in his chair and answered all the duke's questions very politely; while Byron looked aside to see what else was going on in the room.

All the waiters at Brooks's were dressed like footmen, in white wigs, white breeches, white gloves, and dark green velvet coats. Above their heads the candles in the crystal chandeliers blazed brightly over the room, their flickering reflections bouncing off the heavy silver and sparkling glasses on the tables.

The old duke finally took his leave, allowing Beau Brummell to exhale a huge sigh of relief. "Now back to *your* our news, Byron, tell me all your news."

"I have no news," Byron replied; and yet as the conversation continued he finally told Brummell about his time away at Newstead Abbey in Nottinghamshire, and his meeting again with his first love, Mary Chaworth.

Brummell's sharp ears caught the sudden low and soft tones of Byron's voice as he spoke of Mary Chaworth, and instantly knew the poor man was still in love with her.

Brummell did not judge, nor voice his opinion on the folly of it, and gave Byron that absorbed and thoughtful attention that one does when a close friend is sharing something very personal.

Yet *why* Byron – with so many sophisticated and beautiful young women in London's high society now throwing themselves shamelessly at him, eager to get into his arms and into his bed – should remain so in love with an unsophisticated country cousin he had idolised since he was seventeen, and *still* be in love with her, was truly baffling to Brummell.

"She is as lovely as ever," Byron said, and then paused, wondering if he should share with Brummell his concern about the occasional bruises on Mary's arms and face – bruises that Nanny Marsden, the housekeeper at Annesley Hall, believed could only be attributed to the behaviour of Mary's boorish husband.

"I told her she will always have a friend and protector in me," he said, "because that husband of hers, Jack Musters, now he is a man that needs —"

"What? Surely you don't mean *'Handsome* Jack' Musters?"

Byron stared at Brummell. "You know him?"

"Musters of Colwick?"

"Yes"

"I was at Eton with him."

Byron sat back, not at all pleased at learning this, but Brummell was grinning. "Do you know why he is called 'Handsome Jack?"

"No," Byron admitted, "because his appearance has always looked fairly ordinary to me."

"It's because of the way he speaks. To Jack Musters, everything is *'handsome'* – whether it is a meal he has just enjoyed, or the sight of a fine horse, or anything else that meets with his approval. He has only one single boring word to express his praise – *'handsome!'* Consequently he is now known by one and all as 'Handsome Jack'."

"Well, that's another conundrum solved," Byron said. "Because I did sometimes wonder why his name always carried that appellation."

Brummell laughed. "It's a mock! Although from what I remember of Jack Musters, he probably still takes it literally."

~ ~ ~

The following day, when Reverend Thomas Nixon, the Rector of Hucknall Church, called at Annesley Hall, Mary Chaworth had a peculiar foreboding as to the reason for his unexpected visit. Although only twenty-eight years old, her disastrous marriage had made her feel as old as Time itself.

Reverend Nixon declined to sit down, insisting gravely that his visit must be very brief. He stood stiffly, saying in a quiet voice: "I believe you are now fully aware, Mrs Chaworth, of your husband's many infidelities?"

Mary lowered her eyes. "Yes, Reverend. Your wife keeps me regularly informed."

"Which my wife did not want to do, I can assure you. Who would want to tell any man's wife such terrible information? But now ... now I'm afraid that it falls upon me to inform you, that a daughter of one of your tenants gave birth to an illegitimate child this morning. A child fathered by your husband."

He was clearly surprised when Mary showed no shock, just a quick intake of her breath.

"What the girl and her parents wish to know," Reverend Nixon continued, "is whether your husband will be prepared to financially support the child, or will it have to rely on support from the parish?"

"The Annesley Estate will support the child," Mary answered. "If you will be kind enough to send the girl or her parents directly to me, it will be arranged."

Reverend Nixon hesitated. "And ... your husband?"

"Is in Yorkshire."

As soon as Reverend Nixon had left, Mary's dignity collapsed into anger and mortification. No more, she would take no more of this from Jack Musters. She had taken enough, *more* than enough! She would not allow herself to be treated in such a shameful way any longer, as carelessly disregarded as the poor girl who had given birth to his child this morning.

For the first time in years Mary felt the strength of a new resolve, seeing a way out, a way forward. Even if she were to live the rest of her life alone, bringing up her children on her own, she would do so with dignity, and without bringing any more shame on the Chaworth name.

~ ~ ~

When Jack Musters returned from Yorkshire and found the doors of Annesley Hall bolted and barred against him, he could not believe it. Not even when he was handed the birth certificate of the girl's newborn child – along with the papers for a legal separation, which Mary had now instigated against him – he would not *believe* it.

Forced to move back into his parents' home at Colwick Hall, he did everything in his power to get Mary to see reason, sending her letter after letter apologising, and then more letters beseeching her to forgive him – and if she did – he promised he would reform his ways from this day on, and would only do everything handsome and proper by her.

In response to her silence he sent her more letters from Colwick Hall, threatening her, lots of threats: he would seek custody of the children. Under the law, the *man* always got custody of the children; she knew that, didn't she?

Mary's silence was like steel – he could not break through it, nor get any response whatsoever. Mary had simply shut her ears and her mind against him. She refused to listen or live with him.

So, as he had done in the past, at the time of her mother's refusal to allow Mary to marry him, he did now what he had done then, and sought the assistance of his own mother.

Sophia Musters, a socialite who spent more of her time in London than in Nottinghamshire, thought it was all such a nuisance now to have to go over to Annesley from Colwick and plead with her daughter-in-law on Jack's behalf.

And on being admitted entrance inside Annesley Hall, *plead* she did, in her most sympathetic voice.

After all, she was a woman too, so she understood. And no one knew better than her what is was like to be deceived and have to live with a man she no longer loved. But a woman must *bear* these things, suffer them, if only for the sake of the children. A legal separation was only one step away from *divorce*. Surely Mary would not even consider such a thing? Was she not a Christian? And even if one were to throw all care for religion away – a divorce would be *social suicide*. Did Mary not realise that?

Eventually Sophie Musters realised that she may as well have been talking to a wall; reporting back to Jack that she had been unable to reach Mary at all, unable to get her to concede to anything.

"Except the children," she said. "Mary bade me to tell you that if you even *attempt* to seek custody of the children, she will get her lawyers to fight you all the way. And she does have proof of your regular adultery, Jack. Proof of *one* illegitimate child at least. So be thankful she does not know about the others."

Jack was heartbroken, still unable to believe it. Mary had always been ... so sweet, so gentle, so *weak*. What had changed her?

Jack refused to sign the Separation Papers. No, he would *not* sign them! He accused Mary of making him the laughing-stock of the county, and then quit Nottingham and returned to his mistress in Yorkshire.

~ ~ ~

The winter of 1813 came in with a day's fall of snow, which quickly turned into slush, and then continued dreary and grey. It was not until she saw the first buds of springtime that Mary finally turned away from the ramshackle debris and sordid fatality of her marriage, and sat down to write a respectful but heart-yearning letter:

My dearest Lord Byron...

"No, no, *no!*" She tore up the page, determined to shut off all further thoughts about Byron. He lived in a different world to her now, and to drag him back into her confused little life would not only be wrong, but unfair.

Jack had left the Chaworth name and her own reputation in tatters. He had demeaned her with his many mistresses and made a child with another woman, and she knew that most people in Nottingham pitied her. She did not want pity – it was a return to honour and *respectability* she craved, and now it was up to her to return those two things to the Chaworth name.

Yet she knew that she loved Byron, the old friend that he was, and the young man he had become – kind, funny, beautiful, the stuff of dreams – but it was all too late for her now, *too late*. She had chosen Jack, and now she must be strong-minded and live with the awful consequences of that choice.

Chapter Two

~ ~ ~

Byron had just arrived at a party given by a London hostess, Miss Johnson, a close friend of the Prince Regent. As usual, admirers immediately surrounded Byron until Scrope Davies and Hobhouse came to his rescue. "I should warn you," said Hobhouse in a low voice, "the Prince Regent is here."

"Here?" Byron turned and looked around. "Where?"

"In one of the other rooms, surrounded by his courtiers."

No sooner had Hobhouse imparted this information when a courtier appeared, bowed low, and then informed Byron that he had been summoned to meet the Regent.

"His Royal Highness desires for you to be presented to him, Lord Byron."

Byron turned to Hobby and Scrope and communed in a whisper. "Damn! He must have heard my name announced."

"So he must," said Scrope Davies, very amused at Byron's predicament.

"Has he not *heard* of all the savage things I have said about him?"

"No," Hobhouse was quite convinced. "His courtiers would never allow him to know anything bad or critical said against him, if only to protect their own backsides from his temper."

"Well, heigh-ho, here goes."

As Byron turned to follow the courtier Scrope Davies quickly caught his arm, a grin on his face. "Byron – if the Prince is holding a glass of wine in his hand, then make sure to stand well back. Remember what happened to Beau Brummell? Wine thrown in his face?"

Byron grinned. "If he does that to me I will *scourge* him with comical lampoons from now until Doomsday."

Hobhouse did not think any of it at all funny, seriously worried for his friend. "After all," he said to Scrope, "it's not as if Byron could pick up a glass and throw wine back at the Regent. He'd end up in the Tower if he did."

It seemed the longest half hour that Hobby had ever endured, drinking and waiting. Even the cool and calm Scrope Davies was showing signs of agitation at the length of Byron's absence.

"I thought when one was summoned to be royally *'presented'* the entire thing lasted no more than three minutes."

Hobby nodded. "Usually no more than five minutes."

Scrope suddenly sat alert. "Ah, here he is back, safe and sound ... and no wine stains on his face or clothes that I can see."

They watched as Byron made his way back down the long room while finding himself forced to stop here and there in conversation with one person after another.

"Does he *have* to charm and jest with everyone who speaks to him?" Hobby grumbled. "Surely he knows we are waiting to know!"

"Ah, well, it looks like he has now been favoured with the Royal Assent."

When Byron eventually joined them, Hobhouse demanded, "Well? What took place? What did he say to you?"

Byron was still somewhat surprised. "The prince's conversation was *very* affable. He seemed to have no idea that I am one of his worst critics."

"No?"

"No, he even complimented me on *Childe Harold,* and from then on we spoke of nothing else but poetry and poets."

"Oh good grief! All this time talking about poetry?"

"His Highness makes the claim, Hobby, that he has read more poetry than any other prince in Europe, and after listening to him quoting Homer and numerous other poets, I think I believe him."

"You do? So tell me – has he read your other poem, *Lines to a Lady Weeping,* upbraiding him for reducing his daughter to tears due to the way he now treats the Whigs?"

Byron smiled. "Even if he has, he obviously does not know who wrote it, especially as it was published in the Chronicle anonymously. So I would say no, he has no idea it was written by me, because he has now invited me to attend his next levée at the Palace."

"His next levée at the Palace?" Hobhouse sat back in disgust. "And will you go?"

"Certainly. I will powder my hair white, fluff out my frills, and then spend the entire event bowing and grovelling like a hobgoblin."

Scrope Davies laughed while Hobby exhaled a sigh of relief. "For a moment I thought you were serious"

"No, but I do seriously need a drink now!"

Within seconds a footman was at his side holding a tray of champagne. Byron lifted a glass and was about to take his first sip when one of the butlers arrived, holding a sealed note on a tray.

"I'm told to inform you that it is urgent, my lord, and the messenger awaits your reply."

Byron read the note, and then looked archly at the

butler. "And how am I supposed to get there in double-quick time? Did the messenger say?"

"Yes, my lord. He said Lord Holland's carriage and driver have been put at your disposal and both are waiting for you outside."

"What is it?" Hobhouse asked.

"I've no time to tell you, so read it yourself," said Byron, giving him the note and quickly following the butler.

"My goodness, why the rush?" asked Scrope, looking at Hobby. "I've never seen Byron quit a room in such a damnable hurry. Is someone dying?"

Hobhouse looked up from the note, excitement on his face. "No, it's the Irish Catholics. Lord Wellesley has brought forward a second motion in the House of Lords for the Catholic question to be given further consideration in this session. The vote is taking place *tonight,* and it looks like the count is going to be *equal.* That's why they have sent in haste for Byron. The Whigs need just one more vote to win it!"

Arriving so late in the proceedings, Byron walked directly into the body of the chamber, to be greeted with smiles of relief from the Whigs.

The Chancellor, Lord Eldon, sitting on the opposite side and seeing Lord Byron enter, scowled and exclaimed loudly to his fellow peers, "Damn! – The Whigs will have it now, by God! The vote that's just walked in will give it to them!"

The motion was carried by a majority of one, causing the leader of the Whigs, Lord Holland, to be very pleased when he and Byron eventually left the House.

"From what I understand," said Lord Holland, "a Select Committee will now be arranged, comprising of peers from both sides. If I put your name forward, will you agree to sit as a member of that committee?"

Byron looked at him wryly. "I think you know my answer."

"Yes," Lord Holland smiled, "I rather think I do, especially as the Irish Catholic question is a matter so very· close to your heart. But now, promise me, that during the debates you will not become satirical against the opposing peers or lose your temper."

"I promise, but I warn you, if I reach the age of fifty and the committee have still *not* reached a resolution, I will resign."

Lord Holland laughed. "And how old are you now, Lord Byron?"

"Twenty-five."

"Then there's hope!"

~ ~ ~

Fletcher, who was already in his nightshirt, was surprised and dismayed when Lord Byron returned so early from the party.

"You told me you would not be back until three or four in the morning. You told me I could go to bed."

"So go to bed."

"It's nigh on midnight."

"Then *go* to bed!"

"No, no, I couldn't do that. I'm a professional London valet now, and we London valets do have our standards. Just tell me what you want me to do, my lord."

"Very well." Byron threw off his cloak. "I want you to go into my bedchamber, lift the pistol from my bedside table, aim it at your head and promptly shoot yourself."

Fletcher gave him one his silent servant stares, before venturing to ask sadly, "Was the party a bad one, my lord? Is that why you left it early?"

"No, Fletcher, I left the party in order to try and emancipate four million people."

"Oh, I see," said Fletcher, not seeing at all. "Will I bring in your evening post, my lord? Just one letter came, but it looks like a lady's hand, so it might be from *you-know-who.*"

"Oh, pray not!" Byron flopped down in the chair at his desk ... Someone had mentioned tonight that Lady Caroline Lamb was back from Ireland, but he had not been given time to dwell on it.

"No, don't bring it in, I won't read it tonight."

"Whatever you think best, my lord."

Later, after shooing Fletcher off to bed, Byron sat down as usual at his bedroom desk to write in his nightly journal ... concluding with a few lines about Madame de Staël, whose books he admired, but whose personality now irritated him beyond measure.

She has been quarrelling with Monk Lewis about everything and everybody. She has not let even poor quiet ME alone, but told Lewis that first, I was affected; and secondly, she complains that I "shut my eyes" during dinner.

What this last can mean I don't know, unless SHE is sitting opposite. If I then do it, she is very much obliged to me; and if I could contrive to shut my ears also, she would be still more so.

In the meantime, I have worse faults to find with her than shutting my eyes – one of which is opening her mouth too frequently. This is a woman who writes octavos, and TALKS folios.

But if I really do have so ludicrous a habit, of shutting my eyes during dinner, as she alleges, I will try and break myself from it, if only to allow myself to get a glimpse of the other diners at the table, and to see my plate.

Chapter Three

~ ~ ~

Lady Caroline Lamb's outrageous persecution of Byron had not been forgotten nor forgiven by London's *haut monde*.

Upon her return to London she had found herself ostracised by most of her own circle. And even those who remained her friends, quickly became tired of her when they discovered her time away in Ireland had changed nothing.

She was still obsessed with Byron, and her oft-repeated lament was becoming a bore –"*He broke my heart, yet still I love him.*"

Apart from her mother and grandmother, only one person found himself feeling sorry for Caroline, and that was Byron's publisher, John Murray.

For some weeks now, since her return, John Murray had become aware that Lady Caroline often slipped into his publishing premises in Albermarle Street and hid herself in the ground-floor waiting room, in the hope of seeing Byron arriving or leaving; but Byron had not visited for some time, so all her time in hiding was wasted.

Rather than reproach her, John Murray decided to befriend her, making his way down to the waiting room carrying in his hand a cup of tea for her.

"Lady Caroline, no good can come of this. If Lord Byron were to find out, he would never visit my premises again."

Caroline meekly agreed to sit and talk with him, and while she talked in that low caressing voice of hers,

Murray could not help noticing how much she had changed while in Ireland. She had lost so much weight, now as thin as a stick, and her eyes seemed huge in her thin face.

"But forging his handwriting in order to steal his portrait from these premises" John Murray said quietly. "You must have known you were committing a felony and could have been convicted of theft."

"Convicted?" said Caroline. "For stealing a portrait? Even though it was a very *small* portrait?" She shook her head of blonde short curls in amazement. "Why, that's nonsense!"

John Murray sighed, knowing that Lady Caroline could not conceive of any member of the aristocracy being convicted of any crime, and certainly not imprisoned or transported for such.

"Do you honestly believe that my grandfather, Earl Spencer, or my father Lord Bessborough, would allow such a thing? And all because of a small painted picture of a poet!"

The "poet" then became the main topic of her conversation, asking John Murray so many questions that he dared not answer, information about Byron that he was sworn not to reveal.

"Why, Lady Caroline..." asked John Murray in a kind tone, "why are you allowing yourself to behave like this? Why are you persecuting yourself in this way?"

The sadness in her eyes and in her voice touched John Murray's heart.

"Because Byron likes others, but I only him."

PART TWO

The Giaour

"His all-absorbing love for Mary Chaworth was the agony, without being the death, of an unsated desire which lived on through his life, and filled his poetry with the very soul of tenderness."

Thomas Moore

Chapter Four

~ ~ ~

In the spring month of May 1813, Byron's Turkish tale *The Giaour* was published, selling out its first edition in three days.

Byron had been inspired to write the story during his travels in the Levant when he became aware of the Turkish custom of throwing any wife found guilty of adultery into the sea, after being tied up alive in a sack.

Although, the young woman who suffered such a terrible fate in *The Giaour* was not a wife, but a slave in a harem, whose death was then avenged by a young Venetian, her heartbroken lover, known to the Mussulmen as "the *Giaour"* – the Infidel.

In Nottingham, Mary Chaworth was transfixed as she read every line about that foreign land and the young man who rowed in a fisherman's boat to its shores, determined to repay murder with murder.

Far, dark, along the blue sea glancing,

The shadows of the rocks advancing

Start on the fisher's eye-like boat

Of Island pirate or Mainote;

And fearful for his light caïque

He shuns the near but doubtful creek:

Though worn and weary with his toil,

And cumbered with his scaly spoil,

Slowly, yet strongly, he plies the oar,

Till Port Leone's safer shore

Receives him by the lovely light

That best becomes an Eastern night.

In his rooms in St James, John Hobhouse was also reading *The Giaour*, enjoying the tale of the infidel, now on land, racing through the night —

Who thundering comes on blackest steed,

With slackened bit and hoofs of speed

Though weary waves are sunk to rest,

There's none within the rider's breast;

And though tomorrow's tempest lower

Tis calmer than thy heart, young Giaour!

On – on he hastened, and he drew

My gaze of wonder as he flew;

Though like a demon of the night

He passed and vanished from my sight ...

Hobhouse read on, wincing uncomfortably when vengeance was paid and —"*his turban was cleft by the infidel's sabre.*"

Hobby unconsciously put a hand to the top of his head, rubbing an imaginary pain, while realising that the entire incident of Hassan's death had passed vividly before his eyes as if he had actually *been* there, and watched it.

He continued reading, for now the Mussulmens' hunt was on — for "*Lelia's love* – the accursed *Giaour.*"

Apart from his opening verses about the tragedy of the formerly great nation of Greece now subjected to

Turkish rule, Byron had constructed the story with three narrators speaking their own personal view of the series of events, but the underlying theme was the difference between Christian and Moslem perceptions of love, sex and death.

Hobby was enjoying it so much he paused to refill his wineglass, already wording in his mind the praise he would give to Byron about *The Giaour* – so much more enjoyable than *Childe Harold's Pilgrimage* – at least there was none of Byron's sly in-jokes in this one!

But, as usual, Byron did not fail to eventually disappoint Hobby further on, when the Giaour spoke his thoughts about Lelia, his lost love, to the Friar of the monastery.

She was a form of Life and Light –

That, seen, became a part of sight;

And rose, where'er I turned mine eye,

The Morning-star of Memory!

Now why did he have to go and spoil it! Ever since Cambridge, Byron had always referred to his first love, Mary Chaworth, as his "Morning Star". That man was just *incapable* of getting away from reality in his writings. Always, always, it came slipping in somewhere.

Hobhouse decided not to read any more, not now that he knew all of the descriptions of Lelia were based on the Giaour's feelings for Mary Chaworth. Only a poet – a *foolish* poet – could hold on to a hopeless love for so long.

Yet, minutes later, after sipping more wine, Hobhouse began to recognize his own biased prejudice and hypocrisy ... for as exasperating as Byron's hopeless love for Mary Chaworth may be to him personally ... was it not those same experiences and memories of his own realities that made other parts of Byron's poetry so vivid and engaging?

After all, like himself, during their travels together through Albania and Turkey, Byron had seen with his own eyes the way women were treated so cruelly by being tied alive in sacks and thrown into the sea. And Byron had also seen – as few other Englishmen had seen – the bloody and awful sight of dismembered corpses of young Greek men killed by the Albanian chief, Ali Pasha.

So in those non-romantic parts of the *Giaour,* Hobhouse had to concede, Byron was writing mostly about what he had actually seen, what he had felt, and not what he had chosen to invent.

He picked up the *Giaour* again and began to read on.

~ ~ ~

Sitting alone in her parents' drawing-room in the northern town of Seaham, Annabella Milbanke had a slight smile on her face as she read the poet's descriptions of true love; surprised and feeling somewhat rapturous by the unexpected religious tone of certain passages.

Yes, love indeed is light from heaven.
A spark of that immortal fire
With angels shared, by Allah given,
To lift from earth our low desire.
Devotion wafts the mind above,
But Heaven itself descends in love,

A feeling from the Godhead caught,
To wean from self each sordid thought;
A ray of Him who formed the whole;
A glory circling round the soul!

Annabella slowly laid the book down on her lap and looked towards the fire, her heart thumping and her eyes glowing like those of a big cat.

Here was the proof! Firstly, that Byron was not an atheist at all – else how could he write these beautiful words about heaven and the Godhead with such feeling?

And secondly ... well, she had suspected it for some time, and although Byron had tried to hide it within the casualness of his short letters to her, she was now certain that her rejection of his marriage proposal to her last summer, had caused him considerable pain and anguish.

How to relieve him? How to let him know that if he were to propose again *now*, she would be his without hesitation.

And then it came to her – she would seek the help of his "Machiavelli" – the person who seemed to advise him and guide him in all things – her own aunt, Lady Melbourne.

In a flush of excitement she wrote to her aunt in a gushing tone, devoid of her usual strict restraint of manner and words, telling her that she had now read 'The Giaour', and –

"The description of Love almost makes me in love. Certainly he excels in the language of Passion. I consider his acquaintance as so desirable that I would incur the risk of being called a Flirt and enjoying it, provided I may do so without detriment

to himself ..."

In London, Lady Melbourne was so surprised by the letter from her prim and proper niece; she had to read the letter twice. And just the *thought* of Annabella acting like a *flirt* made her smile in disbelief. How very amusing!

Chapter Five

~ ~ ~

In her bedroom at Melbourne House, Caroline Lamb read every word on page after page of *The Giaour*, weeping when she read the lines —

The hour is past, the Giaour is gone;

And did he fly, or fall alone?

Woe to that hour he came and went!

The curse for Hassan's sin was sent

To turn a palace into a tomb:

He came, he went, like the simoom —

"Yes, yes ..." Caroline sobbed, "*my* Giaour has gone, my *infidel* ... my cold and heartless infidel!"

She threw the book furiously against the wall. Yet the following day she was back in John Murray's establishment on Albermarle Street, but this time standing in his office.

"Oh, yes," she told him, "the heart of a libertine is like iron. And Byron has the *coldest* heart of any libertine."

Well, if she wanted to believe that Lord Byron was cold-hearted, she must be allowed to do so, but John Murray felt bound to protest —"Lord Byron is not a *libertine!*"

"Yes, he is.*"*

She walked slowly in front of his desk, running her finger along the edge. "Oh, not like Casanova, or the scandalous Earl of Rochester ... not like them ... but Byron is a free-thinker who refuses to be restrained by the rules of society, as do all libertines."

"And as *you* also refuse to be restrained," John Murray wanted to say, but instead he found himself slightly smiling as he remembered something Byron had once said to him about London Society ... "*You may call a man a profligate or a libertine and he will smile at you – but tell him his neck-cloth is not folded correctly and he is likely to call you out for a duel.*"

He looked at Lady Caroline and saw that she was staring at him, her whole manner completely changed to one of insipidity; even her voice was weak as she asked humbly, "Will you tell the Giaour I wish to see him?"

"I will, Lady Caroline."

"I know not his new address. Do you know it?"

"No," John Murray lied. "He comes and he goes and I am as wise as you are. All my business with him now is done through his book agent, Mr Dallas."

"But when you see him, you will tell him ... and give him my love?"

"I will, Lady Caroline."

~ ~ ~

Byron was away from London, on a short visit back to Newstead Abbey, in response to a letter from another Mr Murray – old Joe Murray, the head butler.

"Well, it's all these letters, my lord," said Joe wearily, pointing to a sack filled with letters. "I don't know what else to do with them. Every day young Rushton carries them up from the Hut, and a fortune it would cost to post them on to you in London."

Byron was frowning at the sack. "You do realise, Joe, that there could be some *important* letters for me in there?"

"Aye, but how am I to know the difference between

one letter and another? How am I to know which letters I should post on to you, and which ones I should not?"

Bryon pulled the sack of letters into the downstairs parlour and sat down to sort through them; constantly sighing miserably at being forced to attend to such a tiresome business.

Since the publication of *The Giaour* letters from all over the country had been flooding into his publisher's office, and now some of those so-called fans were writing directly to him at Newstead Abbey.

"It's an audacity, my lord, writing to you here at your private home," said Fletcher. "Yea, verily it is. A downright *cheek* of some people I'd say!"

Byron shrugged. "Stop your prattling, Fletcher, and open some of these letters. I want you to look at all the seals on the back and see if any of these letters are from someone I know – someone *you* know that I know – and if so, place them to one side."

"And what will I do with the others?"

"Place them on your *other* side, so I will know those are the ones from strangers."

Byron continued reading quickly through the tiresome letters, often quite ridiculous ... although some were very amusing, and those letters he put aside to actually answer – yet the very worst of the letters came from some very high-ranking young ladies in England who, in their nervy gushiness, sought to hide behind big and unnecessary words which were, in any event, used incorrectly ... "*may I beg you to extrapolate a lock of your hair and send it to me...*"

At that very moment young Rushton came hurriedly into the parlour.

"Joe Murray said you needed my help with the sack of letters, my lord."

Byron stared at him. "Have you washed today?"

"Aye." Rushton, bewildered, looked down at himself and then touched his face. "I'm clean. I'm always clean, my lord, in the way you instructed."

Byron stood up, walked to the window and peered out at the sunshine. "It's a warm day, Robert, would you agree?"

"Aye, my lord, very warm."

"So here's what I want you to do. You know the huge waterfall down near the back end of the lake? I want you to go down there, strip off and stand under the waterfall until you are as clean as a freshly-bathed baby."

Now it was Fletcher and Rushton who were staring at Byron, and then at each other.

"But my lord," said Fletcher, "it's always only *you* that bathes under that waterfall. No one else is allowed to go near it."

"And I'm clean," Rushton insisted. "I don't need to wash again."

"Do as I say, Robert. Get some soap and wash yourself from head to toe under the beautiful cool streams of the waterfall. It's much quicker than hefting in buckets of water for a bath."

Fletcher was lost in the bafflement of it all, and also feeling great sympathy for young Rushton who had now left the room – until his lordship turned from the window with an amused grin on his face. "I'll make it up to him with a nice silver florin when he gets back. That should please him."

Fletcher stared. "A nice silver florin would please *anyone*, my lord."

"And it's not really a hard task, is it? Not on a humid day like this. Personally, I love going under the showers of the waterfall."

Fletcher remained befuddled until his lordship finally explained why he had given Rushton such a task; and the two of them were still laughing when Robert returned and Byron let him in on the jest.

"Do you mind, Robert? I would consider it a great favour."

Even without the eye-popping silver florin that Byron handed to him, Rushton saw the funny side and laughed his agreement.

"It's a sin, mind, deceiving people," Rushton said, sitting down on the chair that Fletcher had positioned in readiness for him. "I'll be bound to ask God for his forgiveness."

"Do that *after* you have done the deed," Fletcher instructed, throwing a towel over Rushton's head and vigorously drying his damp hair. "Now, my lord, how many locks do you need?"

Byron had sorted through the letters. "Of the ones I have read, I would say about twenty."

"So it's a good thing our Robert here has a good thick head of hair."

"And dark, like my own," Byron agreed, and couldn't help laughing again. "Just think, Robert, all those high-ranking young ladies who will soon be clasping a lock of *your* hair to their heart and cherishing it forever."

Joe Murray, who had been let in on the jest while Robert was away at the waterfall, stood at the door unnoticed amidst all the laughter.

Smiling, he returned to the Servants Hall and said to Nanny Smith: "Fame hasn't changed him. He's still jesting, still up to his tricks."

Nanny Smith, with her very tender conscience, did not think it funny at all. "Those poor young ladies ... all being hoodwinked."

Joe laughed at the very thought of it. "Say what you will, if you must – but you have to admit, when his lordship is away, and during his long absences, our dull life here at Newstead has few laughs in it."

Chapter Six

~ ~ ~

Upon his return to London, Byron found himself busily answering letters from Lady Melbourne.

Now that Caroline was back, letters were flying back and forth between the two of them: Byron's letters full of anxiety and irritation, because – not knowing his new address – Caroline had taken to finding him out and following him wherever he went, through the streets, looking back to see her ducking into a doorway, and then haunting whatever house in which she knew he was a guest – waiting outside until all hours, and then besieging him when he tried to enter his carriage.

And he in turn was shocked by the drastic change in her appearance.

"I am being haunted by a skeleton!" he wrote to Lady Melbourne.

She replied full of sympathy and advice, informing him that this was the *new weapon* being used by her daughter-in-law, starving herself and paling her face with a smidgeon of white powder to make her look so desolate in her love for him, that he would eventually take pity on her and take her back into his heart and back into his bed.

In their shared dislike of Caroline, and their shared revulsion at her shameless behaviour, the two had become firm friends and allies, although Byron now looked upon Lady Melbourne more as a mother-figure, who always seemed to have his best interests at heart; and for that alone, he adored her.

"In any situation that perplexes you," she wrote,

"write to me and I will always advise and guide you as I would my own sons. And, as always, it will be confidential, and always 'entre nous' – between us."

~ ~ ~

Byron was struggling to read and understand a letter from his sister Augusta – always a confusing and slow process – due to her hasty scrawl and her habit of jumping from one subject to another before getting to any point or conclusion.

Now she was upbraiding him for a rumour she had heard that he was flitting from one woman to another and acquiring a reputation as a bit of a *roué*

Sighing, he lifted his pen to reply —

My dearest Augusta,

You may perhaps have heard that I have been fooling away my time with different "regnantes" but what better can be expected from me? I have but one RELATIVE and her I never see. I have no connections to domesticate with, and as for marriage I have neither the talent nor the inclination.

I hope all my nieces are well, and increasing in growth; but I wish you were not always buried in that bleak common near Newmarket.

Your most affectionate brother, BYRON

All this letter writing was becoming ridiculous, Byron decided, because, in truth, he scarcely knew his half-sister. If Augusta was to approach him on a street he was sure he would not know her from any other stranger.

They had met only twice, and that was as far back as eight or nine years ago, when he was still a schoolboy at Harrow. Until then he had not even known he had a half-sister, and his delight was short-lived because soon after their last meeting she had married George Leigh and became his prisoner, having child after child and becoming more muddle-headed by the year. Reading her letters now was a form of mild torture, either a hurried scrawl that he could not decipher, or a long rambling gossip about God knows who or what?

Still, she was his father's daughter, his own half-sister, and for those two reasons alone he was prepared to forgive her anything.

Chapter Seven

~ ~ ~

That *'bleak common near Newmarket'* was an isolated house, with eight paddocks, surrounded by miles of empty fields, in a district aptly named as Six Mile Bottom.

Inside the house, Augusta Byron Leigh was even more distracted than usual, engrossed in the care of her growing family, while feeling she was sinking into a pit of desperation – sinking under the burden of her husband's debts.

She had only one kitchen maid, one parlour-maid, a nanny and a cook, because that was all the staff she could afford, often doing the housework herself while the maids looked after the three children; although when one or other of the children was sick, or needed comforting or nursing, it was always Augusta who rushed to their care.

And at night, when the children were soundly asleep in their beds, Augusta constantly spent those quiet hours sitting at her table sorting out the mounting bills; constantly pushing her hair back from her forehead in frustration as she tried to find a way to save a penny or a pound here and there, because now the creditors were daily clamouring at her door and becoming more angry in their demands with each week that passed without payment.

Fortunately she had the perfect excuse to fend them off, telling them the truth – her husband was not at home – but then George was rarely at home these days, travelling up and down the country from one race meeting to the next, trying to make enough money to pay off their debts, while Augusta was left to manage the household on a mere three hundred pounds a year which had been left to her through an annuity by her late grandmother, Lady Holderness.

Three hundred pounds a year might seem a fortune to someone of the middle or lower class, but Augusta's name still held the title of 'Honourable' and therefore she was seen as an aristocrat, not only by her creditors, but also by her relations and friends who expected her to live and dress like an aristocrat, something she could no longer do.

Not since she had married George Leigh, a former Hussar and equerry to the Prince of Wales whom her guardian, Lord Carlisle, had not liked, yet had allowed Augusta to marry him.

These days, though, Augusta often found herself thinking back to beyond her time living with her guardian, Lord Carlisle ... to those days in her childhood living with her grandmother, Lady Holderness ... believing now that she herself must have been the *least* favourite of Lady Holderness's four grandchildren. She *must* have been, else why leave her so little, and the others such a lot?

Or was it because of her father, John Byron, whom Lady Holderness had detested?

Probably.

And yet, now that she was a mother herself, Augusta could understand her grandmother's hatred of John Byron, whether he deserved it or not. It was all such a sordid story, yet one that Augusta had been forced to live with all through her growing years.

Lady Holderness's most beloved and beautiful daughter, Amelia, had married Francis Osborne, now the Duke of Leeds, and went on to have three children by him; two sons and a daughter. The marriage had been a good one, until Amelia met and fell desperately in love with a young army officer, Captain John Byron, finally abandoning her husband and three children to run away to France with him.

London Society had rocked with the scandal of Lady Amelia's desertion of her husband; and Lady Holderness had never quite lived down her daughter's disgrace. For a man to leave his marriage and children was one thing – but for a *wife* to do it was simply intolerable.

Lady Holderness had suffered silently through the public scandal while her daughter was divorced by her husband, who was also granted custody of the children.

As soon as the divorce was finalised, Amelia married John Byron in France, writing letters full of happiness home to her mother, begging for her forgiveness, which she eventually got; but she did not return herself until a few weeks before she was due to give birth to John Byron's first child.

The happiness of Lady Holderness's reunion and reconciliation with her daughter was short-lived. Amelia died giving birth to Augusta, and from then on John Byron had left the child in the care of her maternal grandmother while he went in search of another heiress and another fortune to ruin.

At least, that was how Lady Holderness had told it.

All Augusta could remember was that every one of her needs had been well taken care of as a child. Although as she had grown older she had noticed the change in her grandmother's attitude whenever her three *Osborne* grandchildren came to visit – so much more loving and so genuinely happy to see them. And those children, Augusta's two older half-brothers and a sister, had been polite, but clearly did not like this *half*-relation who lived in their grandmother's home.

It was not until a maid reported to Lady Holderness that Augusta spent most of her time crying in the summerhouse that her grandmother instructed her other grandchildren to *try* and be more kind to Augusta, reminding them that their mother had been Augusta's mother too —"You all had the *same* mother!"

After that, the three Osbornes had tried, they really had *tried* ... but the fact remained that *they* were the children of the Duke of Leeds, and their mother was a lady never spoken of in their father's household, and this *half*-sister of theirs was part of the reason for that.

And so life went on, with Augusta doing her best to be of no trouble to anyone, shy and timid and tolerated by her snooty Osborne relations, while she in turn always did her best to try and make them like her – even when the boys sneakily said horrible things to her about her father. "I'm so sorry," was her regular reply.

She was always "so sorry," always so ready to accept in a contrite way whatever they said, if only to prevent any quarrels. All disagreements unnerved her, and all confrontations terrified her.

Lady Holderness had ensured that she was privately educated to a high standard in all female subjects, but not in preparation to be an aristocratic young lady of leisure like her half-sister, but more in preparation for the career that had been chosen for her, as a junior Lady-in-Waiting at St James's Palace.

After the death of her grandmother, Augusta, at the age of sixteen, found herself shunted over to the care of her new legal guardian, Lord Carlisle, a distant relative on the Byron side; and from then on she spent most of her time living in one or other of two households: up in Yorkshire at Castle Howard with Lord Carlisle and his family – or, whenever she was needed and sent for – down in London as one of a troupe of Ladies-in Waiting to the Queen.

Both were enclosed worlds, very private, no commoners allowed. And in both worlds Augusta was well aware of her place. In Lord Carlisle's Castle Howard she knew she was regarded politely as an aristocratic *dependent;* and when at St James's Palace, a royal servant.

Yet she faced it all like a true Christian, because that was how her grandmother had brought her up, to accept whatever trials the Good Lord sent to one, and to always be kind to others.

And Augusta was always kind, to everybody; kind and caring and happy to be so, because over the years Augusta had convinced herself that most people in her life had truly been so very, very *kind* to her.

"Mrs Leigh?"

Startled out of her thoughts, Augusta's eyes moved up from the table of receipts and bills to stare at the children's nanny. "Yes, Flora, what is it?"

"Miss Georgiana says she won't go to sleep until she gets one more kiss from *you*."

Augusta smiled and immediately stood up. "The little imp!"

She nodded to Flora as she headed towards the stairs. "You go and have some tea. I'll stay with her until she nods off."

"Thank you, Madam." Flora stood watching her mistress rushing up the stairs, thinking as always how lucky she was to be employed here. True, aye, Mrs Leigh could often be forgetful and a little confused in her manner at times, but that was because she was driven so frantic these days. But she was also an *easy* mistress, never told you off, not even when you was in the wrong, which made working here a real easy doddle.

And Flora knew that the rest of the staff agreed with her on that.

Chapter Eight

~ ~ ~

Two weeks later Augusta arrived unexpectedly in London.

In the lobby of the apartment building in Bennett Street, she hesitated, nervously timid at the thought of meeting her *other* half-brother whom she had not seen for years. She had been a girl of twenty then, dressed in a fashionable red velvet costume with her long brown hair topped off by a cute red hat – but look at her now!

She paused to look at herself in the mirror on the lobby wall and saw a much older person, twenty-nine now, almost thirty. Her face looked pale and strained, and her simple cotton dress and brown-corded jacket were more suitable for country lanes than London town.

The sound of footsteps on the stairs accompanied by voices startled her, turning her head to see two young men walking into the hall.

Immediately her shyness made her turn her back and lower her head, pretending to search inside her purse, but through the wall mirror she covertly watched them...one was short and strongly-built and speaking somewhat angrily with a frown on his face; while his companion, taller and extremely handsome, was a rather blasé young man, responding to his friend's complaints with an expression of unconcealed amusement.

When they had gone, Augusta took a deep breath of relief, because, like her *other* half-brother, Lord Byron, who had once told her in a letter that he "*hated strangers*" Augusta hated them too. All strangers terrified her, until she got to know them better. If they were nice, she liked them, but if they were not, she avoided them.

She moved towards the stairs and was about to head up to the first floor of apartments when a voice halted her – she turned and saw a man emerging from a door, dressed like a porter.

"May I help you, Madam?"

Augusta became flustered. "I-I've come to see Lord Byron."

"Is he expecting you?"

"Yes."

The porter looked dubious. "He made no mention of any visitors to me."

"I'm his sister."

"Indeed? Are you indeed? Have you visited Lord Byron here before?"

"No."

"May I have your name, Madam?"

"Mrs Leigh."

"I'm still obliged to escort you up."

Augusta meekly followed him up the stairs to the apartment. When his knock on the door was answered by Fletcher, the porter said. "This lady, Mr Fletcher, says she is Lord Byron's sister."

Fletcher stared somewhat suspiciously at the rather plainly dressed person in front of him. She was not at all like the usual glamourites who called on his lordship claiming to be his sister or cousin.

"Mrs Leigh," the porter added.

"Mrs Leigh ..." Fletcher blinked at the name, and then recognition dawned. "Oh, the *Honourable Mrs Leigh*. Yes, yes, I have posted many letters to you! Come in, pray come in, Mrs Leigh. Lord Byron is out, but he will be back shortly."

Augusta was led into the large drawing-room where Fletcher fussed over her, ordering Mrs Mule to bring in a tray of tea, which she did – both of them smiling a lot as they told her they had heard so much about her from Lord Byron, and now it was a rare pleasure to finally meet her.

Augusta smiled a lot too, feeling most welcome here; and later, when she had relaxed and had waited for quite some time in the drawing-room, she began to feel even more at home amongst her brother's comfortable sofas and furnishings ... yet the more she gazed around her ... she could see quite a lot that could be improved.

Fletcher carried in another tray of tea and caught her in the act, his face shocked, and then absolutely *outraged*. "Mrs Leigh!"

Moments later he heard Lord Byron's voice in the hall, speaking to Mrs Mule, and Fletcher rushed out to complain to him.

"My lord, you will *have* to speak to your sister. What she has been doing in there ... well, at the very least, it's rude!"

Byron was surprised, not only by the unexpected arrival of Augusta, but at the fury on Fletcher's face. "Why, what has she been doing?"

"*Tidying,* my lord! I went in there just a minute ago and found her *tidying* your drawing-room. All the cushions were neatly-placed, not thrown here and there on the sofas as you like them."

Byron was still laughing when he entered the drawing-room, and Augusta was wide-eyed with shock to recognise him as the blasé young man she had seen earlier downstairs ... but there was nothing blasé in his manner now. He looked delighted, coming straight to her and enclosing her in such a strong hug she was literally struck dumb with astonished happiness.

"At last!" he said. "My sister finds some time for me at last."

Augusta drew back, and stared into his face. "But ... since I last saw you ... you have changed so *completely* ... in every way.*"

Byron looked at her archly. "And it would be strange, wouldn't it, if at twenty-five I still looked like a teenage schoolboy?"

Augusta was still amazed. He was impeccably dressed in dark, well-tailored clothing, his linen immaculately white, and his hair even darker than she remembered it.

"Everything about you is so smart, so elegant, and so ... *finished.*" She ran her hands down the sleeves of his fine jacket. "Who styles your clothes?"

"Oh," Byron thought about it, "well, a few years ago I would have had to say Beau Brummell; but now, I would have to admit that my style is heavily influenced by Hamlet."

"Hamlet?"

"Yes, you know ... the part in the play that speaks about the true *'glass of fashion* – rich but not gaudy'."

"Rich but not gaudy," Augusta repeated, and that was exactly how Byron looked now.

"Come, sit down," he urged her, "and tell me everything, all your gossip. I want to find out if, in normal conversation, you still talk in that damned *crinkum-crankum* way that you do in your letters."

Augusta laughed. His criticism made her feel even more at home than all the polite but lukewarm hospitality that was usually shown to distant relatives upon their short-notice arrival.

Byron was genuinely delighted to actually *see* his

sister again, after so long; although he found her conversation to be *exactly* like her letters – muddle-headed and hurried and jumping from one subject to another.

"I'm just so nervous about it all," Augusta explained. "First meeting *you* again, after so many years, too many really, too long – and then agreeing to do *that,* which I also have not done for such a very long time."

"Doing what? I thought you had come to London to see me."

"Oh, did you? Well, yes, I *did,* and I have wanted to come and see you for so long, I truly have, most certainly. But you know, with the children ... and then *this* gave me the perfect opportunity to kill two birds in one journey."

His puzzlement was visible. "That? This? Augusta, what the devil are you talking about?"

Augusta stared at him, also puzzled. "Did you not receive my last letter?"

"Yes, I did, but it contained nothing about *that* or *this.*"

"Did it not? Then it cannot have been my *last* letter to you..." Frowning, she sat thinking for a few seconds. "Oh, goodness, I do believe I must have forgotten to post it."

"So why not just *tell* me now, whatever was in the unposted letter?"

So she told him. "You were still a small boy living with your mother ... but do you remember, later, when I visited you at Harrow, telling you that I lived in the care of Lord Carlisle?"

"Yes, when Lady Holderness died you were a genteel relative in need of shelter and Carlisle took you into his family."

"Which was very kind of him, but he only agreed because my distant family connection to him was on the *Byron* side."

"Kind? He was supposed to be *my* legal guardian too, but he avoided me like the plague. I saw him only once."

Augusta's smile was sympathetic. "Byron, when I visited you at Harrow, I did explain the reason why. He was terrified of your mother."

"Everyone was terrified of my mother." Byron shrugged. "So, pray move on and get to the point, Augusta, I *beg* you."

"Well, during that time I became acquainted with the royal family, and on occasions I was sent to help out as a lady-in-waiting to the queen. And now I have been asked to help out again, on a temporary basis."

"As a lady-in-waiting?"

"Yes."

Byron stared at her, truly surprised; but then he remembered that, of course, Augusta had her own connections to the aristocracy. And she had been brought up by her grandmother, Lady Holderness; a close friend of the queen.

"What about your children?" he asked. "Who will wait on them?"

"Oh, they have their nanny and the maids and George has come home to master the household in my place. He is very good with the children, and I shall be away for only a few days or weeks at a time, whenever someone at the palace is ill or needs a few weeks off to visit family. It is a temporary position, on a regular basis."

"A temporary position on a regular basis? Do you mean that whenever the palace summons you to occasionally replace someone, you must go?"

"Yes. That is what I have agreed."

"And George? Your lord and master? What does *he* think of your new career?"

"He understands, and he is grateful. You know our situation, Byron, and how desperately we need extra money to support us."

Byron did know, but now he also knew that George Leigh lived less for his family and more for the excitement of horse racing. Not only did he breed and sell horses, he also gambled on them.

"Augusta married a fool, but she would have him," Frederick Osborne had confided to Byron some months earlier; but as he had never met Augusta's husband, Byron was left without a comment either way.

Not wishing to be too personal at this stage, he turned the conversation back to the subject at hand.

"I suppose the king *is* truly mad, otherwise his son would not be acting as Regent. Perhaps the old queen is now bats also, have you thought of that?"

Augusta tutted her disapproval: "Byron, they are both very old, so it is wrong to judge them so. The queen's mind is still as sharp as a knife, but her body is frail. And I always did like her, so it will be a pleasure to help her."

"How many ladies-in-waiting does she have?"

"Oh, quite a few, although most have served her for a long time and are much older than me. At almost thirty, I think I will be the youngest."

Byron did not like it – did not like the thought of Augusta being financially forced to work at all.

Yet, later that afternoon, he showed only support when he accompanied her to St James's Palace for the purpose of becoming acquainted with her new apartment, and being shown around the parklands and gardens.

"So you see, Lord Byron," said the lady doing all the showing, "your sister will be quite comfortable here during her periods of service, and the gardens are truly very relaxing in spring and summer."

"Why did she insist upon addressing all the information directly to me?" Byron asked when they returned to Bennett Street, causing Augusta to laugh.

"Oh, it's so unexpectedly superb to have such a *clever* brother who is now a famous poet. I'm sure the palace female staff will constantly *plague* me for information about you."

"When do you start?"

"In three weeks. So I can stay in London for only a few days, no more than a week at the most, before I have to go back to Newmarket and get the children arranged and my bags packed."

"Good. Stay for a week so we can get to know each other better." He stood up. "I'll arrange for Fletcher to get you lodged in a nearby hotel."

"Goodness, no! A hotel? Why, the *expense* ...*" Augusta trembled at the very thought. "No, you heard what she said, that particular apartment is mine from today onwards, so while I'm here I shall lodge in my room at the palace. I *have* lodged there many times in the past, you know, so I won't feel strange in any way. No, not at all."

After a silence, Byron agreed. "And it *is* just a short walk from here to there. So we can spend every day together, and I'll take you out on the town and allow you to have some *fun* for a change."

~ ~ ~

In the days that followed he discovered a few new things about his half-sister. When he took her out into town she was full of delight and laughter, losing her shyness as she enjoyed herself. The strain and paleness was gone from her face, and she was even beginning to look younger than she did upon her arrival; but then, as she said, it was her first holiday from home in years.

He also discovered, to his amazement, that she had the same absurd sense of humour as he; noticing the ridiculousness of certain people or situations even before he did – both laughing in quiet hysterics at things other people may not have thought very funny at all – such as a London dandy strutting along Mayfair holding up a black umbrella to protect his complexion from the sun.

"I am invited to a party at Lady Davy's tonight," he told her. "If you would like to go with me, I do *have* an invitation for you."

"A party?" Augusta was not at all sure ... "It's been so long..."

"Then it's high time. And if you come, you will meet again some people you already know, and you can talk to whomever you please."

"Yes, but..."

"And I will watch over you as if you were unmarried and in danger of always being so," he grinned. "Now do as you like, but if you choose to array yourself by half past ten, I will call for you."

"Array myself?" Augusta's face was such a picture of panic and embarrassment; Byron finally understood all her shilly-shallying.

"Oh! I don't suppose you brought a gown with you, did you?"

Augusta hesitated. "N-no, I don't believe I did." She had not been to a party for years.

"Never mind, I'll buy one for you. I'm sure we can get

something already made up in Bond Street."

The gown Byron eventually selected for her was in the style that most young ladies wore these days, consisting of slender drapes of blue muslin, cut in the empire line with a ribbon under the breast, and the neckline so low, and so revealing, it made Augusta blush wildly at the very thought of wearing such a garment.

"As lovely as it is," she insisted, "it is *not* suitable for me."

She found a dress she liked much better, tried it on, then came out of the dressing room and showed it to her brother.

Byron made a face. "My choice was better."

"For a female younger than I, and unmarried perhaps," Augusta replied quietly, "but I could not go out in public with half my bosom on display."

Which was exactly how Lady Caroline Lamb was dressed at Lady Davy's party that night, wearing a gold muslin dress that had been wetted down with water to make the fabric cling to her body and become see-through, and the strips of muslin that barely covered her breasts made Byron wonder why she had bothered to put a dress on at all.

Caroline saw his look, and mistook it for appreciation, flouncing past and ignoring him and his new female, while at the same time smiling at everyone as if she was blooming with careless happiness.

Augusta, meanwhile, in the bustle of a high society party, did not bloom at all. She was as shy as an antelope, her large blue eyes nervous as she gazed around her, speaking only when she was spoken to, while remaining by her brother's side very closely, as if all the lights and dancing and bright fashions of the women were now very strange to her.

Very proudly Byron introduced Augusta to everyone, enjoying the surprise of those who had no idea he had a sibling. It was especially gratifying to him because from the first time he had entered London Society, he had met so many members of so many large families – all *born* to love each other because of their shared name and blood – while he stood alone without appearing to have a living kith or kin to his name.

So it was a pleasure to be able to introduce Augusta as "*my sister*". He even proudly introduced her to Miss Annabella Milbanke, but most especially to Lady Melbourne, who immediately took Augusta under her wing.

"Let me take you off and introduce you to some of the ladies, dear? I'm sure you will find they are all quite charming. Come, and you too, Annabella."

Byron bowed to Miss Milbanke, who responded with a prim dropping of her eyelids, before following her aunt, while Byron's eyes followed her.

"A *cold* dish she would have been," he stood thinking, "and certainly not the right woman for a man who likes his suppers *hot*."

Lady Crewe broke into his thoughts. "Will you join us in the music room, Lord Byron? Gell and I are on our way there to hear Lady H give evidence of her musical talent at the pianoforte."

"And the flute," said Sir William Gell. "Apparently we are all to be treated to a beautiful rendition on the flute by a gentleman I have never heard of."

Byron always enjoyed the company of Gell and Lady Crewe, two middle-aged people who were usually good fun, and as well as that — "Oh I *love* to hear the sweet notes of a flute," he said, "so lead the way, my lady, lead the way!"

The three of them entered the music room to find it packed, all chairs and sofas occupied, leaving them no choice but to remain standing at the back of the room.

Lady H approached the piano as stiffly as a white stick. She was not Lady Holland, and Byron had no idea which "Lady H" she was.

Before he could ask lady Crewe, another woman walked over to the pianoforte to join Lady H, announced as a 'Miss Somebody', or a name similar to that.

He bent sideways and whispered to Lady Crewe, "What did they say her name was?" but Lady Crewe's only response was to hush him: the music was about to begin.

The piano struck up as the two ladies swung their hands down to play, but it seemed that the person giving the most "evidence of her musical talent" was Miss Somebody, a lady of about fifty and the dominating player of the recital, sitting on the piano-bench nearest to the audience and constantly flashing imperious glances around the room as she played, her spectacles glinting away in the lights of the candelabra on the piano – *green* spectacles.

His amusement at her self-grandeur got dangerously worse when he looked at the way she was dressed – bunched-up in a gown of a heavy red and green brocade-type fabric – which was very similar to the old embroidered bag used by the Keeper of the Privy Purse in Parliament.

This threw him into a fit of silent laughter, forcing him to lower his head and keep it lowered until Lady Crew nudged him with a whisper, "Why are you laughing?"

"She reminds me of the Privy Purse," he whispered

back.

"The Privy Purse?" Lady Crewe stared at Miss Somebody, and then she too lowered her head with a splutter of chuckles, whispering to Gell, until the sounds coming from the back of the room were like an eruption of the whooping-cough as all three tried to strangle their laughter – which was now impossible.

Byron quickly stepped out of the room, followed as quickly by Lady Crewe and Sir William Gell, all hurrying towards the door leading to the garden where they could release their laughter without causing offence.

"Oh, Byron, you are such a *bad* boy," Lady Crewe remonstrated. "Why do you always make me laugh at things when I'm supposed to be grave and sedate?"

Gell decided they all needed a drink and called over a footman. "If you would be so kind, my good man, it's champagne for these two, and a brandy for me. We all need to gargle our throats rather quickly."

They remained sitting in the garden under the torchlights, sipping their drinks, until more guests filed out into the coolness of garden.

"Is the piano recital over?" Lady Crewe asked one of the ladies.

"Yes, thank heavens, but the gentleman with the flute is now about to commence with *his* party piece. I believe he is a foreigner of some sort."

"Oh, the *flute!* I don't want to miss the flute." Byron stood up, looking at Lady Crewe and then Gell. "Are you coming to hear the flute-player?"

"No fear," Gell replied. "Lord knows what peculiar thoughts you may have about *him* that will send us all scuttling out of the room in a hurry again."

"As long as he's not wearing *green* spectacles," Byron laughed, and took himself off to the music room, which he found half-empty.

The musician was seated on a chair at the top of the room; a stout little man wearing a white wig with his head lowered, while his hands fiddled with the top of the flute.

Byron saw an empty sofa at the side of the room and sat on the farthest end of it, near to the musician, eager to hear the mellow notes of the flute wafting towards him.

Waiting, Byron's eyes were fixed on the flute-player while for some long minutes he continued to fiddle with the flute, which, surprisingly, was made of glass. Never in his life had Byron seen a *glass* flute before.

The flute-players bushy white eyebrows twitched as if he was puzzled in some way, and the fidgeting and fiddling went on until most of the people in the room were beginning to lose patience. Some of the older ladies waved their fans irritably.

Unaware that another guest had sat down near to him on the sofa, Byron sighed, sat back, looked around and saw Annabella Milbanke sitting a few inches away from him. He looked at her with some surprise, and gave the usual acknowledgement.

"Miss Milbanke."

"Lord Byron."

Both returned their eyes to the musician who was now holding up the glass flute towards the lights of the candelabra and waving it slightly, so that all could see the inside of the glass tube very clearly.

Impatient and curious, Byron turned his head to look at Miss Milbanke. "What is he *doing* with that glass flute?"

Annabella smiled. "I believe he intends to play it."

"And does he intend to let us *see* all the notes as well

as hear them?"

Before Annabella could reply, a fluttering mass of feminine gold muslin and blonde hair plonked herself down on the edge of the sofa between them, wriggling her bottom backwards until she had squeezed and elbowed Annabella farther down the sofa; then she sat back and threw her arms out to rest along the top of the sofa, displaying her half-covered breasts.

"Oh, la la Lord Byron! If I had known you were going to be here tonight, I would not have come."

He could see that Caroline was slightly drunk. She drew in her arms and leaned close to him, a teasing smile on her face as she said in her low caressing voice, "*Mon cher* ... do you wish me to go away?"

"No, no," he said casually, "pray allow *me* that privilege."

He stood and walked out of the room, leaving Annabella scowling at Caroline.

He finally found Augusta with Lady Melbourne and other ladies in the garden room. As soon as she saw him Lady Melbourne swiftly drew him aside to speak quietly.

"I tried to find an opportunity to warn you earlier, but could not do so in the presence of your sister. I'm afraid the Prince Regent has insisted that the social ban on Lady Caroline be lifted. He and the Spencers have always been very close, so it's no surprise. I have other things to tell you, but not now – not until we can have a more private *tête-à-tête*."

Augusta crossed over to where they were standing and touched her brother's arm. He looked at her regretfully. "I do think we should leave now," he said. "Would you mind?"

"Of course she would mind!" Lady Melbourne insisted. "Do let her stay a little longer. She has been contentedly listening to all the scandalous gossip of the ladies, and amusing me by blushing charmingly throughout."

"Then I shall certainly take her away. Come, Augusta."

Augusta paused to give a perfect curtsy to Lady Melbourne, who smiled as she watched her leave the room, concluding that Lord Byron's timid sister, with her big innocent blue eyes, may not possess the aristocratic title or sophistication of a true 'lady', but she most certainly had all the passive requirements for a lady-*in-waiting*.

In the carriage going home, Byron was very apologetic. "Did you think I had abandoned you and left you for too long in the care of Lady Melbourne?"

"No, not at all, I found Lady Melbourne to be an extremely cheerful and *comforting* companion."

"Isn't she?" Byron nodded. "I always find her so. Yet Caroline Lamb and the rest of the Ponsonbys and Spencers have secretly nicknamed her *'the thorn'.*"

"I can't think why." Augusta was surprised. "I could determine nothing prickly about her at all. Quite the opposite."

Byron sighed. "I do love that woman, in a filial way. I'm sure if I lived in the same house as her, listening to her calm guidance and advice every day, I would never again take a step wrong."

Augusta saw the sincerity of his expression, and thought she understood the reason why. "Do you now think of her as some sort of good-mother replacement?"

"No. Although I have occasionally wished that she was my aunt." He looked at Augusta and smiled. "Not any more, though. Not now I have my very own *sister.*"

Augusta's face was flushed and pleased. She had not

expected to be liked so much by her half-brother. Or to be so much *appreciated* by him. It was all so very different to the attitude and manner of her other half-siblings – the condescending Osbornes.

~ ~ ~

Byron's sister was the subject of discussion when Lady Melbourne, her daughter-in-law, and Annabella Milbanke returned later that night to the ground-floor drawing room in Melbourne House.

"My goodness, being Byron's sister, one would not expect her looks to be so plain," said Caroline. "There was nothing particularly striking about her that I could see.*"*

Annabella remained silent, looking at her cousin-in-law with disdain.

"Why are you looking at me like *that?"* Caroline demanded. "Looking at me in that prim provincial way of yours."

"I am looking at you with pity, Caroline, because you are not capable of possessing one unselfish thought in your head."

"And what do *you* possess? Here you are, past your twenty-first birthday and still no suitor in sight. Your coming-out *husband-hunt* season last year was a flop and now you are back down in London to try again."

"Annabella received three marriage proposals last year," said Lady Melbourne, "and you do know that, Caroline."

"Three proposals, and all jokes," Caroline replied. "One from that idiot, Augustus Foster; another from that effeminate fool, William Bankes –and the third from Lord Byron was made only and solely to hurt *me*."

"Ladies, ladies, stop being so cruel to each other,"

Lady Melbourne ordered. "And Caroline, I would be obliged if you would refrain from criticising Lord Byron's sister. I found Mrs Leigh to be a very nice person. A little plain in her dress, perhaps, but in all other ways, I found her to be very sweet and gracious."

"A little *plain* in her dress?" Caroline retorted. "Her dress had a high neck and long sleeves and was *black*. What woman other than a Quaker would wear black to a party?"

"Black *velvet,*" said Lady Melbourne, "and I thought she carried the colour off very gracefully, especially as she topped it off with that beautiful pearl choker."

"Yes, I noticed that pearl necklace," said Annabella. "I thought it quite beautiful."

Lady Melbourne nodded. "Mrs Leigh told me her brother had bought it for her earlier today, from a jewellers in Bond Street."

Caroline had poured herself another drink, seething with irrational jealousy against Byron's sister. She tipped back half the contents of her glass into her mouth in one gulp, shuddering with fury.

She had seen Byron and his sister leave, and had seen the attentive way he had placed her wrap around her shoulders; seen the tender way he had smiled at her before escorting her out – as if she was someone *special*. And yet he had abruptly left her own sweet self abandoned on the sofa in the music room to go in search of *her* – his precious plain-looking sister.

She said scathingly: "When the two of them first arrived, I wondered whom Byron had brought in, and where on earth he had met her, because at first sight she looked to me like a blushing *nun* on her once-a-year day off from a convent."

"And yet..." said Lady Melbourne thoughtfully, "when

she and I spoke together, although I agree she looks nothing at all like her brother, there was something about her that reminded me of him ... a facial expression perhaps, or the way she phrased some of her words ... no, no, none of those," she shrugged, "but there was *something* so like, yet I can't put my finger on what it was."

Annabella knew what it was. She had seen it straight away. It was her smile.

Chapter Nine

~ ~ ~

When Augusta left London to return to Newmarket, Byron could not help worrying about her.

During their many conversations and occasional heart-to-heart confidences, he had learned just how desperate the Leigh's financial situation had become. It seemed wrong to him that his sister should be forced to pinch every penny – wrong that he should have to watch her constantly pushing her hair back in a stressful way as she spoke about it. No wonder she had become so muddle-headed down there in Newmarket.

Yet not once would she countenance a word of blame against her husband, excuse after excuse coming to her lips. George had paid a lot of money for a good horse that had turned out bad, a worthless investment. He had hoped that particular horse would sire a few good racers, but they could not get him to breed. One of George's favourite Greys had broken a leg and had to be shot. A mare had slipped on ice ... and all leading to financial calamity.

He was in debt himself, but he had to help her, no matter what it cost, especially as her children were also *his* nieces.

He dashed off a quick note.

My dearest Augusta,
Can you tell me how much George owes? I shall be able to make some arrangement – for him – but at all events you and the Children shall be properly taken care of – what I do for him now, might be seized &c, – so anything done for yourself would be

safer and more advantageous to both.

ever yrs—B

The next few hours were spent answering the demands of the day's post, from his publisher, his attorney, Lady Melbourne, two or three friends, and then the last, from Miss Annabella Milbanke.

I have received from lady Melbourne an assurance of the satisfaction you will feel in being remembered with interest by me. Let me then more fully explain this interest, with the hope that the consciousness of possessing a friend whom neither Time nor Absence can estrange, may impart some soothing feelings to your retrospective views.

He was puzzled ... *retrospective views?* She had to be referring back to his former rash and stupid proposal. He read on –

You have remarked to my aunt about the serenity of my countenance, but mine is not the serenity of one who is a stranger to care, nor are the prospects of my future untroubled. It is my nature to feel long, deeply, and secretly, and the strongest affections of my heart are without hope. I have disclosed to you what I conceal even from those who have most claim to my confidence, because it will be the surest basis of that unreserved friendship which I wish to establish between us –

Unreserved friendship – what was he to make of that? From a woman he had seen no more than two or three times and who was almost a stranger to him. Oh, women were the devil to understand!

He continued reading her letter, and then answered it very politely, ending by replying to some of her questions – questions which he truly thought to be rather too *un*reserved in their inquisitiveness.

You ask me if Augusta is "shy – <u>to excess</u>?" Yes, as I tell her, she is like a frightened hare with new acquaintances.

As to my "honest" opinion of your aunt, Lady Melbourne, I am not perhaps an impartial judge, but she is doubtless in talent a superior – a supreme woman – and her heart I know to be of the kindest. Her defects I never could perceive, as her society makes me forget them & everything else for the time – & so you see that I am therefore unqualified to give you an unbiased opinion.

Yrs truly
Byron

By return of post she sent him a second letter, informing him that her stay in London was over, and she was returning North to her home in Seaham, but sincerely hoped that their correspondence of friendship would continue.

Again he answered her letter very politely, yet could not help reflecting on the oddity of it all in his journal:

A very pretty letter from Annabella, which I have

answered. What an odd situation and friendship is ours! Without one spark of love on either side, and produced by circumstances which in general lead to coldness on one side, and aversion on the other. So she is clearly a very superior woman.

~ ~ ~

Later that week, in response to his letter offering financial help, Augusta replied with a four-page letter full of gratitude, and relief, and more rambling gratitude, until finally at the end she disclosed the amount the Leigh's needed immediately to repay the creditors – £3,000 – an enormous amount.

Byron made the cheque payable to Augusta, sealing the letter as a knock on the door was followed by Fletcher breezing into the room.

"Another letter for you, my lord. It came on the five o'clock."

Byron rolled his eyes, wondering why London had to have *four* deliveries of mail every day.

"If I read it, I will feel obliged to answer it, so hold on to it until the morning."

Fletcher nodded, knowing that if his lordship did not answer a letter immediately, he usually forgot to answer it at all.

"It's very thin and light," Fletcher said, his fingers feeling the square of vellum, "so I don't think it's from a woman, and if it's not, then it might be important."

Byron had to smile at Fletcher's logic. "Oh very well." He took the letter, opened it, saw it was indeed just a few lines, and read ...

My dearest Lord Byron,

If you are coming into Notts, please call on a very old
and sincere friend most anxious to see you.
Mary.

His heart felt like it was beating a thousand beats a
minute, his eyes wide. He read the note over and over in
the growing dusk of the room, finally looking across to
the window and seeing it was dim and shadowy outside.

Fletcher watched him as he stood up and moved
across the room, opened the cabinet and – unusual for
him at this early time of the evening – poured himself a
glass of brandy, sipped it, and then carried it to the
window where he stood pondering.

"Is anything amiss, my lord?"

"What?" Byron turned at the voice, startled, as if he
had completely forgotten Fletcher's presence in the
room.

"Is there anything amiss?" Fletcher repeated. "Or will
you still be going to the party?"

"What party?"

"You have invitations to three tonight."

"Do I? And which one have I acknowledged and
accepted?"

"All three, my lord. You have agreed to go to the first
at nine, the second at ten, and the third at eleven."

"No, no," Byron shrugged, "I'm not in the mood for
all that gadding about ... No, I think I'll go down to
Brooks's for supper and spend an hour or two with a few
of my friends, and then return for an early night."

"No parties?" Fletcher's face expressed rigid offence.
"But I've already pressed and laid out your evening
clothes."

"And I will wear them to Brooks's. One can't walk in
there dressed in boots and a riding jacket. Why are you
sulking?"

Fletcher wanted to know what was in the letter, and Byron knew he did.

"Is there a reason for this sudden change in the arrangements, my lord?"

"Only that I have some business with the steward at Newstead. So tonight, Fletcher, I would be obliged if you would pack enough clothes for us both for a week or two in the country."

"Newstead? We're going home to Newstead?" Fletcher was all smiles now. "Was your letter from Owen Mealey then?"

Byron sipped his brandy. "Tell me, Fletcher, beyond the daily requirements of my wardrobe and organising my small household, is my private business any of *your* business?"

"No, my lord."

"Then all you need to know is that we should be ready to leave London as early as possible in the morning."

Fletcher made an attempt at a placating smile, rueful and affectionate. "You can rely on me, Lord, Byron, I'll have you up and out by dawn."

"But before you do," Byron picked up the letter to Augusta, "can you get this posted in the nine o'clock mail tonight?"

PART THREE

Sweet Surrender

'I could have added a page to their history (Byron and Mary Chaworth). Musters, the man, left her and went to Paris. I saw him at Calais, on his route, and he told me he had separated from his wife for life, and that Byron was the cause of their separation.'

Beau Brummell

Chapter Ten

~ ~ ~

Newstead once more — breathing in the fresh and better air of the country; the birds singing at full pitch; the wild rambler roses showing off their blooms, releasing their scent into the warm July air — riding over to Annesley, still wondering why she was "most anxious" to see him.

The maid who answered the front door went to fetch Nanny Marsden, who came puffing along the hall with a big smile on her face, greeting him very warmly, taking his hand in both of hers and shaking it for so long, so gratefully, and so vigorously he began to fear his arm might be tugged off.

"Ah! Now, this *is* a pleasure, my Lord Byron! And I know it will be a pleasure for my young lady too. A friendly face is just what she needs right now, and you was always her most *favourite* friend."

Byron frowned. "Is something wrong?"

"No, not as I could say. Excepting ..." Nanny Marsden lowered her voice to almost a whisper, causing him to lean closer. "She's been too much on the quiet side of late, sad-like, sitting alone in her courtyard or the apple-orchard and doing nothing but reading those two books of yours."

"Perhaps ... perhaps she is missing her husband?"

"Ah! That brute! No, he's been here a few times since the separation, but she will *not* receive him, not under any circumstances. It was never a good match, y'know, right from the start, but I suppose she told you all that, when you was here last."

Byron knew it would not be prudent to reply. "May I see her? Is she up in her sitting-room?"

"No, last I seen her she was out in the apple-orchard inspecting the trees. She reckons there will be a good showing of apples come September. Now *you* know well where the apple-orchard is, don't you, my Lord Byron? Can you find your own way there, or shall I call someone to take you?"

"No, no, I need no guide." He gave Nanny Marsden a quick smile before turning away to leave the house and wander over to the orchard where he had spent many afternoons with Mary in the past.

His steps slowed as he entered the orchard, wandering through the trees along one twisted path to another, until he saw her. She was standing sideways to him, bending down, as if picking up something from the grass.

He paused, and remained where he was, smiling lovingly upon her, because there she was, looking as young and as natural as she had looked in their younger days, her brown hair tied loosely at the back of her neck and not a hint of rouge or powder on her face, an unadorned country girl wearing a lilac dimity dress and a white apron tied around her waist.

Whatever she had picked up from the grass, after a glance, she threw it away, standing up fully and looking straight ahead into the distance as if listening for a far-off noise. She turned her face to him, then turned away – and quickly looked back at him again – seeing him, her eyes opening wider and a slow smile coming on her face.

We met—we gazed—I saw, and sighed.
She did not speak, and yet replied.

She walked towards him, blushing and smiling and glad to see him, her two hands lifting towards him.

Their hands met, and he clasped both of hers in his, seeing then the dark hollows under her eyes, and knew she had been suffering, "sad-like" as Nanny Marsden had said.

"You wrote," he said, "so I came."

She was still smiling. "I wanted to see you."

"Yes, but why?"

She paused, as if considering her answer, while he watched her and felt an urgent desire to kiss her soft open mouth, to touch his own dry lips to her soft pink lips in a loving and lustful way.

"I wrote to you because ..." She shook her head, vague, confused, as if the reason why was strange, even to herself.

"I just wanted to *see* you again."

~ ~ ~

The magnificent promise of a very hot summer came to pass only a week later. At Annesley there was a strange thrill and quickening in the air. The sun was beaming, the corn was turning gold, and the young mistress was not sad any more.

The dreams of all his yesterdays, the romance that should have been his, so long ago, had now blown into flame. Within days of his return they had become lovers. Their love was now mutual, but secret; it had to be.

It was the romance, of the most romantic period of my life. The love of better things and better days. The unbounded and heavenly ignorance of the rest of the world and its ways. The moments when we gather from a glance, more joy, than from all future pride and praise, which never can entrance the heart in an existence of its own, of which another's heart is the zone.

Strangely, there was no gossip at all. The servants in both households of Annesley and Newstead all seemed to have been struck by an incurable form of lockjaw.

Only Fletcher – who now had the regular job of riding back and forth between Newstead and Annesley carrying letters and messages from one to the other – dared to open his mouth to speak to Joe Murray about it:

"He's always been mad on her, and now she's even madder on him."

Joe quickly hushed him up as if he had uttered a blasphemy. "You'd better not let his lordship hear you speak like that, else you'll be out of his service and quick. You know how he feels about his privacy and tittle-tattle."

Fletcher almost jumped in fright, glad of the reminder. "Aye, the way he just dismissed Susan Vaughan and not another word said about her, but *I* meant no harm, Joe, no criticism neither. Why would I? His lordship has always taken good care of me. Like a father to me he is."

Joe couldn't help laughing. "How can he be like a *father* to you, when he is six or more years younger than you?"

"I mean he's *good* to me, that's all."

"Even so," Joe warned, "a *good* valet keeps his mouth closed at all times. Remember that."

Chapter Eleven

~ ~ ~

Very early one morning in late-July, not long after the sun had risen, a young man named William Howitt was riding between Newstead and Annesley on one of the upper hills, when he saw a dark-haired young gentleman walking through one of the fields below.

He knew he was a gentleman from the style of his clothes, brown leather boots, brown breeches and a beige riding jacket, but he was not riding; he was walking beside his horse, holding the reins, and he walked with a slight limp.

He reigned his own horse to a halt and stared, certain it was Lord Byron, but if it was, what was he doing up and out at this time of the morning, when the sun was barely risen ... and coming from the direction of Annesley?

For one excited moment he had the impulse to charge his horse down the hill and introduce himself, eager to tell the poet what an honour it was to actually *meet* him in person, but his own good breeding restrained him.

One did not accost a gentleman on his own land, especially when that young gentleman had his head lowered and appeared to be engrossed in his own thoughts ... He was not even sure if it *was* Lord Byron, and if it was not, then what a blundering fool he would make of himself.

Never once did the young gentleman look up or around him, but a minute or so later Howitt saw him mount his horse, and then knee his horse into a gallop towards Newstead.

Arriving at Annesley Hall, and riding under the arch, Howitt looked around him but very few people seemed to be up and about, apart from a young stable-man who came wandering out from one of the stalls, looking at him curiously, obviously wondering who he was.

"This is private property, sir, and trespassing is forbidden."

Howitt jumped down from his horse and explained who he was and why he had ventured under the arch. He was from Derby, still at college, and was writing a book about the rural life of England and its ancestral houses.

"I can only visit these houses in my summer holidays, you understand, so I was hoping to get a good view of Annesley and its lands before any of the household had risen."

"Aye, but you've come inside the boundary, sir, so you're still trespassing."

"Yes, but if I came back later, do you think the master of the house would allow me to view the inside of Annesley Hall?"

"Nay, sir, it would not be allowed. The mistress would not like it. You can ride around the hills and fields and take a good look at the house from the outside if you like. I'm sure the mistress wouldn't mind that, so long as you keep a respectable distance."

Howitt was disappointed, but pressed on. "If I wrote and requested an appointment with the mistress, do you think she would receive me?"

"I couldn't say, sir, because I'm not the one to ask, but if you stay here I'll ask the housekeeper for you."

Howitt stood in the sunshine of the courtyard and waited patiently, thinking about his book. His ambition was to ride all over England and view every rural ancestral house that existed, so it would take him years to write, but the finished book would be a gem, and like no other book of its kind.

The housekeeper herself came out to see him, a stout woman of about sixty years, looking him over carefully, and seeing that he was a young man of the upper middle class, she greeted him respectfully. "Good morning, sir."

Once again he explained his reason for being there, and why.

"Ah! A book about the history of Annesley Hall?" said Nanny Marsden. "Well, if you were to put your petition in writing to Mistress Chaworth, I'm sure she will give you a nice reply."

And that was that. Reluctantly he turned to leave, then swiftly turned back. "Do you know, I thought I saw Lord Byron earlier, riding his horse towards Newstead and coming from this direction."

William Caunt and Nanny Marsden glanced at each other, and then both quickly shook their heads.

"No, me duck! It must have been someone else you seen to be sure," said the housekeeper. "We haven't seen Lord Byron around these parts for years. Down in London he lives now. One of the high set!"

Howitt was disappointed; yet glad he had not made a fool of himself earlier. "I was so sure it was him there."

William Caunt was curious again. "Do you know Lord Byron then?"

"No, I have never had the honour of meeting his lordship, but I am a great admirer of his poetry."

"Then what made you think it was Lord Byron you saw, if you have never before seen him?"

"Well, he does own the adjoining estate, and yes, I have *seen* him, in a way, so I do know what he looks like."

Howitt then explained that during his summer holidays the previous year, he had called at Newstead Abbey hopıng to see Lord Byron, but as his lordship was down in London and not in residence, he had explained to an old gentleman named Mr Murray about his book, and that gentleman had very kindly escorted him on a tour of the Abbey.

"The only part I was not allowed to view was the wing containing his lordship's private apartments."

William Caunt was amazed. "Joe Murray allowed you *inside* the Abbey?"

"Not immediately. On the first day I called he refused most belligerently, but then I was told in Newstead Village that Mr Murray was famous for having a strong passion for his pipe, so when I returned a few days later, I brought him a gift of a large pouch of excellent tobacco which I had purchased in Nottingham; and to my delight he relented, and turned out to be a very kind gentleman. I was even served tea and cake by a maid before I left."

Nanny Marsden was looking at Howitt with narrowed eyes. "That don't say how you know what Lord Byron looks like, if he wasn't there at the time of your calling."

"No, but while I was in the Abbey last year, I saw his portrait, on one of the walls. I must admit I stood looking at it for quite a long time, at the author of 'Childe Harold's Pilgrimage', that's why I thought the young gentleman I saw this morning was he, because of the similarity."

"We all make mistakes, sir," said Nanny Marsden dismissively "So if you write your petition to Mistress Chaworth, I'm sure she will send you a firm reply. A good day to you, sir."

She turned her back abruptly. "Come along, William,

we have our work to do."

William Caunt waited until he had watched the young man ride off, and then caught up with Nanny Marsden in the kitchen, a small grin on his face.

"When I lived at Newstead, Lord Byron had a favourite saying that he would tell to Joe Murray over and over. Do you want to know what it was?"

Nanny Marsden looked at him. "A saying? So what was it?"

"I *hate* strangers."

"Aye," Nanny Marsden nodded. "I suppose most people do – especially when they come calling at this early hour of the morning. Did you ever know the like? I'm sure the young man meant no offence, but how would he like it if folk came knocking at the door of *his* family home and asked if they could traipse around it for a gawk."

"For a book."

"A gawk or a book, all one and the same. One sees and one tells."

William Caunt was still grinning. "At least now I've got something to twit Joe Murray about. I'm sure his lordship don't know that Joe allowed a stranger *inside* Newstead Abbey."

"Bribed by a pouch of tobacco!" Nanny Marsden shook her head at the weakness of men and their cravings.

~ ~ ~

That evening, after ensuring that all the stable lads had been fed, followed by the house servants, Nanny Marsden climbed the stairs to find out if the mistress and her visitor were ready to be served a light supper in the dining room.

Throughout the past hour Nanny had occasionally heard the sound of the piano playing, but now, on reaching the landing, all she could hear from the mistress's sitting room was laughter.

Knocking on the open door and receiving a call to enter, she stepped inside to see Lord Byron standing by the piano, the side of his body and his elbow leaning against it in a casual way, and Mary sitting with her fingers on the keys.

"Nanny, Lord Byron has been telling me all about the antics of some of the *Haut Ton* down in London."

"London, oh my!" Nanny Marsden replied, for London was a glamorous place to all country folk.

"There was a time, years ago," Nanny Marsden said wistfully, "when I was a lass of sixteen or so, I used to dream night and day of getting a position down there in one of those grand houses in London."

"Did you, Nanny?" Mary looked surprised. "Was that before *I* was born?"

"Aye, long before; but I never got past the Nottingham turnpike."

"Then you were lucky," Byron said, seeing the sad glimmer of a lost dream in Nanny Marsden's eyes. "It might not have been the glamorous life you imagined. In fact, I would think most servants in those grand houses in London are wishing they could change places with you, and live a quiet life in the country."

"Why so?" Nanny Marsden looked at him curiously. "Do the High Set treat their servants badly then?"

"No, not badly, but in my experience some do treat their servants somewhat carelessly. The older ladies are the worst, the difficult old *dowagers* that all servants dread. I'm sure some of them were born before Henry the Eighth, but pretend to be *merely* in their eighties."

"How d'you mean?" asked Nanny Marsden. "Carelessly? I can't imagine it."

"Then I will show you," Byron said, remembering an incident that had taken place while he was waiting in the hall of Holland House for Lord Holland.

Within minutes he had Mary and Nanny Marsden in fits of laughter by doing a very good mimic of one of those grand old dowagers issuing instructions in a contralto voice to one of the butlers, his hand waving in the air as he did so.

"Holman! You there! Yes, you, sir! I am eighty-six years old and my selfish family is shamelessly neglecting me, so I want you to arrange a small soirée for me next Thursday evening. What? How dare you tell me your name is not Holman! So if you are not Holman, where is the damned fellow?"

"Mr Holman retired from service at the end of last year, my lady."

"What? Retired? But surely he knew that I was relying on him to arrange my soirée for me? Oh, bother! Why is it always the damned servants who are the hardest to please?"

"Indeed, my lady."

"Well, get to it, man! Find my address book and send out some invitations for me."

"Beg pardon, my lady, but how many invitations shall I send out?"

"Oh, not many, a small gathering is all, with only the best of the select. So let us say ... no more than five hundred or so..."

Mary's head was bent over the piano keys in laughter, while Nanny Marsden lifted the corner of her apron and dabbed it to her eyes, not at all sure if she was laughing or crying. His lordship had played the two parts so funny, but it was Mary's laughter that brought tears to her eyes ... oh, it was so good to see her young mistress *laughing* again.

Chapter Twelve

~ ~ ~

Throughout the summer Byron had flitted back and forth between London and the country, confusing his friends by always seeming slightly vague about his past movements and future plans, making it impossible to pin him down to a certain attendance at any soirée or party – which infuriated Madame de Staël.

Wherever she went, to dinners or balls, the French novelist always kept an eye out for the sleepy-eyed young poet, and when he did not appear, she was sourly disappointed.

It was not him personally that she was interested in, for she always had her own French young lover in tow; although at forty-seven she was not totally immune to Byron's personal attractiveness, which was in part sexual, in part intellectual, and the other part she admired so much was his *politics*.

And why not, eh? She had read his speeches to the English Parliament. She had listened to him in serious conversation with other men, and she knew he was as much influenced by the political principles of *Jean-Jacques Rousseau* as she was. He was an English lord yet he thought a democracy or even a republic would be a fairer system of government for the English people. *Bon, bon, bon!* She approved, she cheered him on, and wondered why he did not speak with her in the same serious way he spoke with the men?

She was unaware that, behind her back, Byron often complimented Germaine de Staël, in a back-handed way, saying that, "Intellectually, she would make a great *man* ... but she was hindered by her gender, and even more so by those ridiculous Turkish turbans she always wore on her head."

"N'importe." Madame de Staël shrugged away her thoughts – No matter! When Milord Byronn became her son-in-law they would have plenty of time to talk seriously together.

And that was the reason why she was constantly looking out for him, because it was *"Byronn"* she had decided, whom she wanted to have as a husband for her daughter Albertine.

~ ~ ~

Byron was late, but arrived in time for dinner, feeling somewhat dismayed when he found himself placed in the chair *next* to Madame de Staël.

"Milord Byronn ..." She greeted him with her usual buck-toothed smile, and from then on the pleasure of the evening went straight downhill.

During the past week, he had spent most of his free time at Newstead reading her new novel, *De l'Allemagne,* which had just been published in English by John Murray, and he had liked it tremendously – but knowing what an egotist she was, he also knew that unless he could twist his face into numerous expressions of awe and admiration, she would simply *refuse to* believe he had liked it. So he did not mention it.

Fortunately the gentleman on her other side kept her talking for a time, while he enjoyed a conversation with Lady Melbourne; until Madame de Staël suddenly caught his arm and leaned into him, speaking in a secretive way ... telling him that, in Paris, she had recently seen the beautiful Lady Oxford walking around with a miniature framed picture of Milord Byronn pinned to her bodice.

"So first, Milady Caroline Lamb, and then Milady Oxford ... so tell me, Milord Byronn, *why* it is, these ladies find it so *'ard* to forget you?"

He looked at her sideways. "Perhaps it's my wit?"

Madame de Staël smiled knowingly. "Last year, you 'ad the *affaire* with the beautiful Milady Oxford, *oiu*?"

Now the sleepy eyes somewhat widened, surprised at the question, and she laughed her amusement.

"Ave you forgot, milord, that I am *French*? And we French are not like the English. We are very understanding of young men's *amours sexuelles*. Even our young *femmes* are brought up with such understanding. So too is my daughter, Albertine. You 'ave met her? No? Oh, so I must arrange the introduction for you."

After that he had no interest in anything else she said, and merely pretended to be listening, lost in his own thoughts with his eyes half-shut and wishing he was deaf, but after a while he heard some familiar words ... words that made him look at her as she talked on.

"*There is nothing real in this world but love,*" she was saying.

"That's from your book, *Delphine*."

She nodded. "And so true, eh? *Our feelings are –*"

"Madame de Staël," he interrupted irritably. "I have already *read* all your books, so when I come out of an evening, I do not need to *hear* them being read to me again."

She stared at him. "You 'ave read *Delphine?* As well as *Corinne?*"

"You know I have. I've told you I have, twice, three times I've told you, so how many more times?"

She shrugged her shoulders in a very *French* way. "And so I 'ave told *you* many times, Milord Byronn, in this life, without *love,* one must choose between boredom and suffering. So what are *you* now – bored? Suffering? Or in love?"

Which completely disarmed him, making him smile in a flustered, almost fragile way, and she laughed with delight. "Ah, *see!* Always I can make you *forgive* Germaine de Staël!"

And she could. His dislike of her was just a thin crust on top of the thick pie of his admiration for her. She was, after all, the woman who had helped to draft the first Constitution of the French Republic.

Yet, as they talked on amicably, Madame de Staël was able to hide the fact that *she* had not forgiven *him* for being so irritably impolite to her, and as soon as dinner was over she sought out the company of Lady Holland and whispered to her about Milord Byronn that ... *"Il est un démon!"*

Lady Holland, now so used to Madame's dramatics, laughed it off and remained amused when Madame went on to complain that Milord Byronn was as haughty and conceited as Lucifer.

"Hautain – oui?"

"Oh, yes," Lady Holland agreed, "very haughty."

"Vaniteux – oui?"

"All men are vain," Lady Holland replied lightly, unwilling to allow this criticism of her favourite guest to go on for much longer; especially as she believed she knew the *real* reason behind all the bitter complaints in Madame's conversation.

Germaine de Staël had come to London convinced she would be received as the *"Literary Lion"* of the English metropolis, but discovered that appellation had already been given to Lord Byron. Still, it was a man's world, and at every function that Madame de Staël had attended in London, she was lauded as much as he was lionized, so why complain?

Later, when her husband joined her and asked what spicy little secrets Madame de Staël had been whispering so heatedly into her ear, Lady Holland was still smiling. "She has now convinced herself that Byron is a bad angel ... *un démon!*"

"Well he's no *saint,* that's for sure," Lord Holland replied, "and he's also not here. He left some ten minutes ago."

~ ~ ~

'My Dearest Augusta, – I have only time to say that my long silence has been occasioned by a thousand things (with which you are not concerned) It is not Lady Caroline, nor Lady Oxford, but perhaps YOU may guess, and if you do, do not tell.'

Yours ever, B.

Chapter Thirteen

~ ~ ~

A day in late August, a hot and yellow sultry day when even the birds seemed too languid to sing, Byron and Mary were walking slowly through the shaded paths of Annesley Wood, on their way down through the trees to Nanny Marsden's empty cottage.

Mary gazed up at the overhanging trees. She enjoyed strolling in the wood, because here in its privacy they were free to hold hands as they walked, unlike on the terraced gardens of Annesley where they were bound to keep a respectable distance, like polite neighbours.

She now smiled at him with the warm delight of the romance inspired by the wood. "I love it here," she said, "because it's so peaceful and comforting. I have always loved this wood, so old, so sweet and serene."

"I think what you love most is the *secrecy* of it," Byron replied. "Why don't we just pack up all our personal belongings and go and live some place abroad?"

"Oh I could not do that," Mary said with some alarm at the very suggestion.

"Why not? You are legally separated. So why are you so *frightened* all the time?"

It was true, Mary was frightened of rumours and gossip, frightened of her Nottingham neighbours who might carry their tales over the river to the Musters at Colwick Hall; and in particular, she was *very frightened* of Reverend Nixon and his wife – the two biggest gossips in Nottinghamshire.

So Byron's proposal was very tempting. "When you

say 'personal belongings' does that include my children?"

"Of course it does. They are a part of you so I will cherish them."

Mary had no doubts about that. She had seen Byron being as playful and as tender with her children as he always was with his animals.

"You are wrong, though," she said quietly. "I am not *legally* separated. Jack still refuses to sign the papers, although my lawyers keep chasing him to do so."

He looked at her curiously. "Why don't you just get a divorce? It's not so terrible as it might seem. Look at Lord and Lady Holland – if *she* had not been divorced, she would still be living a miserable life with a man she detested, a man who was unfaithful to her every week of the year. Now though, *now* she is happily married to a man she loves, and who truly loves her in return."

"Really?" Mary had not known that one of the Hollands was a divorcee. "And yet they still hold a respectable place in Society."

"Most certainly they do." Byron smiled. "And *she* is *five* years older than him."

Mary sighed, knowing he was referring back to the time she had considered him to be too young for her, even though the difference was only *two* years.

Yet the reference back to that time reminded her now of something she needed to tell him, something she knew he would not be happy to hear.

"Byron, I will not be free to see you or receive you at Annesley, not for at least three weeks. My cousin, Ann Radford, is arriving in the morning."

"Ann Radford?" Byron looked away. He had always hated Ann Radford, that *she-cat* of a female who, in their younger days, had never lost an opportunity to exert the influence of her own cunning mind over Mary's weaker one.

"I always hated Ann Radford," he said frankly, "and she hated me."

"No, she did not hate you, Byron, she *liked* you, very much, but you always made it clear that your preference was for me."

"And rightly so. That cousin of yours was always a fright of a sight, with those small beady eyes of hers always watching me. And when I learned that it was *her* who kept urging you to marry Jack Musters, I thought it was because she hated *me.*"

"No. It was Jack Musters who kept urging me to marry Jack Musters."

"So, if Ann Radford likes me so much, why cannot I call to *see* you, if only as a friend and neighbour?"

"No, *no.*" Mary's body was gripped by a tremble of shivers at the very thought of it. "If Ann Radford sees you and I together, in any way at all, she will *know,* Byron, she will *know*!"

"Then why don't you just *tell* her?"

"No, *now* is not the time! Because of my situation you promised, Byron, that you would keep everything *secret,* that you would tell no one about us, that you would not even write about it in your *journal,* not yet, not yet – you *promised.*"

In the end, Mary's distress was such that he relented and held her, and agreed to do whatever she wished, and if her wish was for him to return to London and not come back to Annesley for three weeks, then be it so.

But they still had the afternoon ... and tried to make every moment last as long as possible. Nanny Marsden's empty cottage was like a small corner of Paradise. Love was a beautiful thing, and no man could have loved her more ... "Are you just a dream ... my precious love ..."

Later, nearing the edge of the wood, at the time of parting, they were both sad, and he made one last plea to be allowed to stay and visit her at Annesley, as a friend, a neighbour. How could Ann Radford know anything?

"No, no..." Mary was too frightened of Ann Radford and her tongue. "No yet, my love, not yet."

She hastily smeared the tears from her eyes and put her arms around him. He held her close and hid his face into her neck, wondering why females always had to make life so *difficult* for the men in their lives. His love for her was so impassioned, so emotional at times, that the last thing he wanted to do *now,* was to leave her and return to London.

Chapter Fourteen

~ ~ ~

In London, Byron found a number of letters waiting for him from his dear friend, Lady Melbourne.

Caroline, she informed him, had gone with William and Augustus to the Melbourne's country retreat of Brocket up in Hertfordshire – *"so please feel free to call here at any time, as it would give me great pleasure to converse with you again."*

He immediately wrote back, telling her he would call on her at Melbourne House within the next week; and Lady Melbourne waited with growing disappointment when a week passed, and still Lord Byron had not called.

It depressed her, knowing and facing the reality that few young men of twenty-five would be very eager to keep company with a lady of sixty-two years, but she had truly thought that Lord Byron was different. He had always shown such delight in her company, always appreciated her guidance and advice in all matters concerning Caroline, leading her to believe that the increasing confidentiality and companionship in their letters was now based on genuine affection.

Then a letter came, and as soon as she had read it, she instantly understood and forgave him.

My dear Lady M, – Feeling feverish and restless in town, I flew off to see some of my friends in Cambridge, but my stay was short, and here I am now on a visit to another of my friends, James Wedderburn Webster, at Aston Hall in Rotherham. Webster has invited me many times, yet only now have I had the inclination.

Webster has now gone the way of most men, married, and settled in the country. His wife, Lady Frances, is a pretty young woman, but in delicate health, and I fear going – if not gone – into a decline. Her sister, Lady Catherine, is here too, but unhappy due to being crossed in love by Lord Bury, the son of Lord Albemarle.

Webster himself is passionately fond of having his wife admired, and at the same time jealous to jaundice of everything and everybody. I have hit upon the medium of praising her to him behind her back, and never looking at her before his face.

Last night, after dinner, by way of a relaxant, he preached me a sermon on his wife's good qualities, concluding with the assertion that in all moral and mortal virtues, she was very like Christ !!! I think the Virgin Mary would have been a more appropriate typification, but it was the first comparison of the kind I had ever heard, and it made me laugh till he got angry, and then I got out of humour too, which pacified him, and shortened the eulogy on his wife.

Lord Petersham is coming here in a day or two, who will certainly flirt with Lady Frances, and I intend to have some comic Iagosism with our little Othello her *husband. I really believe the girl is a very good, well-disposed wife, and will do very well if she lives.*

> *Yrs, dear Lady M – BYRON*

As he had always done in the past, when writing to his mother while abroad, Byron confined the subject of his letters to match the interests of the recipient of the letters. To his mother he had only ever written about the fashions and oddities of the *women* of other countries, the style of their clothes and houses etc., and the *weather* of course; his mother had always insisted upon knowing about the *weather* in foreign climes.

And so now also, he wrote to Lady Melbourne solely on those things he knew would interest her, the day-to-day events in a gentry country household – and although every word he wrote was true, he related the same events to different people in different ways.

Hobhouse, for instance, simply *detested* Webster; and whenever he saw Webster in London, Hobby would cut him dead by crossing the street, leaving Byron standing on the pavement wondering *which* friend to annoy or appease?

So no letter from here to Hobby then; because forgiveness would be out of the question.

Nor could he write to Scrope Davies either, that rake of dashing vivacity and "*fierce embraces*" who made conquests of so many women, had not liked Webster either, but even *worse* – he had met Lady Frances before she had married, and the effect she had on Scrope was catastrophic.

He could still remember the day Scrope had called in on him in London, flushed and excited and begging to know – "*Did you ever see Lady Frances? She is the only person I ever saw who has everything the eye looks for in a woman. She has that incredible beauty which the eyes glide over with sheer delight."*

But it was not to be: the silly girl had turned down the glorious Scrope, a Fellow at Kings but also a notorious gambler, preferring instead the more reliable wealth of the big-headed and small-brained James Wedderburn Webster.

Which left Byron wondering why *he* was here? Fraternising with the enemy? Although he knew why, and there were *three* reasons why: firstly, it was somewhere to go to get away from himself; secondly, it was a journey of only thirty miles or so away from Newstead and Annesley; and thirdly, it was the *address* of the place which had piqued his curiosity.

When James Wedderburn Webster and his new bride had lived in Dorset during the previous two years, Byron had never once answered an invitation or felt any inclination to visit them, but — *Aston Hall* in *Rotherham?* Now that was a place certainly worth a visit.

On the first day of his arrival, he had sat down in the library and dashed off a note to Augusta:

I am at this moment residing in Aston Hall in Rotherham, in the very house where MY father John Byron, and YOUR mother Lady Carmarthen, did all their secret romancing.

The novelty of finding himself in such a place delighted and amused him. And, if nothing else, the annoyance of Webster would distract him from his constant thoughts about Mary ... she would not even allow him to write to her at Annesley ... not while Ann Radford was there, because his seal on the letter would betray who had sent it.

Before going to bed he wrote in his journal: —

*I have been pondering on the miseries of separation,
that – oh, how seldom we see those we love! yet we live
ages in moments when we do meet.*

~ ~ ~

Lady Melbourne loved reading Lord Byron's letters,
because he wrote to her in the same voice in which he
spoke to her, and at times she could almost believe he
was in the room with her.

*My dear Lady M., – Today I was told by my friend
Webster that his Countess (mistress) is, he says,
"relentless." What a lucky fellow – but I don't lay this
down as a general proposition.*

*All my own prospects for amusement are clouded,
for Lord Petersham has sent an excuse; and so there
will be no one to make Webster jealous of but the
curate and the butler – and I have no thoughts of
setting up myself. Lady Frances evidently expected to
be attacked by me, and seemed prepared for a brilliant
defence. My character as a roué has gone before me,
and now my careless and quiet behaviour has
astonished her so much, that I believe she is beginning
to think herself ugly, or me blind – if not worse.*

*To return to Webster – I believe his mistress is
mercenary, and yet I know he can't at present afford to
bribe her. I told him his pursuit of her would get*

known, and he must expect reprisals, and what was his answer? – "I think any woman fair game, because I can depend upon Lady Frances's principles – SHE can't go wrong, so therefore I may."

So I asked – "Then why are you so jealous of her?" And he responded "Because – because – zounds! I am not jealous. Why the devil do you suppose I am?"

I then numbered some very gross symptoms he had displayed, even before her face, and even before the servants, which he could not deny.

Every now and then he has a fit of fondness for his wife, and kisses her hand in front of his guests; which she receives with the most lifeless indifference, which struck me more than if she had appeared pleased or annoyed.

Her brother told me last year that she married to get rid of her family (most are ill-tempered) and that she had not been OUT at the balls etc for two months before she accepted Webster.

You have enough of them, and me for the present.

Yrs ever, B.

What he did not mention to Lady Melbourne was that throughout his time with the Websters, he had been suffering great pain in his right leg. It was a familiar pain that came and went, depending upon his exertions, exacerbating his limp, or lightening it again when the pain eased. It was also a pain that he never mentioned or drew anyone's attention to, often hiding it behind jests and laughter. Only Joe Murray and Fletcher knew when he was in pain and, strangely, both of those men always knew it without being told.

Fletcher came to his aid now as he sat down on the side of his bed with a sigh of relief, glad the socialising of the day and evening were over.

Kneeling to unlace and remove the shoe, Fletcher then, unbidden, removed a small bottle of ointment from his pocket and began to gently massage the afflicted foot. "You should not have gone riding for so long today," he said, "and then all that *standing* for hours in the garden party afterwards. I was watching you with some concern, my lord. All that riding and standing would have put a strain on any man's legs."

Byron sighed tiredly and agreed. "True, but I must not complain. As the respectable Mr Job says in the Bible –'why should a *living* man complain?' ... I really don't know ... except it be that a *dead* man can't."

"Nor do anything else neither."

"And yet," said Byron thoughtfully, "the said Job in the Bible *did* complain, incessantly, non-stop, until his friends were tired of him and his wife finally urged the pious patriarch to *'Curse – and die!'* The only time, I suppose, when some relief is to be found from swearing."

Fletcher fingered another small amount of ointment and began to smooth it into his lordship's right ankle, so much thinner and weaker than the left one – no wonder his lordship felt great pain when he was forced to stand on it for hours.

Oh, aye, his lordship suffered much; more than people knew, or would ever know, or even have a suspicion of it, so good was his lordship at hiding his pain in the presence of others.

And yet that man *Webster,* their host, the first thing he said to his lordship when they arrived – and in front of the ladies too – "Well, Byron, how goes along that right foot of yours?"

And his lordship, his face unchanged, answered, "Oh, it goes along much the same as ever, walking beside the left, just like your own."

Still, even Fletcher could see that Webster their host was jealous of his lordship, because Webster knew him so well, had known him since their younger days, so he would also know that a damaged foot was the *only* jibe he could make against his lordship, because his foot may be flawed, but the rest of his body and form was perfect.

Why, even in Greece, when his lordship had stripped naked to attempt the swim across the Hellespont, many of the Greek men had stood to admire him, and some had even been so bold as to declare that his lordship had the best *signor* they had even seen.

Oh, aye, that Webster was mad jealous of his lordship; but now, to Fletcher's knowledge, his lordship himself had only ever shown jealousy when talking of one other man – and that man was Shakespeare.

"Leave it now, Fletcher, my ankle feels greatly eased, so no more of your ointment. Remove the left shoe, bring over my moccasins, and then take yourself off to your bed."

"Are *you* not going to bed now, my lord?"

"No, not yet." Byron looked over to the small desk which his hostess had very kindly provided for him. "There are letters over there, sent on from London, which need to be read and replied to."

When Fletcher had gone, Byron moved over to the

desk, deciding he would ignore the letters and write in his journal instead.

I have missed a day; and as the Irishman said, "have gained a loss." Or did the Irishman actually say – "I have gained BY the loss"? N'importe – I believe with Robin Hood — "By our Mary (dear name) thou art both Mother and May, I think it never was a man's lot to die before his day".

He looked at the page, wondering why he was writing such nonsense? How long had it been now? Almost two weeks. So one more week and he could return to Nottingham and see her again.

A knock on the door surprised him. His call to enter was ignored ... forcing him to get up from his chair and limp across the room, silently cursing Fletcher for being so damned deaf when he should be listening, and yet always listening when he should be minding his own business.

He opened the door – his face showing his complete surprise at the sight of Lady Frances, holding a candle.

She smiled, speaking in a whisper, "Lord Byron, I merely came to ask if you have everything you need?"

He thought about it ... well, some laudanum might eradicate the pain in his leg and give him a good night's sleep.

"I do, yes, Lady Frances, thank you."

"Are you quite sure?"

He was quite sure that he would be called out in a duel tomorrow if her husband knew she was at his bedroom door.

"Yes, you have been most kind, and ..." He hesitated, because there *was* something he felt he needed right now ... some bedside companionship.

"Would you mind," he said, "if I asked you for the loan of one of your dogs?"

"One of our dogs?" Lady Frances stared and repeated. "One of our dogs?"

"An old one will do. For a little silent company."

"Well, I suppose I could send up one of our poodles."

"Thank you. I have an extreme fondness for all dogs, no matter the breed."

She abruptly walked away with her candle, leaving him to close the door, limp back to the chair at his desk, feeling now so very tired of all this socialising.

He picked up his pen and wrote in his journal:

"One gets tired of every thing, my angel", says Valmont. And the 'angels' are the only things of which I am not now a little sick.

Chapter Fifteen

~ ~ ~

At last, the waiting was over and he was back in Nottingham, back at Annesley Hall, lifting the brass knocker on the front door.

He waited for some minutes, glancing up at the windows. Usually she knew when he was coming and watched for him from one of the windows and then came out to meet him ... but not today. Yet he had sent her a note to say he would be calling this afternoon.

He knocked again, wondering where was the footman or a maid or even Nanny Marsden? Were they all in the apple orchard gathering up the last of the September apples?

His head was turned, looking towards the apple orchard, when the front-door suddenly opened and there in its frame stood Ann Radford – a dark, tall, fierce-looking female at the best of times, but today her face wore a thunder of loathing.

"I regret, Lord Byron, that *Mrs* Chaworth is not at home today."

So the she-cat was still here! And by the look of her, as tyrannical as ever.

"Oh, not at home?" He tried to collect his thoughts. "Has it been necessary for her to go away somewhere?"

"No, she has not gone anywhere, but she is '*not at home*' to you, Lord Byron; not today, not tomorrow, nor any day in the future. It is God's will."

She shut the door, leaving him standing there, confused and dazed and wondering what had happened?

Mary could not have changed her mind or killed her love for him since he had last seen her. No, he would *not* believe that.

He knocked again, and kept on knocking impatiently until Ann Radford opened the door again.

"Lord Byron, I thought I had made it very —"

"I insist upon seeing her!"

"You have no right to insist upon anything *within* the boundaries of Annesley, Lord Byron. Please remember that *this* is not Newstead."

"And *this* is not God's will – who on earth came up with that claptrap? *You,* I suppose!"

She stared at him coldly. "My cousin is a good and delicate creature who has suffered enough from men destroying her peace and good intentions. Like all men, like Satan, you have attempted to lead her astray, but you have not succeeded, because she now sees her folly and is repenting her sins."

"*What* sins? She spent a few months in happiness and was at last beginning to rejoice in the life that God gave her – until *you* came along and spoiled it. What did you do? Did you cunningly tease the information out of her, and then turn on her and *damn* her as a sinner?"

The door slammed in his face again, and he was left in his confused rage, and nothing else to do but return to Newstead.

~ ~ ~

He was almost at Newstead when he heard the sound of a horse behind him and looked back to see William Caunt coming after him at a gallop.

He turned his own horse around and cantered back to meet him until both drew rein, and Caunt handed him a letter.

"The mistress sends her sincerest apologies, my lord, and asked me to give you this."

Byron ripped open the letter and sat reading it while William Caunt watched his expression darkening with every line that he read, finally reaching the end and exclaiming with some bewilderment, "God damn!"

"Is there a reply, Lord Byron?"

"No." Byron turned his horse around. "No reply."

Caunt watched him galloping off towards Newstead, and then slowly turned his own horse around, wondering what it was all about?

All that William Caunt knew for sure was that Miss Radford had been upsetting the mistress something badly this past week, and – according to the maid Sarah – whenever the housekeeper Mrs Marsden had sneaked halfway up the stairs to listen to what Miss Radford was saying, she had always come back down with sadness on her face and shaking her head at the woe of it all.

~ ~ ~

At Newstead, Fletcher was lying lazily on his back under a tree near the old Monks Pond, certain that his lordship would be away for hours; so it was with some surprise that he heard the sound of hooves flying past.

Curious, Fletcher moved to his feet and came out of the trees, walking towards the back of the house to find his lordship's horse standing loose and untethered and the reins hanging down.

"Is his lordship back already?" he asked Joe Murray in the Servants' Hall.

Joe nodded. "And he said he is not to be disturbed for the rest of the day."

"Not even by me?"

"Well, he didn't mention you by name in particular,

only that he was not to be disturbed."

"Something is not right," Fletcher said, "I'd better go up there and find out what."

"No!" Joe ordered. "If his lordship said he's not to be disturbed then he's not to be —"

Fletcher was gone out the door, causing Joe to turn to Nanny Smith in annoyance, "Since when did Fletcher stop taking orders from *me*?"

Fletcher was taking the stairs two at a time, his curiosity killing him, as well as his concern.

On reaching his lordship's door, he knocked his usual knock, waited, and when he heard no call for him to enter or go away, he slowly opened the door and looked inside.

His lordship was leaning against the frame of the window, his head turned away from the door.

"My lord?"

Fletcher moved closer, and as he drew nearer to the window he saw that his lordship's face seemed to have a fire on it, but it was only the light of the sun.

And moving closer still, he saw that his lordship's blue eyes were luminous with tears.

"Ah, what has she done now?"

"She did nothing. She did not even come out to see me."

Fletcher was baffled, unable to understand or make any sense of it. "But she does *love* you, my lord. We *all* know that."

"Not according to her letter." Byron waved his hand towards some torn-up pieces of paper on his desk.

"It seems she *was* in love with me, but now she is more in dread of the Devil, and is repenting all of her sins ... and mine."

Fletcher stared, and Byron looked away again. "Her

wish is for us not to meet or see each other again ... for the sake of *both* our souls."

"Women and their holy dreads!" Fletcher exclaimed irritably. "Sally was just as bad, always prophesying my doom in Hades for drinking liquor. But I would have thought that Miss Chaworth —"

"Is very weak," Byron said quietly. "And Ann Radford was always as cunning as a fox, although Mary could never see it."

"Cunning as a fox? In what way, my lord?"

"In every way, but mainly in protecting her comfort through Mary's money. She's not even a true *cousin* of Mary, just some distant orphaned relative of Reverend Clarke who eventually married Mary's mother after she was widowed. I used to think Ann Radford was younger than Mary, because she always looked to me like a little black cat with her small staring eyes and enormous teeth when she yawned. But now she looks like a *huge* fierce cat and she's not younger than Mary but older."

Fletcher was staring at his lordship, realising he must be feeling greatly upset to be talking so openly about other people to *him* in this way. But come to think of it, Fletcher had never liked Ann Radford neither, and nor had his wife Sally liked her, but they had not known her well enough to suspect that she was *cunning*.

"Even in our younger days," Byron continued, "Ann Radford was always begging money and clothes from Mary. She would come into the small sitting-room at Annesley where we were sat, or down into the courtyard, and show Mary a magazine page with a *'beautiful'* dress and keep on *meowing* excitedly about the dress until Mary finally rushed off to beg her mother to order it for Ann. And then, a few months ago, Mary told me the reason why Ann Radford no longer resided at Annesley, was because she had kept saying how much she yearned for her *own home*, so Mary bought her a house somewhere."

"Aye, I did hear she had her own fine house now, but I didn't know Miss Chaworth had *paid* for it."

"And no doubt Mary is paying all the bills as well. Where else would a spinster like Ann Radford get money from?"

Fletcher's head was nodding with realisation: now he understood, and all too clearly, because did not *he*, in the same way, depend upon his lordship for a living? Although *he* had always *worked* to earn it.

"I've never liked cadgers," Fletcher said, but Byron was not listening.

"So I can understand why Ann Radford must have got into such a state of terror when she learned I had asked Mary to leave Annesley and live abroad with me. What of her income then? Who would pay it?"

Fletcher's head was still nodding. "But ..." he said, "what *I* can't understand, is why Miss Chaworth is paying so much heed to *her* now, instead of you?"

Byron looked at Fletcher as if wishing he could hit him. "Don't be such a fool! That's what *cunning* people do. They slyly find out all the soft spots and weaknesses of a person, and then *use* them to get that person to trust them, and trust them implicitly."

"Well, not being a cunning person myself," said Fletcher, slightly aggrieved, "I didn't know that."

"If the truth be known, Jack Musters probably encouraged Mary to buy the house for Radford, to get rid of her out of Annesley."

Fletcher was nodding again. "They do say he detested her."

"And now he is gone, and *she* is back to rule the roost.

And Mary is a bigger fool than you are. Ann Radford always *hated* me, I could see it in her eyes. Yet how cunningly she fooled Mary with her lies – it was not *me* Radford liked – it was Mary she *loved*."

Fletcher frowned, puzzled. "What d'you mean?"

Byron opened his mouth to answer, and then closed it again, remembering where he was, and *whom* he was speaking to ... "No matter," he said dismissively. "I don't know what I'm saying or even what to *think* about this."

He took a deep breath, and then stood looking around the room in a long thoughtful silence.

"Mary has had the wits frightened out of her by the wrath of Radford's religion," he said. "And now Radford has probably convinced her that I am the son of the Devil himself."

"And we all know *that's* not true!" Fletcher declared. "So what are you going to do?"

"I don't know ... I can't force myself on her ... or force my way into her home ... so what can I do? Except take myself and my black soul back to London."

~ ~ ~

While Fletcher went off to arrange the carriage and then pack their bags, most of which had not yet even been *un*packed, Byron sat down at his desk and picked up his pen, slowly writing one last letter to the only girl he had ever truly loved.

My dearest Mary. My only beloved, precious Mary. Why have you done this to me? Why have you played with my emotions, yet again, even though you know, and know it well, that I love only you, always you, ever you.

I was ready to be your slave, but not your fool. And so, in accordance with your wishes, I can now comfort you with the promise that you will never see me again.

BYRON

Fletcher came back into the room and saw the tears running down his lordship's face, and decently pretended not to notice; but it upset him to see his young master so hurt, so very hurt. Love was a terrible thing when it all went wrong, and now Fletcher was glad that *he* would be having nothing more to do with it, not with love, not now Sally was gone ...

The memory of his beloved lost Sally brought tears to Fletcher's own eyes and his sniffs got louder as he continued packing the bags.

Byron, as he always did in times of great emotion, felt the need to write away his sorrow by bundling it all up into poetry.

"Leave that, Fletcher, we will return to London when I am ready and not before."

"But, my lord, I thought – "

"Leave me alone, Fletcher, go away, scram, *basta, chásou!*"

Fletcher left the room in a huff, returning to the Servants' Hall and Joe Murray, still sniffing. "He's not the only one with heartaches, no, not the *only* one."

"What now?" Joe asked.

"I was doing my best for him, like I always do, and he repays me by telling me to get lost in three different languages – English, Latin and Greek!"

"Heartache?" Joe frowned. "Are you going to tell me what's going on, Fletcher?"

Some hours later, when the dimness of the evening

had set in, Joe made his way up the spiral stone steps to his lordship's apartments, and poked his head around the door. "Some food, my lord?"

Byron shook his head and kept on writing; and a sad and lonely figure he looked to Joe, sitting there at his desk scrawling away with his pen, lost in his own thoughts and words.

"At least," Joe thought consolingly, as he made his way back down the stairs, "he's had the presence of mind to light the candles on his desk, and not keep on writing in the dim dusk like he used to do."

Pages had been written, so much of it scratched out and rewritten, and now Byron was writing it all again neatly in a fair copy, line by line ... a story in poetry, set in the East, a place he knew so well ... about the love of a young man named Selim, for a girl he was not allowed to love, named Zuleika. To lift the veil from her face, and leave it lifted, that was his dream, but first he must get past her Moslem father.

"Son of a slave"– the Pasha said –

"From unbelieving mother bred,

Vain were a father's hope to see

Aught that beseems a man in thee.

Thou – when thine arm should bend the bow

And hurl the dart, and curb the steed,

Thou – Greek in soul if not in creed

Must pore where babbling waters flow,

And watch the unfolding roses blow.

He wrote on into the night, finally accepting a glass of wine from Joe, but then his tears formed again as he wrote once more the lines ...

Zuleika, child of Gentleness!
How dear this very day must tell,
When I forget my own distress,
In losing what I love so well ...

The following morning, when the carriage was ready to leave, Joe Murray was furious but he managed to hide it. He waited until Fletcher had climbed up top with the driver, and then wished his lordship a safe journey.

"I'm told there are lots of hungry footpads on the highways now," Joe said, "so you'll drop me a line to let me know you got down there safely, will you?"

Byron nodded. "I will, Joe, as soon as we arrive back in Bennett Street."

Joe stepped back in his stiff butler way, his chin high as he watched the carriage rolling off down the drive ... but as soon as it was out sight he dropped his shoulders and rushed back inside to vent his fury on Nanny Smith.

"Did you see him? Did you see his face? Heartbroken he is, *heartbroken.*"

Nanny Smith nodded, dabbing the corner of her apron to her eyes.

"I saw it once before," Joe said furiously, "and him just a lad going back to London with tears in his eyes, and all because of *her!* And now she's gone and *cut* him again! Cut him off with only a letter, Fletcher says."

Joe drew in his breath. "So now I'll say it once, and I won't be saying it again – the name of Mary Chaworth must never be mentioned again in this house – not while I'm in charge of it. And now I request the same pledge from *you,* Mrs Smith."

Nanny nodded her agreement, if only to calm Joe

down, but she knew there was more to this tale than had been told.

All she knew now was that she felt as sorry for Miss Chaworth as she did for his lordship, and she didn't know why.

Perhaps Nanny Marsden would be able to tell her when she went over there next, but she would not be going to Annesley for some time, not with the risk of Joe Murray finding out.

She turned as Bessie came into the Servants' Hall to know if the linen on Lord Byron's bed and Fletcher's bed should be changed now?

"Aye, Bessie," Nanny replied. "His lordship always likes clean linen ready and waiting in case he comes back without warning. So we may as well do it today as tomorrow. You go up and make a start and I'll be up shortly to help you."

"He won't be back," Joe said gloomily, sitting down and sucking on his pipe. "Not here to Newstead, and not for a long while."

"Aye, happen so," Nanny Smith agreed, and left Joe to commune the rest of his thoughts to his pipe, while she made her way upstairs to help Bessie change the beds.

~ ~ ~

The carriage was nearing the end of the mile-long leafy lane when it suddenly halted.

Byron lowered the window and looked out to see what was happening ... Robert Rushton was dismounting from his horse, and now rushing up to the window, sheer surprise on his face.

"Are you leaving Newstead, my lord?"

"Yes."

Going back to London?"

"Yes, why?"

"I've just been to the Hut to collect the post, and this letter for you here – it's marked urgent."

Byron took the letter and saw the word '*Urgent*' written on the front.

He quickly opened it and saw the letter was from James Webster, begging him to "*pray return*" to Rotherham if he was still at Newstead, as he urgently needed his help.

Damn! The last thing he wanted to do was spend any more time with Webster ... but then he sat back and gave it some thought ...

London would still be dull and half-empty now until the summer season was over. Scrope Davies was away in Harrogate. Hobhouse was down in Whittington Park with his siblings. Brummell was God knows where ... and Webster needed his presence and help very urgently.

He shrugged, deciding he may as well go, especially as it was less than thirty miles away ... so a speedy short trip, instead of a long thought-provoking journey.

He looked at young Rushton. "Now, was it not a good idea of mine, Robert, to make you attend school for two years?"

Rushton smiled his boyish smile. "Aye, my lord."

"Otherwise you would still be unable to read, and so would not have known that this letter for me was urgent."

Rushton nodded. "I'm reading more books now, my lord, big books."

"*Big* books?" Byron's eyes widened. "Such as?"

"I mean in size, my lord, big books in size – *long* books."

"Such as?" Byron repeated. "Did you finish Robinson Crusoe?"

"Aye, I finished that six months ago, but that was only half as long as the book I'm reading now."

"Which is?"

"Tom Jones."

"*Tom Jones?*" Byron almost spluttered. "Where on earth did you get a book like *that?*"

"From your own library, my lord – you said I could go in there."

Robert's face was beginning to flush, until he remembered, "It had your name written in pencil on the inside, my lord, and the date, so you must have read *Tom Jones* when you were –"

"Sixteen, yes I know, and more harm it did me than good at that age." Byron was grinning, until he remembered Susan Vaughan, and realised the harm to young Robert had already been done.

"Robert," he said, "before you get back on your horse, will you tell Fletcher and Hughes that we are not going down to London after all, but *up* to Aston Hall in Rotherham."

PART FOUR

Lady Frances

"Her letters show that she was (or fancied herself) very much in love with him ... her manner to me was very flattering, and her eyes played off most skilfully – but this is evidently her habit – the fishing always going on."

Thomas Moore

Chapter Sixteen

~ ~ ~

Arriving at Aston Hall, the "*urgent help*" that James Webster needed was nothing more than Byron's approval of a *political pamphlet* Webster had written and hoped to publish.

"Will you read it, Byron, and give me your honest opinion? You are better than I at this sort of thing."

Byron's fury was abated solely by the excited arrival of the poodle dog that had kept him company during his last visit. "*Nettle!*"

"And Nettle has been pining for you," James added. "After you had left he lay down on his paws and refused to eat a bite."

Byron stopped playing with the dog, looking at Webster. "And he can reside with me while I am here?"

"You can keep him. I give Nettle to you as a gift," James said generously. "On condition you help me with the wording of my pamphlet."

Lady Frances appeared, and seemed as excited as Nettle to see him. "Lord Byron, how *delightful* to have you with us again."

"Lady Frances," he moved to bow over her hand, but she moved both hands up to his shoulders and gave him a light kiss on each cheek as if greeting a beloved brother.

He quickly glanced at her jealous husband who, strangely, did not seem at all perturbed by his wife's affectionate behaviour. Not a bit, he seemed more joyous than anything else.

As they escorted him into the house, Byron sighed,

slightly amused as he found himself thinking – "Well, as they say in Nottingham, "*there's nowt as strange as folk.*" And James Webster, he concluded, was the strangest of them all.

~ ~ ~

Within a few days, Webster had returned to his old jealous self, and once again Byron was writing to Lady Melbourne.

My dear Lady M., – Well then, to begin, and first a word of mine host. He has lately been talking AT, rather than TO me, before the party presently here (with the exception of the women) in a tone, which, as I never use it myself, I am not particularly disposed to tolerate it in others.

This morning when he got me in private and alone he insisted upon boring me about his Countess. I told you I thought she was mercenary, and now I think she must be a diablesse and he has not bid high enough. When he asked for my opinion, I told him I would not give a Birmingham farthing for a woman who could or would be purchased – nor indeed for any woman – that is to say, unless I loved her for something more than her sex.

This must have annoyed him, because now tonight after dinner, when the women had left the room, he literally provoked and goaded me in front of the men by something not unlike bullying, indirect to be sure, *but obvious goading, that "he <u>would</u> do this, and he would do that" etc.,etc., and <u>he</u> thought that "any woman" was <u>his</u> lawful prize. Ooons! who is this strange monopolist?*

Then he proposed to me a bet, that he, for a certain sum, "wins any given woman, against any given homme, including <u>all friends present</u>", which I declined with becoming deference to him and the rest of the company. Is not this, at the moment, a perfect comedy?

Reading the letter in London, Lady Melbourne did indeed think it a comedy; laughing at the audacity of this self-loving friend of Lord Byron.

And yes, who was this monopolist, so full of his own prowess and self-esteem? And how long had he been buried away in the backwaters of Rotherham? Had he not been in London lately? Did he not know that Lord Byron was not only the Idol Poet of the day, but was now a romantic *icon* amongst all the young ladies of London's high society; and not only the young ladies, but all of their *maids* as well.

When Lord Byron arrived in any household – it was an *epic* event in the eyes of all the servants – all tripping over each other to get a closer look at him; and those maids he troubled himself to turn his blue gaze on, often swooned clean away.

No wonder most houses were using only their butlers and footmen to greet-in-the-hall and serve-in-the-dining-room now, although some of *them* were just as bad as the females.

As Lady Holland had so perfectly and laughingly phrased it one day, when some of the hostesses were complaining about the ridiculous behaviour of their servants with regard to Lord Byron – "*He kills the girls and thrills the boys*, and unless we lock them up we cannot stop them from staring."

It was a fact that wherever Byron arrived, he immediately conquered. Was it his charm, his smile, his beautiful looks, or his poetic genius – who could say? It was all down to some strange and fascinating charisma that Byron possessed.

And so this fellow, Webster ... he was now playing a very dangerous game if he thought he could taunt and bully Byron, and get away with it. Lord Byron's good manners went only so far – as Caroline had found out to her cost.

Lady Melbourne smiled to herself as she wondered what Byron would do next? He had a very *wicked* streak in him, she knew. But would his good manners prevail?

She felt immeasurably delighted that he had chosen herself, a woman of sixty-two, to be his guide and special *confidante* – and now she could not wait to receive his next letter.

~ ~ ~

In Aston Hall in Rotherham, during dinner, Lord Petersham had – twice now – referred to Byron and Webster's "*time at Cambridge*", and yet Webster had made no attempt to correct him. And when Byron sought to do so, Webster quickly spoke over him and denied him the opportunity.

Byron sat back in his chair, realising that Webster was clearly fearful of anyone knowing that he had *not* attended Cambridge, or indeed any university at all.

Then Lady Frances asked Byron a question about their time together at Harrow. "Is it true, Lord Byron, that while you were both at Harrow, it was James who gave you the most help with your Latin?"

Byron stared at Webster who quickly knocked back the last dregs in his wine glass and declared, "The Irish Catholics *must* be given some equality! On that I agree with Lord Byron, and that is what my *pamphlet* is all about."

Lord Petersham responded and took up the discussion while Byron sat back with his head lowered and a slight smile on his face as he realised that if he wished now, in this present company, he could get his revenge and expose Webster as a liar and a fraud and smash him down in one minute flat, because nothing of what he had obviously told others about himself was true.

He glanced at Lady Frances ... even his wife believed he had been educated at Harrow and Cambridge!

Well that was sort of true, because Webster *had* attended Harrow in 1800 at the age of twelve, but only for one month, before being thrown out due to his intolerable behaviour, and from then on he had been schooled at home by a tutor. Byron had not entered Harrow until the following year, so their paths had not crossed.

Lord Petersham was addressing him directly. "And was it at Harrow, Lord Byron, that you and James first became friends?"

"No..." Byron looked at Webster, saw the frantic expression on his face, and *no* – he couldn't do it.

"James entered Harrow a year before I did."

"And the two of you have been friends ever since?"

Byron nodded. "We have been friends for a long time."

Webster began to gabble then, distracting Petersham

and everyone else, allowing Byron to sit back quietly and think back on everything that James was trying so desperately to hide.

Webster and he were the same age, twenty-five, but they had first met in their teenage years in London, in the *fight* clubs.

In those days, while still at Harrow, Byron would go down to the gym of Gentleman John Jackson to learn how to fight his adversaries at Harrow, and to fight them hard. His limp had always made some of those Harrow toffs see him as an easy knock-down, but they soon learned that was not so.

Gentleman John Jackson had been the British bareknuckle boxing champion from 1795 until 1800, holding the title undefeated for five years, and under Jackson's training Byron had punched and sweated every weekend away, until he became a skilful hard hitter; and as the years passed he and Jackson became friends, going to the fight clubs together to watch the contests. Jackson had retired from the game and Tom Cribb was the new champion, and Cribb was their man.

One Saturday afternoon, at a fight club in Leicester Square, Bob Gregson, the promoter, introduced a new "young blood" to John Jackson and asked him to train him. "*He's got potential, but whether a future champ or no, it's too early to say.*"

That recommendation made Byron take a hard look at the youth, around the same age as himself, seventeen or so, and that was when and where he had met James Webster.

After that, the two of them frequently met in Jackson's gym, where Byron would watch him spar and wonder where Webster had ever got the notion that he could be a champ? But then he soon learned that

Webster had many notions, and all of them notions of grandeur in one form or another. He was always very deferential to Byron's rank, always calling him *Lord* Byron; and then he changed his own name to *James Wedderburn Webster,* saying to Byron, "It sounds so much better than plain James Webster and adds more gravity to my personage, don't you think?"

A pest of the first water, is what Byron thought of Webster, yet he could not help feeling sorry for him. He was an outrageous braggart and an absolute fool, but there was also something of the lost animal about him.

The only thing he found truly repugnant about Webster was his love of money. He would do *anything* for money. So instead of becoming a champion boxer, he became a champion pedestrian, walking and running great distances for money. For a wager of 500 guineas, an enormous sum, Webster had taken up the challenge and walked non-stop from Ipswich to Whitechapel, seventy miles, with Gentleman John Jackson travelling in an open carriage beside him to ensure no cheating. He covered 65 miles in 19 hours and so was left with five hours to do the rest at a stroll. Webster would have willingly walked from John O'Groats in Scotland to Land's End in Cornwall, if there was money to be gained from it.

A week or so later he took up another bet for 600 guineas to ride his mare non-stop from London to Brighton which he managed to do in 3 hours and 19 minutes, which led Byron to reckon he had rode at an average of 16 miles an hour, earning him the new nickname of "Bold Webster". The fact that his poor mare was half dead at the end of it, Webster tried to remedy by feeding her a tankard of red wine, after which, she collapsed and expired.

Within a month though, Webster had lost all his winnings to his walking rival, Captain Barclay, by betting him a thousand guineas that he could not walk a thousand miles in a thousand hours. A man could live very well for a year on a thousand guineas, so Barclay took the bet and kept walking until he had won it.

While Byron was at Cambridge, Webster joined the Army and then dropped out in order to join the Navy, and after a short spell on a 65-ton man o'war, *HMS Lion,* he dropped out of the Navy to go to Lincoln's Inn to study to become a lawyer, which also did not last long.

But then, at the age of twenty-one, just a few days before Byron had set sail for Greece – Webster, upon reaching his majority, had inherited a fortune, married a daughter of Lord Mountnorris – and now here he was in the great mansion of Aston Hall in Rotherham – Lord of the Manor with gold knobs on.

"Damn it, Byron, are you *asleep?"* Byron looked up and Webster looked outraged. "The *ladies* are about to leave the room!"

Byron scrambled to his feet and stood with rest of the men as Lady Frances, her sister Lady Catherine, and Lady Sitwell departed, wishing he could depart too.

Fuming now that Webster had barked *at* him, instead of addressing him politely, Byron contemplated whether to draw him aside into the corridor and give him a swift punch in the jaw, or to leave here at first light in the morning ... but then, with a sudden and really *wicked* thought, he decided to exact his revenge upon Webster in another way.

~ ~ ~

At his desk in London, John Murray finished reading

the pages in front of him and looked up, amazed. What a truly *unpredictable* young man Lord Byron was.

Only last week he had said in a letter that his determination was not to write any more poetry, and yet today in the post had arrived this beautiful piece of poetry from him, *The Bride of Abydos,* the tragic love story of Selim and Zuleika, sent from Newstead.

What had brought about this change of heart, John Murray could not even begin to guess. Despite their growing friendship, Byron was still a mystery to him in many ways. The only thing he knew for certain was that when his emotions were stirred, Byron could be extremely potent.

~ ~ ~

In Aston Hall, especially during luncheon and dinner, whenever Webster's face was turned away from him, Byron occupied himself in looking long and thoughtfully at Webster's wife, Lady Frances; and that young married lady of twenty years old, who was well aware of him looking at her so thoughtfully, was beginning to get in a bit of a dither, blushing and trembling and knocking over her wine glass.

Yet Byron remained remote from her, keeping his distance; while also keeping in mind Webster's boast that *he* could, "win any given *woman* against any given *homme*, including *all friends present."*

The man really needed to be taught a lesson in how to treat one's friends and guests.

Lord Petersham had been flirting outrageously with Lady Frances from the moment he had arrived, while Byron looked on with amusement, and Webster looked hugely gratified while whispering to Byron – *"She won't go wrong, so he's wasting his time. Come and have a game of billiards with me."*

In the Billiard Room, before the game had even begun, Webster dashed off to add "*a very important sentence*" to his infernal political pamphlet, shouting over his shoulder, "I'll be back. I'll be back in a mo! You get in some practise while you're waiting!"

Byron picked up the stick and lazily started potting one ball after another ... "*get in some practise*" ... damned cheek! He had been playing billiards since he was thirteen years old, from his first term at Harrow.

He was still leisurely potting the balls, when Lady Frances walked in.

"Lord Byron ... may I join you in a game?"

He looked at her with some surprise. "You play billiards?"

"Oh, yes," she said softly, "I am very good at billiards, and far better than *il marito.*"

Italian for – the husband.

"And il marito,*"* he said*, "*will be back at any moment to play a game also."

"Then may we ... may we play until he returns?"

Byron smiled. "If you wish."

And the game began.

~ ~ ~

My dear Lady Melbourne, – In these last few days I have had a good deal of conversation with an amiable person, whom (as we always use initials in letters) I will denominate Ph. Well, these things are dull in detail. Take it once, I have made verbal love, and if I am to believe mere <u>words</u> (for there we have hitherto stopped) it is returned.

The place of her declaration was a billiard room, where she asked me a very odd question – "how a woman who liked a man could inform him of it when he did not perceive it?"

We went on with our game (of billiards) without either of us counting the hazards, until I then took a very imprudent step with pen and paper and answered her.

My note was received and read, and deposited inside her bodice to a place not very far from her heart, when who should enter the room but the person who ought at that moment to have been in the Red Sea, if the Devil had any civility. But <u>she</u> kept her countenance, and the paper; and I my composure.

(I am at this moment interrupted in the library by the <u>Marito</u> and write this before him, he has brought me his political pamphlet in manuscript to decipher and applaud, I shall content myself with the last; oh, he is gone again)

My note produced an answer, a very unequivocal one too, but a little too much about virtue and the ethereal process in which the soul is principally concerned, which I don't very well understand, being a bad metaphysician.

I need not say that the arrogance of Webster has tended to all this. If a man is not contented with a *pretty woman, and not only runs after every little country girl he meets, but absolutely boasts of it; he must not be surprised if others admire that which he knows not how to value.*

Ever yrs, B.

P.S. 6 o'clock – This business is growing serious, and I think "Platonism" is in some peril. There has been very nearly a scene, almost a hysteric, and really without cause. Her expressions of love astonish me, as she had first appeared so cold.

She says she is convinced that my own first declaration was produced solely because I perceived her previous penchant, which by-the-by, I neither perceived nor expected. I really did not suspect her of a predilection for anyone, and even now in public, with the exception of those little indirect yet mutually understood LOOKS of hers, her conduct is coldly correct.

Yet this evening, in the midst of our mutual professions – or, to use her own expression, "more than mutual" she burst into an agony of crying. Had anyone come in during her "tears" and my subsequent tender consolation, all would have been spoiled. Fortunately we managed to restore sunshine, but we must be more cautious.

She later managed to slip me a note before Webster's

very face, yet she is a thorough devotee and takes prayers morning and evening, besides being measured for a new Bible once a quarter.

I hear his voice in the passage; he wants me to go to a ball at Sheffield, and is now talking to me as I write.

~ ~ ~

In London, during the following week, Lady Melbourne's eyeglass was constantly being lifted and lowered as she read and laughed her way through a number of Byron's letters. To seduce a man's wife in response to a wager, or out of revenge, was shocking; yet she knew Lord Byron was *wickedly* enjoying himself.

My dear Lady Melbourne,– you must pardon the quantity of my letters, and much of the quality also. Anything, you will allow, is better than my dwelling on the <u>past</u> *– but you won't pity me, and I don't deserve it anyway.*

Nearly a scene (always nearly) at dinner. As it is necessary to separate the ladies at table, I was under the necessity of placing myself between Lady Sitwell and mine hostess's sister Lady Catherine.

I was seated, and in the agonies of conjecture about whether the dish before me needed carving, when my little Platonist exclaimed, "Lord Byron, THIS is your place." I stared, and before I had time to reply, she repeated, "Lord Byron, change places with Catherine."

I did, and mine host roared out, "Byron, that is the most ungallant thing I ever beheld."

Lady Catherine, by way of mending matters, answered, "Did you not hear Frances ask him?"

HE has looked like the Board of GREEN Cloth ever since, and is now mustering wine and spirits for a lecture to her, and a squabble with me. He had better leave it alone, for I am in a pestilent humour at present, and I shall certainly end by disparaging his eternal political pamphlet.

Monday afternoon

We are going to Newstead, the whole party of us, for a week, in a few days, and there the genii of the place will be perhaps more propitious.

Her eyes are always looking at me, captivating me, but HE haunts me – here he is again, and here are a party of purple stockings come to dine. Oh, that accursed pamphlet! I have not read it; what shall I say to the author now in the room? Thank the stars he is now diverted by the mirror opposite, and is now observing, with great complacency, himself – he is gone!

I mentioned to you yesterday a laughable occurrence at dinner. This morning HE burst forth with a homily on the subject to the TWO sisters and myself, instead of talking to us separately.

You will easily suppose with such odds he had the worst of it, and the satisfaction of being laughed at into the bargain. Serious as I am – or seem – I cannot easily keep a straight face.

Your letter has arrived, but it was evidently written before my last three were delivered. Adieu for the present. You are right, she is "very pretty" and not so inanimate as I imagined.

Yrs ever, BYRON

Chapter Seventeen

~ ~ ~

Joe Murray was delighted to see his lordship arrive back at Newstead, and with a party of friends too, and all seemed so merry; although he did not take kindly to Mr Webster walking into the hall and bellowing to the servants: "*Your welcome for Lord Byron! Stand by and bow.*"

"He is being humorously sarcastic," Byron said to Joe, but Joe Murray was not appeased. He did not like sarcasm, not in his hall, and not anywhere else within Newstead Abbey.

The Abbey became a flurry of activity as the cooking began and guest rooms were being prepared. Yet before they had even climbed the stairs, Webster and his wife began a dispute about their apartments at Newstead. A dispute that continued in front of his lordship; and even – to Joe's horror – in front of some of the *servants*.

Lady Frances was insisting to her husband that she wanted her sister to share her bedchamber.

Joe listened as Mr Webster responded by giving his wife a long lecture on the subject, maintaining that "none but husbands have any legal claim to divide their spouse's pillow."

His lordship looked uncomfortable at such an embarrassing scene, and seemed about to say something, but at the same moment Lady Frances turned and said to him in a sweet voice, "*N'importe,* this is all nothing."

My dear Lady M.,

I write to you from the melancholy mansion of my fathers, where I am as dull as the longest deceased of my progenitors. I hate reflection on irrevocable things, and won't now turn sentimentalist.

Today at Breakfast (I was too late for the scene) he attacked both the sisters in such a manner, that one had left the room, and the other had half a mind to leave the house; this too in front of the servants and the other guest! On my appearance the storm blew over, but the details were told to me subsequently by one of the sufferers.

I shall not quarrel with him if I can avoid it. I must remember the advice given to me in a letter by a sage personage while I was abroad – take it in their English – "Remember, milord, that 'delicaci' ensures every success."

Yrs ever, B.

P.S.– I begged you to pacify Caroline, who is now pettish about what she calls a "cold" letter in response to hers so friendly. She has evidently been too long quiet. She threatens me with growing very bad, and says that if so, I "am the sole cause". This I should regret, but she is in no danger; no one in his senses will run the risk, until her late exploits are forgotten.

Joe Murray was like a hawk, watching everyone and everything and wishing his lordship had not brought

Wedderburne Webster to Newstead.

It seemed as if his lordship was wishing it also, because now Joe saw that he was not spending much time with his party of friends, choosing instead to go off alone on long walks with his dogs.

This disturbed Joe, who was hoping that now his lordship was back at Newstead, he was not looking towards Annesley and fretting himself again about Mary Chaworth?

~ ~ ~

The buff-coloured kid gloves lay on her dressing table like a cherished memento. She would not allow her maid to put them in a drawer; she wanted them *there,* where she could see them, and occasionally clasp them to her heart in fond memory ... the buff gloves that Byron had brought back to her from Newstead.

She sat down on the dressing-stool and looked at herself in the mirror. She was still wearing her dark-green riding habit, still wearing her black hat and black kid gloves, but her face was stark white, like the face of someone who has just received a shock.

And she had just received a shock. Upon hearing that his lordship was back in residence at Newstead, she had been unable to resist the impulse of riding over there, to dear Newstead, just to the edges of the trees overlooking the pond of the back gardens of the house, safely hidden behind the branches where she could watch in case Byron came outside.

And he had come outside, but not alone; a young woman was holding onto his arm and the two of them were strolling together, talking to each other and chuckling together, as if sharing some private jest.

Mary could not believe it ... so quickly he had found

another. He looked content enough, and had evidently forgotten her completely.

And then there was just dimness and a chilling sense of loss as she quietly turned her horse around and rode slowly back to Annesley.

Now her face stared back at her from the mirror, like white marble, as she desperately wondered ... *How can you mend a broken heart? ... How can you stop the pain?*

"Oh, there you are!" Ann Radford entered the room and instantly rushed to put a hand on Mary's shoulder. "I hope you did not ride too far, dear?"

Mary eyes lifted slowly from her own face to look at Ann Radford's face through the mirror. "I did, yes, far enough to see how stupid I have been."

Ann placed her hands to the side of Mary's face and murmured, "Oh, your face is so *cold*. Riding out in this autumn weather is not good for you. What you need is a hot drink."

"I need *him*," Mary said, and melted into tears as if in mortal pain. "You should *not* have made me send him away with such brutal cruelty."

"Cruelty?"

"*Yes,* to myself!" Mary cried. "Cruelty to *myself!* He was my dear friend! And I loved *everything* about him."

"Nonsense! What you felt was nothing more than sinful infatuation. Mary, listen to me, you have been unwell, and are still recovering, and in that state one can have any amount of sentimental thoughts about people in our past. Illness makes us think foolish things."

Mary was crying silently now, and Ann Radford's high hard face looked hurt, and her voice filled with reproach.

"I am hurt and shocked that you could think I would ever advise you to do anything that was not in your best interests."

Mary lifted her tear-stained face and Ann Radford nodded her head wisely. "Already I have heard that he arrived back at Newstead with a party of friends that includes Lady Catherine Annesley, who is only eighteen and unmarried, and they say Lord Byron is courting her."

"Lady Catherine Annesley?" Mary stared in front of her, remembering that even in the distance of her view from behind the trees ... there *was* something familiar about the young woman holding onto Byron's arm. She shuddered at the thought.

"If Byron is courting her, then I hope she is not like her older sister, Lady *Frances* Annesley ... or Webster as she is now ... I last saw her two years ago in London and I thought her to be very cold-blooded and extremely vain."

~ ~ ~

Having dressed for dinner, Byron was in his bedroom reading a letter from his attorney, John Hanson, when Fletcher entered holding another letter.

"Lady Frances slipped this into my hand and whispered that I must give it to you immediately."

Byron smiled wryly. "No doubt she is making some special menu requirement for dinner."

"It's sealed," Fletcher pointed out, "see, the red seal on it? So I don't think it's anything to do with the menu for dinner. And anyway, dinner is already cooked and ready to be served."

Byron looked at him. "Fletcher, would you be so kind as to do me a great favour?"

"Aye, my lord, just say it."

"Scram!"

When Fletcher had left the room Byron broke open the seal of the letter, his eyes widening as he read it ... from all outward appearances he would never have guessed that Lady Frances could be so fearfully romantic.

" ... If you knew how my heart leaps on seeing you after a separation of only one hour, for till I knew you, I knew not what it was to adore a person ...

The gong was banging for dinner, and as host Byron had to get down there first.

He placed the letter aside and made his way down the stairs, and with every step he could feel his growing guilt about James Webster, irritating idiot that he was. He had won over the heart of his wife, received her declaration of love, but would he cuckold him and take her? Would he?

Throughout dinner Lady Frances said little, but kept giving him those *looks* of hers that would interfere with any man's concentration, until Webster lost his patience.

"Byron, what the devil is *wrong* with you tonight? If you start a sentence have the decency to finish it. You have me all in a muddle with your starting and stopping and then pausing to make a long inspection of your plate as if it was the only thing of interest in the room."

"James, really..." said Lord Petersham, somewhat disturbed, "that is no way to speak to our kind host."

"Oh, he *knows* I don't mean it in a rude or bad way. We are old and good friends and a man never had one better. At least, *I* never have."

Surprised at this declaration of close friendship,

Byron looked at Webster. "Did you say you are returning to Rotherham tomorrow?"

James nodded. "Yes, and you will return with us I hope?

"No. Tomorrow I must return to London on business. My attorney demands it."

Lady Frances dropped her fork and then fumbled with her napkin. A moment later she flashed a strange look at her husband, as if she despised him.

Byron's attention returned to his plate, thinking how terrible it must be to find yourself married to someone whom you had grown to despise.

While Petersham and Webster gabbled away, and Lady Frances had her head bent, Byron gave her an underlook and wondered how he *really* felt about her ...

She was very beautiful, so much so that any man would be attracted to her, and surely she was the most *agreeable* female he had ever met, perpetually saying to him, "Rather than you should be angry," or "Rather than you should like anyone else, I will do whatever you please, I won't speak to this person, or that person or the other if you dislike it," and continually throwing herself upon his discretion in every respect that it completely disarmed him. And all the loving little kisses she gave him in secret were like a comforting balm to his heart after the pain of Mary's dismissal.

"But I am really wretched with the perpetual conflict within myself," he wrote later that night to Lady Melbourne. *"Her health is very delicate, and she is so thin and pale and seems to have lost her appetite so entirely that I doubt her living much longer. This is also her own opinion. But these fancies are common to*

all who are not happy. If she were my own wife, a warm climate should be the first resort for her recovery. "

On his way back down to the Blue Room, where Webster and Lord Petersham were drinking brandy and talking so boringly about the *three-per-cents* and other more competitive interest-rates ... Byron almost collided into Lady Frances in the dark passage.

"I have been waiting for you," she whispered. "We cannot part tomorrow, we cannot."

"Frances ..."

Her hands touched his face." I am entirely at your *mercy*," she whispered. "I give myself up to you ... I am not *cold*, whatever others may say, but I know I will not be able to bear the reflection on my loss of virtue afterwards. Yet what else can I do? When I feel about you as I do?"

She moved her lips up to his and kissed him. "Now, take me to your room and act as you will."

"Frances ..." He was at a loss as to what to do next. There was something so very *peculiar* in her manner, and the *tone* of her voice ...

And yet, she seemed very surprised when he said, "Frances ... your husband is sitting and waiting for me in the room below. I must go down."

She dropped her head onto his chest and fell into another agony of tears. "Oh, don't betray me now after all our closeness! Don't say I have made a *fool* of myself."

He comforted her and kissed her and felt very relieved when Lady Catherine came along the passage looking for her sister.

"Frances ... are you there?"

Lady Catherine held up her candle and looked very suspicious when she saw them standing together; and then her expression changed to one of amusement.

"Frances, *I* am going to bed. Will you retire also, or –"

"Yes, yes, I am coming..." Frances wiped a hand over her wet face. "I was merely confiding my sorrow about the death of poor Primrose to Lord Byron. And he, being a dog-lover also, understood my grief and was very kindly consoling me."

The amusement was back on Lady Catherine's face as she put an arm around Frances to lead her away saying, "Goodnight, Lord Byron. And thank-you for comforting Frances in her time of need."

Byron turned up his eyes as they departed, and then quickly made his way downstairs to join the men, certain that Lady Catherine had not been fooled by her sister's excuse. What *was* strange though, was why Lady Catherine should be so *amused* by it.

Upon entering the Blue Room he was greeted by a narrowed look of suspicion from Lord Petersham. "Ah, there you are! James has been waiting to have a very serious talk with you."

"No, no," James said stiffly. "I shall choose my own time."

"Then I wonder why you did not choose your own *house* also," Byron replied irritably. "I am the landlord here at Newstead, so if you have something to say to me, Webster, then say it."

Lord Petersham appeared very surprised at Byron's response.

He quickly stood up and knocked back the last of his brandy. "The hour is late, so time for me to retire. Goodnight, gentlemen."

When Petersham had left, in the long silence that

followed, Byron stood with his hand on the mantelpiece looking at Webster. "Well, out with it."

Webster leaned to refill his glass from the side-table, and then sat back with a gloomy hangdog look on his face.

"Yes, I do want to have a serious talk with you, Byron, and I may as well do it now ... " he took a sip of his drink, "but this is all very embarrassing for me."

"How so?"

"Frances ... I'm sure you have noticed how unhappy she is, constantly weeping, but it really is *not* my fault. The girl is an *Earl's* daughter and so has very expensive tastes and requires a certain standard of living ... and now ... well now she wants me to go down to London and arrange a purchase for her, but I really do not have the cash ... not at the moment, and not for a month or two."

Byron frowned. "So this serious talk with me ... is about *money*?"

"Not for me, for *Frances;* and as you and she seem to have become such good friends, and you and I have long been good friends ... I thought you might consider helping me out with a loan?"

Chapter Eighteen

~ ~ ~

The following morning two carriages stood outside Newstead Abbey, waiting for the guests to depart.

There was no sign of James Webster so Byron occupied himself saying farewell to Lady Catherine, and then to Lady Frances – who clasped his hands in her own and whispered to him desperately – "*We must not part for long, we cannot.*"

Before he could answer, Webster appeared and walked towards Byron's carriage. "I'm going south with you, Byron. Lord Petersham has agreed to escort the ladies back to Rotherham."

Byron stared. The *last* thing he wanted or needed now was Webster travelling all the way back to London with him. He said: "You made no mention of this last night."

"No, but now I also have business in London, and so I decided I may as well go with you and have some company on the journey."

Byron could think of no way to refuse him, and stood watching as Webster kissed his wife's cheek in farewell, and then laughingly chided her for her tears. "Why are you crying, Frances? I will be back in a few days!"

Francis nodded, and slowly walked towards her carriage, while staring tearfully at Byron and raising her hand in a slight wave.

"You see how she *dotes* on me," Webster said as the two carriages moved off.

He made himself comfortable on the seat opposite and then sat back with a sigh. "Byron," said he, "I owe to you all the most *unhappy* moments of my life."

Byron looked at him wryly. "Tell me how, so I may sympathise."

"You saw it for yourself – how the poor girl *dotes* on me, and now that I have quit her for a week she is absolutely overwhelmed with grief at my absence – in a worse state than I ever saw her in before, even before we married!"

"So how am I responsible for that?"

"How? The answer is *sex!*" said Webster. "And my unhappy lack of it lately. Frances will never agree to have sex if we have guests in the house. She has a particular aversion to it on those occasions."

"It was you who asked me to return to Aston Hall," Byron reminded him.

"Yes, but you stayed so long! And then Frances made us all come over to Newstead for another week; and then your talk of a ghostly monk frightened Catherine so much that Frances felt duty-bound to sleep with her sister, and now she is deprived of me for even longer. You saw her tears. You saw what a state she is in."

Under any other circumstances, and with anyone else, Byron knew he would have stopped the carriage and thrown the insolent idiot out of it; yet he could not help feeling sorry for Webster and his delusions about his wife. Even Lord Petersham had slyly commented on her lack of interest in *il marito*.

"No matter," Webster said. "Why let *any* woman come between two men who have been friends since their youth. Let's enjoy our journey in good companionship and may all else be forgotten."

~ ~ ~

"You fool! You absolute fool!"

Now back in London, John Hobhouse was beside himself with fury when Byron gave him a full and truthful account of it all.

"And pray, why have you told *me* all this?"

Byron shrugged. "Because you, Hobby, are the one man from whom I keep no secrets."

"You fool!" Hobby said again. "You were used and manipulated and played perfectly like a game of cards. And now I'm wondering which one made the bet? Was it *him*, or was it *her*, or did both of them plan it together?"

Byron hadn't a clue as to what Hobhouse was suggesting. He moved Leander aside and sat up on the sofa. "What are you talking about?"

"High-class prostitution."

"*What?* " Byron stared at Hobhouse as if he was mad.

"It could be," Hobby said, "or something very like it. My guess is that she would never have given herself to you, and the sister came along the passage right on cue."

Now it was Byron who was outraged. "Hobby, how the devil *dare* you even suggest such a thing about Lady Frances? I ask – how bloody *dare* you?"

Hobby's face remained grave. "I would say the true *dare* was for one thousand pounds. That *is* what Webster took off you in the end – a cheque for *a thousand* pounds?"

"No," Byron replied, somewhat stunned at the possibility of truth in what Hobhouse was saying. "I agreed to loan him the money, of course I did, because he is an old friend and he appeared to be financially desperate."

"And you were feeling guilty for flirting so dangerously with his wife..."

Byron was frowning. "But now you have made me think more about it ... there *was* something odd about her behaviour that night ... And later, after agreeing to the loan, when I returned from my room with my cheque book, Webster asked me if I would write out *two* cheques; one for five hundred pounds made out to Lady Frances, and the other for five hundred pounds made out to himself."

"Then they were *both* in on it," Hobby decided. "A winning cheque for each of them. And do you see now how the game was played, Byron? He sends you an urgent letter asking you to return to Rotherham, and when you do, *he* keeps goading you with small insults and large bets that *he* could win any given woman over you; and *she* in the meantime weaves you into her web with her eyes and tears and kisses."

Byron still found it hard to believe.

"And then," Hobby said, "upon hearing you are returning to London the following day, she even goes out of her way to offer you *more* of her charms, compromising you, and all only minutes *before* he has the nerve to ask you for the astronomical sum of one *thousand* pounds. An average family could live well for three or four years on that amount."

Byron's face had turned very pale. "It's not the money, it's the *trickery* ... that's if there was any trickery. This is all guesswork on your part."

"Well, let us look at the evidence," said Hobhouse, who was now studying to be a lawyer as well as a politician.

"James Webster, upon reaching his majority of twenty-one," Hobby continued, as if he was standing in a court, "inherited a large sum of money from the East India Company, which should have gone to his father, but as he was deceased it went to his son James instead, which allowed James to aggrandise himself by marrying the daughter of an Earl."

Byron was not really listening, more absorbed in thinking he was the world's biggest fool.

"After two years of marriage, the Websters had spent the lot on horse-racing and high living, leaving them flat broke, and Webster finally had to go to Scrope Davies looking for a loan."

"Scrope Davies?" Byron was startled. "Scrope has also loaned money to Webster?"

Hobby nodded. "He will never get it back. Neither will you. You both fell at the feet of Lady Frances, and that's the price Webster has made you pay."

"No, no," Byron shook his head, finding it all too absurd to believe – "the Websters hold a lot of wealth in *assets*. Aston Hall and its estate, for a start. That must be worth a fortune."

"It is, to the owner, but the Websters are merely renting it."

"Renting it?" It was just one shock after another. Byron stared at Hobby who seemed to know everything. "Do you know, are their *dogs* rented too? Because Webster *gave* me one as a gift."

"Another dog?" Hobhouse looked around him. "I see only Leander, so where is it?"

"At Newstead."

After a long silence, Hobhouse said consolingly, "You are not the first, and you won't be the last. Who was the guest who tagged along with you all?"

"Lord Petersham."

"And did he have schoolboy eyes for Lady Frances also?"

"Even more than I."

"Then God help him, because Webster will have him fleeced to the skin before Christmas."

Hobby stood up, still furious. "So you now take this as a lesson, Byron, to have nothing more to do with the Websters. Come, I'll buy you dinner at the Cocoa Tree to cheer you up."

Despite all efforts, Byron found it impossible to feel cheerful, still unable to believe that after all his humorous jesting about Webster in his letters to Lady Melbourne; the final joke was on him.

Later that night, he wrote a last letter about the Websters to Lady Melbourne, finally conceding –

"Perhaps I was her dupe. Or perhaps I duped myself. Or maybe with all women I am a born fool. In future I shall have non't to do with any of them."

PART FIVE

Sister Of My Soul

*'For thee – my own sweet Sister – in thy heart
I know myself secure - as thou in mine.'*

'Epistle to Augusta' – BYRON

Chapter Nineteen

~ ~ ~

Byron was soon back in the swing of his London social life, his only female companion at society parties and soirees being his sister; although when he dutifully dropped Augusta off from his carriage outside St James's Palace, and always before midnight, never once did it occur to Augusta that he was not going straight home to bed and sleep himself.

She had no idea that as soon as he had left her, he always headed straight for the Cocoa Tree Club, where he enjoyed himself wining and jesting with his friends and some of the young *belles* at the club, until five or six in the morning.

Minor events that he rarely remembered to log down in his journal.

Tue. 30th

Two days missed in my logbook. They were as little worthy of reflection as the rest.

Sunday I dined with Lord Holland. Large party. Holland's society is very good; you always meet someone worth knowing.

Why does Lady Holland always have that damned screen between the room and the fire? I, who can stand cold no better than an antelope, was perished, and could not even shiver. All the rest, too, looked as if they were just unpacked, like salmon from an ice basket.

When she retired, I watched their looks as I removed the screen, and every cheek thawed, and every nose reddened with the anticipated heat and glow.

Today (Tuesday) a very pretty letter from Madame de Staël. She is pleased to be very pleased with my mention of her in my last notes. I spoke as I thought. Her works are my delight, and so is she herself, for — half an hour.

She adulates and flatters me very prettily in her note, but I KNOW it. If all she says is true, she should have thought of it before she told Lady Holland that I was "un démon."

Fletcher knocked and popped his head round the door. "Mr Moore is here, my lord"

"Then show him in."

Tommy came in carrying a bag of fruit and muttering apologies.

"My dear Byron, I know I should *not* have taken it upon myself without asking your permission first, but I promised a friend that I would introduce you."

"Then do so." Byron looked towards the open door. "Is he here with you now?"

"No, he's in jail."

"In jail?"

Moore nodded. "I'm on my way to see him."

"In his prison cell?" Byron put down his pen and sat back. "So I suppose that bag of fruit is for him. Who is this lucky man?"

"Leigh Hunt. You may have heard of him?"

"No."

"He and his brother owned the *Examiner,* a liberal newspaper in which they courageously made a savage attack on the morals and politics of the Prince Regent, which resulted in both of them being arrested and sentenced to two years' imprisonment."

"In this land of liberty and free speech?" Byron was outraged. "What did they say about him – HRH?"

Moore shrugged. "Oh, nothing more than what everybody already knows ... that he was 'a violator of his word, and a libertine who was head and ears in debt and disgrace'.

"Which prison are they in?"

"Leigh Hunt is in Horsemonger Lane Jail. His brother was sent to Clerkenwell."

"And to which prison do you request my company?"

"Horsemonger Lane."

"Then let us go!"

On their way out Byron paused to help himself to a bottle of brandy from the drinks cabinet. "No offence, Tom, but I think a man in prison would enjoy a drop of this more than a bag of fruit."

Upon entering the jail, Byron was surprised to find the man whom he later nicknamed "*the wit in the dungeon*" to be comfortably in possession of two rooms, freshly wallpapered and painted – with books, paintings and even a pianoforte around him; as well as a little trellised-garden in the yard outside. And even more amazing, was the fact that Leigh Hunt was still editing the *Examiner* from his prison quarters.

Leigh Hunt was highly flattered, a bundle of smiles and delight at finally meeting Lord Byron; while Byron stood looking around him with some perplexity.

"Is *this* what prison is like for everyone?"

"This is all thanks to a very lenient and *liberal*

governor," said Leigh Hunt. "And my friends, of course. They were determined to make me as comfortable as possible, especially Shelley." He looked at Byron. "Have you met Shelley? Percy Shelley? He is a poet like yourself."

"No, I have never met him, but I have *read* him. Although what I read was not poetry, but a pamphlet entitled *'The Necessity of Atheism'*."

Leigh Hunt chuckled. "Shelley was kicked out and sent down from Oxford for writing that. What did you think of it?"

"Well..." Byron shrugged, "it would put a stop all the squabbling between the various religions I suppose."

"Shelley is a great admirer of yours, Lord Byron. Of your politics *and* your poetry, as I am also."

"And yet it is *your* politics that has brought me here. Would you like some brandy?"

They drew up chairs around the table and Tom Moore sat back and listened while Byron and Leigh Hunt talked about nothing but English politics for over an hour. Byron's primary concern was still the fate of the textile workers in Nottingham and Yorkshire, but he could see no way of holding back the progress of machinery.

"Progress in anything cannot be stopped," Byron said, "but some sort of arrangements should have been made for the protection of the unemployed workers, especially those men with families and children to feed."

Leigh Hunt smiled. "You sound just like Shelley. And I agree, I agree, I have four children myself."

Later Tom joined in, matching his wit against Leigh Hunt, causing much laughter between the three, especially when Byron sent out for dinner to be brought in from a nearby cookhouse, although he did not eat a morsel of it himself.

"That's the finest feast I've had in months," said Leigh Hunt, reaching for more brandy, "although my wife regularly brings me in one of her meat pies."

His wife arrived a short time later, with two other women, and all three seemed to have been rendered speechless at the sight and name of Lord Byron.

Thomas Moore could see that Byron was immediately uncomfortable under their stares, and although Leigh Hunt begged them to stay a while longer, Tom insisted very abruptly that they must leave.

And once outside Moore was fuming. "I told Leigh Hunt, I made it *very clear* to him, that should *you* come to visit him with me, then in deference to your privacy, he must *not allow* any other visitors to be present."

Byron looked at Tommy with high amusement. "The man is in jail, Tom. What else did you expect him to do? Tell the turnkey to inform his other visitors that he was '*not at home today*'"?

Tommy began to realise the ridiculousness of his grumbling, agreeing with Byron that Leigh Hunt was to be applauded for sticking by his principles and refusing to recant even a word about the Prince Regent.

Byron said: "The facts are that the Prince of Wales *did* betray all his Whig allies by switching to the Tories as soon as he was made Regent. So he *did* violate his word to the Whigs about Catholic emancipation. And we are not talking solely about the Irish Catholics, but *English* Catholics too. How can his rule and sovereignty be on a *national* scale when half of the English people are denied many political rights because of their religion?"

Arriving home, Byron had such admiration for Leigh Hunt in sticking to his principles, he immediately wrote a letter to the Fortnum & Mason's store, requesting a hamper of wine and a selection of cooked meats and the finest cheeses to be sent at regular intervals to Mr L. Hunt at Horsemonger Lane Jail.

And while he was writing his order to Fortnum's, the "lenient" governor of the Jail was writing down an account of the length of Lord Byron's visit to the politically *radical* prisoner, Leigh Hunt; and then immediately dispatched it to the government office of Lord Liverpool, where it was noted down for future use.

~ ~ ~

Hobhouse was silently furious with Thomas Moore for dragging Byron off to a jail to visit an out-and-out *radical* against the government. Moore was Irish, so he would already have been recorded as a "dissenter" whether he was one or not; but Byron needed to be more careful.

"How sad," Hobby said sarcastically, when Byron told him that Thomas Moore had returned to his wife and cottage in Derbyshire.

"His wife is pregnant again and, if it's a boy, they intend to name him Byron after me."

"How typical," Hobby sniffed. "And no doubt Moore will add Holland and Jersey and a few more lords to the boy's name before he's finished."

"Oh yes, Tommy loves a lord," Byron grinned, showing Hobhouse that he was not completely unaware of Moore's social-climbing tendencies. "But he's a good man, and a genuine friend to me, so I'll not hear you say another word against him."

"More like *you* are a genuine friend to him. Are you going to Lady Jersey's bash tonight?"

"Yes, and I will be escorting Augusta."

Hobby was not a bit surprised. Ever since the heartbreak of Mary Chaworth, which had sent him rebounding into the arms of the dubious Lady Frances Webster, Byron now appeared to trust only one woman, his sister, Augusta.

Chapter Twenty

~ ~ ~

As a Lady-in-Waiting at St James's Palace, Augusta's manner was always quiet, respectful and strait-laced in every way; but once her period of duty was over, she usually spent her time off in the company of her brother, with whom she laughed a lot.

"You would have laughed," Byron would say, when relating some amusing incident to her, "*our* laugh, the Byron laugh."

Augusta was thoroughly enjoying all the humour and laughter, especially as her husband, George Leigh, was more prone to frowning than smiling, although in fairness he did have a lot of worries to suffer.

And yet, Augusta thought with some resentment ... all her husband's *money-worries* did not prevent him from having his own valet at his side wherever he travelled, nor good clothes of the highest quality.

And when he *was* at home – unlike Byron, he did not take any time to inquire about *her* life, or *her* problems in any way. Nor did he go to any great effort to cheer her under the gloom and weight of it all – no, all the worries were *his* to suffer, and *his* alone; while she was expected to simply keep house, bear children, and somehow make a shilling stretch as far as a pound every day of the week.

So no wonder she was enjoying herself up in London in the amusing company of her kind and caring half-brother, who had spared no expense when insisting on getting her measured for a fine new wardrobe of evening clothes to wear – even if he did turn up his eyes at some of the "dowdy" styles she chose.

Augusta had her own reason for not choosing the slinky styles of the day. Within a month or two of first coming up to London, she had suspected that she was pregnant again, but that was a secret she intended to keep to herself for as long as possible. She was enjoying not only her work at St James's Palace, but also the company of the other Ladies-in-Waiting, as well as the *pay* she received.

She would wait, she had decided, until she returned home at Christmas before informing George that another child was on the way; but in the meantime she would enjoy every last minute of her time here in London in the company of the brother she now adored.

~ ~ ~

Of all people, no one knew better than John Hobhouse how much Augusta's affection for Byron was reciprocated in full – having been obliged to listen to him so many times referring to Augusta now as the "*sister of my soul*" or "*my second self.*"

Hobhouse felt and always showed respect for Augusta, because she was his friend's sister, and with himself she was always polite and sensible in her manner, which he liked: but there were other times, when Augusta and Byron got into one of their mutual humours, Hobby saw Augusta change before his eyes, laughing hysterically like a girl of twelve or fourteen, which often made Hobby wonder if she was not only Byron's half-sister, but also a half-wit.

She certainly was not an intellectual or *clever* woman, and she made no pretence of being such, habituated as she was to looking after people and serving them. And in the same way, she now spent a lot of her time fussing over Byron with motherly concern for his welfare.

So much so that at a party one night, Lady Jersey whispered to Hobhouse: "*She acts more like his mother than his sister.*"

And Hobby could not disagree.

~ ~ ~

Lady Caroline Lamb's absolute *detestation* of Augusta Leigh was based on no fault of the woman herself, for Caroline did not know her, but her very presence in the salons of London society infuriated Caroline.

"Why is it," she said crossly to Lady Melbourne, "that whenever one sees Lord Byron these days, he is *always* in the company of his sister?"

Lady Melbourne frowned, because she too was beginning to fret that her role as Lord Byron's personal *confidant* was being usurped by Augusta Leigh, whose advice he now appeared to value more than her own.

Or was she merely imagining it?

True, he was no less her friend and still wrote a companionable letter to her regularly, but even in those letters she could detect that he was becoming more and more under the influence of his older sister.

In his last letter he had even referred to Augusta as being "quite lovable" which was a bit high-flown. But then, the dear boy was still excited by the novelty of having a sister, or indeed, any *relative* at all.

She looked at Caroline. "Lord Byron's relationships are nothing to do with you, Caroline. None of *your* business, do you understand? And I would be obliged if you did not raise your voice in my drawing-room."

Caroline stared. " I did not raise my voice."

"You did, or very nearly did."

Caroline shrugged at the ridiculousness of being accused of something she only "*nearly*" did.

"Will Lord Byron be attending Lord Holland's Christmas Ball, do you know?"

There was a pause before Lady Melbourne replied: "No, he will not. He has been invited to spend Christmas in the country with his sister and his nieces."

~ ~ ~

At Newmarket, Byron was somewhat surprised when he finally met his brother-in-law, Colonel George Leigh.

George was at least ten years older than Augusta, so around forty or so, and he possessed none of the *dash* of the gambling and race meeting *rake* that he had expected to meet. George Leigh was staid and solid and a real *ex-colonel* of the 10th Hussars in every way, right down to his very neat and elegant moustaches.

George Leigh was also surprised when he met Lord Byron, for he was expecting to meet a delicate-figured poetry-fop who would instantly start sneezing and complaining about the cold of country houses. A poetic brother as weak and fluttery as his sister.

Yet Lord Byron was quite masculine, not only in his looks, but in his conversation, which elated George enormously.

They were sitting at dinner when George said to Byron, "No doubt Augusta told you about my problem with the prince?"

Byron shrugged. "I think everyone suffers a problem with the prince, sooner or later. He's that kind of man."

"Well, he accused me of the most dreadful thing, and being the Prince Regent everyone felt duty-bound to believe him. I doubt there is a man in his circle who does not consider him infallible."

"Not Beau Brummell," said Byron. "And *he* knows HRH better than most."

Ten minutes later George was howling with laughter as Byron passed on some of Beau Brummell's funny anecdotes about the Prince Regent; while Augusta sat smiling, pleased to see her husband and brother getting on so well.

And also the children ... Augusta smiled as she watched Byron the following day, playing in the fields with his nieces, the youngest two excitedly screaming their laughter at their new "*Uncle By*".

Byron enjoyed his games with the children, but his favourite was seven-year-old Georgiana, because although being the oldest, she was the shyest of the three. In some ways, she reminded him of himself when he was a red-faced shy boy, and there were moments when he even imagined that she *looked* like him.

So how to bring her out of her red-faced shyness with him?

He finally brought her out of her timidity by faking a bout of lameness, and asking her to hold his hand in order to help him limp back to the house.

She did so, holding his hand very tightly for fear he may fall, and from then on she became like a doting little mother to her "Uncle By", and forgot her own shyness completely. So, clearly her mother's daughter, and nothing at all like George Leigh.

On Christmas Eve, Byron discovered that his family and blood connection to Georgiana and his two other nieces was closer than he had realised, when Augusta finally remembered to tell him that George Leigh was not only her husband, but also her *first* cousin.

"Your first cousin? I thought you married some *distant* cousin?

"No," she shook her head. "So George is *your* first cousin also.

"Mine?" Byron was shocked. "How can that be?"

"George's mother was Lady Frances Byron, our father's sister, and our paternal aunt."

And there Byron saw the connection to Lord Carlisle, whose mother had *also* been a Byron, and the reason why Lord Carlisle had been formerly designated as legal guardian to both himself and Augusta in their separate childhoods.

"You married our father's *nephew?* Your *first* cousin? Of the same blood?"

Augusta's face was blushing with embarrassment, as red as Georgiana's face had been; and perhaps her embarrassment was the reason why Augusta had not told him this before.

"We were in love," she said quietly.

Augusta was fiddling with the ring on her finger, a frown on her brow. "I'm not sure why ... but in those days I saw George as my saviour ... up in Yorkshire at Castle Howard, living with the Carlisles, an orphaned *dependent* relative whom nobody really wanted ... I was beginning to think I would go mad with misery ... until I met George, who is *also* related to the Carlisles. He was with the 10th Hussars then, the regiment stationed quite close to Castle Howard, and when he occasionally came to visit, he and I ... and well, you know the rest."

Byron remained silent, taking it all in, until he replied, "I remember now, when I was at Cambridge, a letter from you telling me you had married a cousin of yours, but I thought then that he was some distant cousin on the *Osborne* side."

The realisation of the close blood-tie between Augusta and George alarmed him, because was it not said that such marriages could lead to impairment in the children?

Augusta looked at him defensively. "It's not against the law, you know, to marry a first cousin. It happens all the time. And the *only* reason why my Osborne half-siblings hated George, was because his mother was a sister to John Byron – *our* father who had taken their precious mother away from them. And the same reason why they always hated *me*, his daughter."

Byron now wondered if that was the reason why Frederick and George Osborne, on the few occasions he had met them, were usually rather cool to him, because he was a *son* of John Byron?

No matter – they were both bores of the first order.

"Is she still alive?" he asked. "George's mother? Our Byron aunt?"

"Sadly, no, she died some years ago. But his father, General Leigh, is still alive, although in retirement, if you would like to meet him?"

"No, no, not especially, but I *would* have liked to have met my father's sister, if only to ask her questions about him."

Georgiana came into the room then, eager to show Uncle By her doll ... a shabby thing that looked quite worn.

"Her name is Amelia."

"Amelia? That's a pretty name."

"Same as Grandma Amelia."

Byron looked at Augusta who smiled. "My mother. I make sure we all never forget her."

Byron thought of the three beautiful dolls he had bought in London as part of the bundle of Christmas gifts he had bought for his nieces, one with blonde hair, one with black hair, and the other a redhead.

"Do you think Amelia would like a new sister?"

Georgiana's blue eyes looked at her mother with some confusion, and then back at Uncle By. "Amelia is a *doll*," she told him.

"I know that, but dolls can have sisters too."

"Can they?"

"Oh yes, and when you are asleep, or not in the room, the dolls talk to each other."

"Do they?" Georgiana's eyes were like two blue moons.

Augusta smiled as she listened to Byron's nonsense, and then left the two of them talking earnestly to each other while she went to check on dinner.

It had to be a special dinner tonight, being Christmas Eve; and thankfully, due to Byron's cheque for £3000, no creditors would be coming banging on the door looking for payment.

Chapter Twenty-One

~ ~ ~

During dinner that night, Byron alarmed George Leigh by announcing his invitation for all the family to spend the week after Christmas with him at Newstead.

"The children will love it," he said to Augusta, "and it is really *their* ancestral home as well as mine."

Augusta had never yet seen Newstead Abbey and was delighted; while her husband was getting jittery in his seat.

"Not me, dear boy, not me, because the day after Christmas is the day the Newmarket races start, and I really *should* attend. There is an Arab mare I am interested in, named Medora, of the *Byerley Turk* breed, and I might get her at a good price. You don't mind, do you, if I stay here and hold the fort while you all go over to Newstead?"

"George, you should come with us," said Augusta. "Byron says Newstead is a house of wonderful antiquity."

"One of the oldest in England," Byron added. "Well, as far back as the eleventh century."

"So it will still be there in a month or two," George replied flatly to Augusta – and then to Byron, "Business, you know. The Christmas period is one of the busiest times in the horse business. No, you all go, and I will see it another time."

Not long after Augusta had left them to their drinks, Byron began to feel very glad that George Leigh would not be coming to Newstead with them, for just like the previous night, his conversation was mainly about horses, and nothing *but* horses.

"All the best breeding horses are of Arab descent," George was saying. "In fact *all* the best horses of any kind are Arab. The Arabian is one of the oldest breeds in the world, high head and high tail, very strong and alert, bred in a desert climate, you see, by the Bedouins."

He lifted the decanter and refilled their glasses.

"But now, the *Byerley Turk* breed is not truly Arabian, but from the Ottoman Empire. *Turk,* you see, and the first one was brought here to England, to Yorkshire, by Captain Robert Byerley, after the Battle of Buda in the seventeenth century, hence the name *Byerley Turk*. I believe it was, in fact, during the sixteen-eighties – 1686 or 1689 – that Robert Byerley brought the first of the breed to Yorkshire, but that was just the start. After that ..."

In the haze of his boredom, Byron's mind began to wander, back to the Ottoman Empire and all the Turks he had known there. Ali Pasha was the worst of them, but he had also met some of the best. The Turks, despite their savage ways in war, also had a gracious dignity about them, which he had liked; and their personal pride in themselves was as high as the sky ... One Turk he had seen in the Levant, had been reputed to be a fearless *corsair* when he sailed out on the seas. *A pirate*, but that fact was never confirmed, because he was not a man to answer questions. His age was no more than thirty, his garb was black, from head to toe, and he was as tall as Beau Brummell, and there was something *forbidding* in his face and in the dark of his eyes ...

Unlike the heroes of ancient race,

Demons in act, but at least Gods in face,

In Conrad's form seems little to admire

Though his dark eyebrow shades a glance of fire...

He came out of his thoughts, and realised George Leigh was still droning on, unaware that he had stopped listening, and now he had to *go* – up to his room and start *writing* – the *corsair* was before his eyes, striding down to the shore –

He pushed back his chair and stood up while muttering an apology, making some excuse, he knew not what, but seconds later he was on his way upwards, thanking Heaven that the Leighs had such a *small* house in comparison to Newstead.

As soon as he reached his door Fletcher appeared, ready to help him undress, but he waved him away, and then called him back – "In what bag did you pack the ink? I see paper and pen on the table but *no ink!*"

"No ink? Oh, that's because it's the new bottle of Japanese ink you bought. I haven't horned it yet."

"No, don't bother pouring it into the inkhorn, just leave the bottle and scram."

When Fletcher had left the room in his usual huff, he sat down at the table, lifted his pen and stared at the white sheets of paper, the *corsair* once more before his eyes ...

He dipped the pen in the inkbottle and began to write at a rapid pace.

~ ~ ~

On Christmas day, George Leigh was also in a grump and huff at Byron's behaviour, for here he was, having set aside this day to be hospitable and companionable to his young brother-in-law, yet the fellow had spent the entire afternoon in his cloak, sitting at a small wooden table under a tree in the field, writing page after page of

God knew what?

"Is he fully sane?" George asked his wife.

Augusta was smiling at the oddity of it all. "The ridiculous thing is that he went out there just to get away from the noise of the children," she said, "but now look – the children are playing and shouting all around him but he doesn't appear to even *hear* them."

Byron came back to reality in time to enjoy Christmas dinner with George and Augusta, and even cheerful enough to bow to the wishes of his little nieces and kiss all their new dolls "goodnight" before the girls were led away upstairs to the nursery.

After dinner, Byron was very relieved that Augusta did not leave the men to the brandy and port in the usual way, but remained sitting at the table to enjoy a glass of Christmas brandy herself, which surely must prevent George from his usual habit of talking about *horses* all night?

He had come to the realisation that he and George Leigh had absolutely nothing in common, and in his own mind he had already given George the nickname of "the drone". Why did some people spout on endlessly about their own particular obsessions?

How would George Leigh like it, he wondered, if *he* sat at the table every night and spouted non-stop verses of poetry by Pope or Milton? Or started a debate on *who* actually wrote the plays about *King Lear* and *Romeo and Juliet* and all the others? Was it truly William Shakespeare? Or was it the reclusive Sir Francis Bacon? And why did Francis Bacon hint in his writings that *he* had written the plays, but Shakespeare had *perfected* them – "*Shakespeare took my words and turned them from copper into gold.*"

Now how would George Leigh like to spend the rest of

the night talking about that?

George Leigh's voice brought him out of the rant with himself, and his words brought a smile to Byron's face, for *tonight,* it seemed, Colonel George Leigh was not ready to talk about horses – but would *like* to know more about the famous Beau Brummell.

"An odd name that, *Beau*, very American."

"His real name is George Bryan Brummell."

"So why do they call him Beau?"

Byron smiled. "Oh, you would have to *see* him to know why."

"He's very handsome," Augusta said. "I saw him once, when I was much younger, working at St James's Palace, and he truly was the *tallest* handsome man I had ever seen."

"And yet he does not *work* for his living," George said curiously. "They say he just parades around London in fine clothes. So what does he *do* with the rest of his time?"

"He designs his own clothes."

"Is that all?"

"I believe so."

"You know him well, do you?"

"Quite well. He is one of my favourite people."

"Is he indeed?" George looked at his wife, and Augusta knew exactly what her husband was thinking, and later he would say it to her, upstairs in their bedroom – "*Now there is fine pair of manly specimens, Gussie, one sitting under a tree writing poetry all day, while the other struts around London doing nothing else at all. What is this world of men coming to?*"

"He likes gambling," Byron said, "somewhat like yourself."

George missed the jibe and his eyes lit bright.

"Gambling, eh? Does he win or lose?"

"He usually wins."

"Wins! A little or a lot?"

Byron sat back in his chair and relaxed. "I would say, over the last five years at least, he and my friend Scrope Davies have each amassed a small fortune for themselves. Both are very good at calculating."

"In what way?"

"Well, at Hazard for example, both know it's easier to throw for a seven than a four or five, and all sorts of other things that I myself still *don't* know."

"Are they honest?"

"Oh, most certainly. Gentlemen in every way. And they both learned their playing skills at Eton."

"Eton?"

"Yes, in the dormitory at night. Once the house master had locked the dormitory door and gone to his own chamber, that's when some of the boys left their beds to gather in the far corner of the room, and that's when the card and dice games began."

George smiled. "Not every different from young soldiers then?"

"No, I suppose not." Byron sipped his drink. "In truth, I would say that Beau Brummell is a *professional* gambler now. It's what he does to earn money. But Scrope Davies is still a Fellow at King's College, Cambridge, although he only goes there now for the autumn term."

George Leigh had never heard of Scrope Davies, so he was not interested in him, but he was now very interested in Beau Brummell, a man who was not a time-waster after all, but a *professional* gambler.

"Is he one of those *born* Londoners, or is he a migrant from another county or shire?"

"A true Londoner. He was born in Westminster, in Downing Street, in house number *ten*."

George and Augusta both stared.

"Are you saying," George asked finally, "that Beau Brummell was born inside *Ten Downing Street* – the official residence of the British Prime Minister?"

"Yes."

Byron was enjoying this; the history of Beau Brummell was far more interesting than the history of horses.

"Was his father a member of the Ministerial Cabinet?"

"No, he was the Prime Minister's *valet*."

They both stared again; until George Leigh, for the life of him, could not understand how the valet of *any* man in *any* establishment could afford to send his son to an illustrious and expensive school such as Eton?

"That would be sons," Byron corrected. "He had two sons, and *both* were sent to Eton."

"Byron, stop it," Augusta insisted, now certain that Byron was making it all up, just like his nonsense about the talking dolls to Georgiana.

Byron laughed, and assured them both it was all very true – "Except, Brummell's father may have *started* his career as Lord North's valet, but he was such an intelligent man, very astute, and so indispensable in every way, that when Lord North became Prime Minister, he made William Brummell his Private Secretary, promoting him to the rank of a civil servant in a governmental position."

George looked dubious. "Did the son tell you all this?"

"No, it was first told to me by the politician and playwright, Richard Brinsley Sheridan. A friend of Lord North at that time."

Augusta was fascinated at the idea of a mere valet rising to such a height, and urged her brother to "Go on."

So Byron went on, and explained to them the details of the Brummell family history, which Beau Brummell himself had explained to him.

"Although every person in London's *beau monde* knows it," Byron added. "It's not something that Beau Brummell is ashamed of, or keeps secret. In fact, his father was a man he is still enormously proud of. Although he does *insist* that his good looks were inherited by him from his very beautiful mother."

"But how did the father," Augusta, asked "become wealthy enough to send his children to a school like Eton?"

"During his time in Downing Street, Brummell's father met many influential people, and was liked and respected by all of them, and some of those influential people gave him the sound financial advice to invest any money he had into property and *land*; and as London then was beginning to boom and stretch to house an ever-growing population, he quickly became quite rich from the profits, enough to buy one property after another until – when Lord North was replaced as Prime Minister by William Pitt – he was finally wealthy enough to buy the Brummell's country estate of Donnington Grove in Berkshire ... and also to send his sons to the nearby school of Eton."

"How incredible." George Leigh looked at his wife. "You see, Gussie, what having influential friends can do for you?"

Augusta frowned. "All they did was give him good advice. The rest he did for himself."

Byron's eyes narrowed slightly as he looked at his

financially hapless brother-in-law. "One piece of advice that William Brummell gave to his sons, which Beau Brummell admits he never did adhere to ... was never to gamble."

This time, George Leigh did not miss the barbed jibe from his young brother-in-law, which so annoyed him, he lit up a cigar.

"Personally I have never wagered money on anything other than the horses. A far more reliable bet in my opinion. One can judge the form and class of a horse, but who can make any judgement on the throw of a dice or the fall of the cards?"

Byron remained silent, and George continued, "This is why I say that the best *racing* horses are from the Arabian or Turkish breeds. They have speed and endurance and *strong bones*. You can tell them a mile off from their finely chiselled bone structure and high-carried tail. What's more, they are good-natured, quick to learn, and always willing to please."

He puffed on his cigar. "And don't forget, the Arabs originally used the breed for raiding and *war*. So hardy, yes. High-tempered, yes. But all a horse really asks from any human is *respect*."

Now it was Byron who was getting jittery in his chair. The drone had started, and who knew when it might end?

"Take the *Byerley Turk* that I told you about last night; a horse that is known for *endurance*. As is the *Barb* breed. And although the Barb is a smaller horse, in bone and body—"

"Pray forgive and excuse me —" Byron was up and out of his chair, rushing out of the room and halfway up the stairs when Augusta caught up with him.

"Byron, are you feeling unwell?"

"Yes, a terrible pain in my head, due to too much food, wine and liquor, and not enough sleep last night. Give my apologies to George, will you?"

Augusta looked up at him searchingly. "Are you sure it was not George's cigar smoke that brought this on?"

He seized on the excuse. "Possibly ... but tell him to carry on. A man should be able to smoke in his own house. I'll just head on up to bed."

She moved quickly up the steps to kiss him on the cheek and wish him a "goodnight"; which thereafter he carried on upwards as quickly as he could – furious at himself for lacking the *endurance* of a Byerley Turk horse.

Twice now he had made a quick exit away from George and his endless horse-talk, and it was no way for a guest to treat a host in his own house.

So it was very fortunate that tomorrow they would all be travelling on to see Joe Murray and Newstead, while Colonel George Leigh would be left to spend his week happily at the Newmarket Racecourse, in more appreciative company than that of his present guest.

PART SIX

The Corsair

"Poetry is a distinct faculty, – it won't come when called, – you may as well whistle for a wind. I have thought over some of my subjects for years before writing a line."

Byron - to Edward Trelawny

Chapter Twenty-Two

~ ~ ~

"This," said Byron, "is where my bear Bruin used to live."

"A bear?" asked Georgiana. "A *real* bear?"

"As real as you or I."

He then told the three girls all about Bruin and his wonderful dancing skills, his love of biscuits and his very handsome looks."

"He *was* handsome, wasn't he, Joe?" Byron grinned over at Joe Murray who was standing outside the wire netting of the long-empty compound.

"How could he be handsome with that long snout of his?" Joe replied flatly. "He was a bear, a *lazy* bear, always having his long naps in his hut after guzzling his biscuits."

Byron mocked a sad face at the girls. "Alas, Joe was always very jealous of Bruin's handsome looks."

"My lord, did you not hear what I said to you? Your sister sent me out to bring the children in, for fear of the cold. And aye, the mildness has gone and there's a bitter nip in the air."

Georgiana took a quick, wide-eyed peek inside the bear's empty hut. "It's so sad we cannot see him now," she said. "I have never seen a bear."

"I have a painting of Bruin in my apartments," Byron told the girls. "Would you all like to see what a noble and handsome creature he was?"

Amidst the yelps, Georgiana turned and led the run back to the house, and Byron grinned again.

"Look at them," he said to Joe, "running like a row of

eager little puppies."

A huge fire was burning in the hearth of the large downstairs parlour; and there Augusta and the children spent their days in relative contentment and warm comfort: the children playing, and Augusta reading; while Byron spent long hours in his small and private sitting-room on the first floor, at his desk, writing his Turkish tale about the Pirate Conrad and his crew.

"Where is Gonsalvo?"

"In the anchored bark."

"There let him stay – but to him this order bear

Back to your duty – for my course prepare:

Myself this enterprise tonight will share."

"Tonight, Lord Conrad?"

"Ay! at set of sun:

The breeze will freshen when the day is done."

A knock on the door, Byron ignored it. Another knock and Fletcher hesitantly entered.

Byron looked at him. "Begone – *now!"*

"I will, my lord, in a jiff I will ... but this letter ... it's just been delivered and it's marked urgent ... and I think it might be from you-know-who."

"I know who? I know a lot of people, Fletcher, so *who* are you referring to? James Webster? Lady Caroline Lamb? Santa Claus?"

"It was delivered by William Caunt."

Byron stared, and almost stopped breathing. "William Caunt ... from Annesley?"

"Aye." Fletcher moved closer and handed him the letter, waiting while his lordship quickly opened it, and read –

My dear Lord, as you are in Notts, please try and call at Edwalton, near Nottinghamshire, where a friend would very much like to see you. — M.

Byron looked at Fletcher. "Where is Edwalton?"

Fletcher shrugged. "I dunno."

Byron looked at the letter again ... "This is no different to the ten or twenty letters that come here from Nottingham's female readers every time I come back to Newstead, and I ignore them all."

"Is it not from Mary C?"

"How can it be? She lives at *Annesley*, not Edwalton. And Mary would write my name in full — Lord Byron — and her *own* name in full, instead of just a mysterious *M.*"

Fletcher was flummoxed. "But it was delivered by William Caunt."

"Perhaps ... perhaps he has a sister, or a female friend living in Edwalton who has begged him to deliver the note because she wants to meet *Childe Harold* or even the *Giaour?*"

"I knew it." Fletcher stiffened as he stared at the window. "I *knew* it was going to snow. It doesn't get this cold without snow being on the back of the wind!"

Byron looked to the window and saw the snow falling rapidly.

"You had better go and tell Joe Murray to make sure the fires in the children's rooms are regularly attended to, and their bedchamber is kept warm at all times."

"And my own bedchamber also." Fletcher was still watching the snow falling. "By morning there'll be some freezing *ice* on the windows, I reckon."

As Fletcher turned to leave, Byron said: "And Fletcher, pray ask Nanny Smith to come up and see me."

~ ~ ~

Nanny Smith arrived a short time later, carrying her usual tray of tea, which she placed on the table by the fireplace. "Shall I pour it for you, my lord?"

"Not for me, but you – you Nanny, you do pour yourself a cup of tea and sit down by the fire."

"No, oh no, my lord, I brought it up for you, so it wouldn't be right."

"It would be wrong to waste it, and I want to ask you about Mary C."

Nanny quickly changed her mind, filling her teacup with extreme care, for her hands were shaking. "Oh no, my lord, I can't tell you anything, because that's a subject I'm forbidden to speak about in this house."

"Forbidden by whom?"

"Joe Murray."

"I hold a higher rank than Joe, and it's *my* house, so I am un-forbidding you."

"Well, in that case ..." Nanny sat down in the armchair by the fire, lifting the cup and saucer with her shaking hands, "but I don't feel right about breaking my pledge to Joe."

Byron left his desk and moved over to stand by the fireplace, his hand resting on the ledge as he looked down at her. "Would it help if we agreed not to let Joe know?"

"It would be a great help," Nanny agreed, and took a long gulp of her tea to calm her nerves, knowing the conversation was not going to be a happy one.

"I really don't know much, only what Nanny Marsden told me, and I had to go over there in secret, without Joe knowing."

"Did you see Mary while you were there?"

"No, how could I? She has moved out of Annesley Hall and taken her children with her."

"Moved out of *Annesley*?" Byron could scarcely believe it. "To where?"

"Edwalton."

Byron stared ... so the note *was* from Mary. He sat down in the armchair opposite Nanny Smith. "Where is Edwalton?"

"Oh, it's a remote and lonely place ... although Nanny Marsden says it is peaceful, very peaceful ... and quiet, very quiet ... just one house there is, surrounded by the trees of Sherwood Forest."

Byron was shaking his head slightly in puzzlement. "And Mary's gone there? Why? Does she own the house?"

"No." Nanny swallowed nervously, looking down at the teacup and saucer now beginning to clatter together in her shaking hands. "It's Ann Radford's house. Mary has moved in with her."

"Ann Radford? That she-cat? *Ann Radford!* And now Mary wants *me* to visit her there? In Ann Radford's house? The nerve of it! The sheer *audaciousness!*"

He hurled himself off the chair in rage, just as Nanny Smith's cup fell off its saucer and dropped onto the floor, spilling what was left of the tea onto the expensive soft blue Persian carpet.

~ ~ ~

It took some minutes for Byron to comfort Nanny Smith and assure her that it was not *her* he was angry with, but – "I can't tell you how much I *dislike* Ann Radford."

"Aye, and there's not many at Annesley Hall that likes her either."

"Is that why Mary moved out?"

"No."

Slowly, with a lot of prompting, Nanny Smith told Byron that Mary had moved out because Jack Musters had moved back in.

"It seems his mother and his lawyers told him it was his legal right to move back in. When he had married Mary and become her husband, he had inherited for himself Annesley Hall and everything else that Mary owned ... so Nanny Marsden says he arrived one day with his lawyers, and when Mary saw the papers the lawyers had brought, she realised she had given up all rights to her possessions on her marriage. She owned nothing. Her husband owned it all."

"Poor Mary..." Byron was fighting the urge to immediately go and see her ... but he knew that he possessed too much pride to lower himself, or lose his dignity, by knocking on Ann Radford's door. But then, he *could* write back and arrange to meet Mary along a nearby path ...

He later discussed it with Augusta. In London he had already confided all about his former relationship with Mary Chaworth.

Augusta begged him *not* to go. "You will only fall in love with her again, you know you will."

Byron was silent, unable to deny it.

"If you *do* go," said Augusta, "not only will you fall in love again, but one step will then lead to another, and Ann Radford will be watching, so then there will be a scene ... *et cela fera un éclat.*"

Byron shrugged, unable to deny the possibility of that also.

Augusta was now deeply concerned for him. "And there has been so much *scandalous* talk about you in the past, Byron, due to your affair with Lady Caroline Lamb. So if it became known that you were also involved with *another* married woman, the scandal would be even worse, leading to your disgrace and dishonour."

"Oh, you don't understand ... and I can't explain." He left Augusta abruptly, not wishing to argue with his sister, not now that he knew she was in the family way again.

He returned to his sitting room and *The Corsair* blocking out all thoughts except those of Conrad and his fellow pirates out on the high seas.

A sail! a sail! a promised prize to Hope

Her nation flag – how speaks the telescope?

No prize, alas – but yet a welcome sail:

The blood-red signal glitters in the gale.

Yes, she is ours – a home returning bark

Blow fair, thou breeze! she anchors ere the dark.

Chapter Twenty-Three

~~~

The snow kept falling and the wind was like a gale, freezing the snow into ice, until all roads out of Newstead became impassable.

Inside the Abbey huge log-fires threw out their blazing warmth into every room and hall. Augusta felt so peaceful and cosy, she began to wish the snow would keep on falling for ever.

"Is it not strange," Byron asked her, "that Ann Radford has changed her mind and allowed Mary to write to me? She must know of the letter, because Mary would not ask me to call there – not if she knew Ann Radford would object or be insulting to me again."

Snuggled up in her armchair, Augusta kept her eyes on the fire while she thought about it.

"It could be," she said, "that if you *did* call there, Ann Radford would let Jack Musters know about it, in the hope of causing a duel between the two of you, and maybe getting rid of *both* of you in one blast."

Byron grinned. "She's bad, but not *that* bad." He paused. "Or maybe she is? God knows with women! All are duplicitous."

He then told Augusta about Lady Frances Webster and the two cheques he had given to her husband.

"I did not expect to hear from either of them again, but within days she was writing to me in London, asking for my picture, and saying surprising things such as, '*If I had your picture to look at, I know I could survive'.*"

Augusta smiled. "Very dramatic ... but you should not have played with her."

Byron shrugged. "A few kisses which did her no harm and me no good."

After a long silence, Byron sighed, "Mary has timed things ill."

"Timed things ill? What do you mean?"

He nodded towards the window. "The snow. If she was still at Annesley ... but it would be impossible for a carriage or even a horse to get through the twelve miles to Nottingham in this, and then out to Edwalton."

"So you will be unable to go." Augusta sat up. "I'm sure she must understand that it would now be very difficult for you to go in this weather."

And sadly, in Edwalton, Mary did understand. Even more so when the days of freezing snow turned into the worst winter Nottingham had seen for decades.

Mary had brought some of her own servants to Edwalton with her, and according to William Caunt – the only servant who had managed to brave and overcome the weather outside – all reports were bad.

The River Trent had frozen over; the market-place was covered in snow with huge mounds of ice piled up in front of every closed shop doorway. Mail coaches were unable to get through, and so any mail that could be delivered was being done slowly, and carefully, by riders on horseback.

One of those riders carried a package *from* Nottingham to be delivered to the publisher, John Murray, in London. The package had the seal of Lord Byron on it, so it was given priority. It contained the first half of *The Corsair*.

A week later, the news became terrifying. Three people had been found along the roadways, frozen to death. Everyone feared that more dead might be found later when the thaw finally came.

Entrenched as he was at Newstead, Byron finally wrote a letter to Mary, apologising for not being able to visit her due to the weather conditions ... while at the same time knowing any visit from him would be impossible, as long as she was residing in Ann Radford's house. He regularly forgave people, it was in his nature to do so – but *never* any person who had insulted him, and for them he could hold a lasting and viperish grudge.

Yet he thought about Mary, often, and tried hard not to do so, escaping from his thoughts and from reality by continuing his tale of the pirate, Conrad, but always, always ... *reality* kept creeping in. He named the woman who was the tragic love of Conrad's life – *"Medora."*

None are evil – quickening round his heart

One softer feeling, would not yet depart;

Oft could he sneer at others as beguiled

By passions worthy of a fool or child;

Yet against that passion vainly still he strove,

And even in him, it asks the name of Love!

Yes, it was love – unchangeable – unchanged,

Felt but for one, for whom he never ranged,

Though fairest captives daily met his eye,

He shunned, nor sought, but coldly passed them by;

Though many a beauty drooped in prisoned bower,

None ever soothed his most unguarded hour.

Yes – it was Love – if thoughts of tenderness,

Tried in temptation, strengthened by distress,

Unmoved by absence, firm in every clime,

And yet – Oh more than all! – untired by time.

In mid-January he finally had the last pages of *The Corsair* completed and packaged and sent by a mailman on horseback to John Murray in London.

A week later John Murray received it, and read it avidly, a smile on his face. He looked up when William Gifford came into the office.

"You must read this immediately, and now that I have the full and completed manuscript, you *can* read it – from Lord Byron."

"Ah, our young poet. So what is he writing about now?"

John Murray smiled. "Oh, it's what our female readers will love – swashbuckling pirates, rich sultans and captive maidens, kidnap and rescue, love and betrayal – but essentially it's about the pirate chief, Conrad, and his love for a beautiful harem girl named Medora."

Gifford was grinning. "So more from the East! The Lakers will never catch up with him now. And Wordsworth will be *spitting* if this one succeeds."

Murray nodded. "And Walter Scott has thrown away writing verse altogether. In future he will be writing novels, and set solely in Scotland."

"That's a pity. I liked Scott's poetry."

"I liked it too, but Scott himself summed it up for me in five words – 'Byron beats me every time'."

~ ~ ~

In the parlour at Newstead, Byron was staring at the date on the new calendar – 1814, January 22nd.

He looked at Augusta. "This day, this date, has now made me twenty-six-years old."

"Your birthday?"

"The anniversary of it."

"You should make a wish," Augusta insisted. "If, on this day of being twenty-six, you could wish for *anything* at all, Byron, what would you wish?"

Byron smiled, as if the answer was obvious. "To still be twenty-five."

Chapter Twenty-Four

~ ~ ~

Augusta had never been happier. She loved Newstead Abbey and the kind and friendly staff who looked after her so well; and it was a rare pleasure for *her* to be the one receiving all the care.

More than everything, though, she loved her brother; whom, she had to admit, often showed more consideration for her comfort and welfare than her husband ever had.

But George was her George and she really did *not* like it when Byron refused to accept George as *his* first cousin.

"I'll not own it! He's *your* first cousin and *you* married him. George being my horse-mad brother-in-law is enough, and *all* that I will own to."

Yet Byron went to great pains to ensure that his letters got sent down to George, informing him that all was well with the children who were happy enough, but Augusta's advanced pregnancy made it unwise for her to travel back to Newmarket until the roads were safe.

The snow and hard frosts continued for another eight weeks, until the middle of March; but during a short thaw in early February Byron took his chance and headed back to London, suffering a broken wheel on the way, but a spare one was soon replaced.

"We may as well keep on going," Byron said to Fletcher, "rather than being stuck here in a damp and freezing inn."

Fletcher agreed. "And I've just given a letter to the mailman who's just gone off on his horse, asking Mrs

Mule to have all the fires lit and glowing for when we get back."

Perhaps it was all the houses, and all the fires burning inside them, that made the streets of London feel so much warmer than the cold countryside of Nottinghamshire.

Byron was happy to be back in the metropolis, and others were very happy to welcome him back, giving him a delighted round of applause upon his entrance at a Ball in Holland House a few nights later.

Byron's surprised look of bewilderment made Lord Holland grin. "*We Whigs* are all very pleased with you, but I would not read the Tory newspapers in the morning if I were you."

"Why not?"

"The poem, '*Lines To A Lady Weeping*' by *Anonymous* ... the Tory newspapers have now discovered that *you* are the author behind it, and are in an absolute uproar."

Byron was baffled. "That poem was published by the *Chronicle two* years ago, and even the Editor didn't know the sender – so how have they found out who the author is *now?*"

Lord Holland caught a passing footman carrying a tray of champagne, scooped up a glass, and handed it to Byron. "All the fault of your *publisher* I'm afraid. He was so eager to send out early copies of your latest production to the papers and other luminaries for reviews – "

"*The Corsair?*"

"Yes, the Corsair, which included some other smaller poems at the back as usual, but in his excitement and haste, Murray also included the *Lines* by mistake."

Byron shrugged. "Then I'll own it. Every word was

true. And what can they do – lock me up in jail?"

Lord Holland stiffened. "Let them dare! They would have the entire Whig Party down on them if they even attempted it."

"Oh, là là! vous vilain!" Lord Holland turned as Germaine de Staël rushed up to Lord Byron, giving him her biggest buck-toothed smile of approval – and then speaking in English, "Oh you bad boy. Oh, you very *bad* boy. *Mal!* "

Byron laughed. "Well, I suppose that is less untrue than your previous description of me being *un démon.*"

"In jest, in *jest,*" she waved her fan over her reddening face, *"une blaque,* that's all."

Surprisingly, he found himself pleased to see her again, and when Lord Holland moved off, he happily spent some time talking with Madame de Staël, catching up on all her news and gossip – although when she laughed, her tongue was stained black, and he knew she had been sucking the nib of her pen again.

"You have been writing today?"

"Oui." She stared at him. "'How did you know?"

"Your mouth is full of ink."

"Psha!" she shrugged her French shrug, "My mouth, it is always full of ink, and my *hands"* – she pulled off a glove and held out her right hand, showing him the ink-stained fingers. "I cannot get it to go, the *ink,* how do you do it?"

"A good strong brush and a bar of carbolic soap."

"Carbolic? What is that?"

"A hard soap with no perfume."

"No *parfum?"* She looked at him as if thinking he was mad to even suggest that she would touch such a thing as a bar of soap with no perfume in it.

"A woman with no parfum in her soap is not a

woman!"

Byron grinned. "And that's why I can merrily use carbolic soap to get rid of *my* ink – one of the many benefits of being a *man*."

"And such a *beautiful* man," said Madame de Staël to Lady Holland later as they watched Lord Byron talking with Miss Bessie Rawdon, "*Bel homme, oui?*"

"Oh, yes", agreed Lady Holland, "and young, very young. At least, at my age, he seems so."

Madame turned fierce eyes on her. "And you *tell* him!"

Lady Holland looked at her curiously. "Tell him what, pray?"

"My *petite* little jest ... him being *un démon!*"

"No," Lady Holland said very precisely. "No, I did not. I told my husband, and *he* must have told Lord Byron."

Lady Holland raised her fan and waved it in the direction of Lord Holland. "There he is – *there* is my husband. Now you go, Madame, and rap him on the knuckles with your fan for passing on your flattery to Lord Byron. Go on, my husband deserves a good rap now and again!"

Madame de Staël stared at her for some moments, aware of Milady Holland's haughty sarcasm.

"You see," she said finally and quietly, "*this* is why we French detest the English."

~ ~ ~

The following morning, Byron instructed Fletcher to get all the newspapers, especially the Tory newspapers. If there was going to be such an uproar, as Lord Holland had said, then Byron could not understand why. He could have written a lot worse about HRH.

For years, while his father was the ruling monarch, the Prince of Wales had been a Whig, and supposedly hated the hard-line Tories. He socialised with the Whigs, and fornicated with some of the ladies of the Whigs, and had no time for anyone who was *not* a Whig.

Promise after promise was made about what he would do when he became monarch and could exercise all the powers of the Crown. He would bring in *reforms* to help the lower classes. He would bring about the emancipation of the Catholics. Yes, yes, he would go against his father's policies, even in that; although he stopped short at the suggestion of emancipating the Jews. "*That would be going too far, eh, what?*"

And even though the slave *trade* had been abolished, the slavery of African men and women was still legal; only slave-*ships* carrying in more cargoes of slaves had been outlawed and their captains liable to suffer harsh punishment if caught. But slavery itself, and being the *owner* of African slaves, was still permissible and quite legal.

But the most *important* thing he would do as monarch, the Prince of Wales *avowed* to the Whigs, was to *get rid* of the Tory government, and bring in the Whigs under the Whig leader William Grenville, who would immediately set all these reforms into motion.

And as monarch he would have the power to do just that, because the system was not that it was the Party who controlled a *majority* in the House of Commons who formed the Government – the Crown played a very influential role, due to the fact of it being *His Majesty's Government.*

Byron had been absolutely outraged when, in 1811, due to his father's madness, Parliament used the Regency Bill to make the Prince of Wales the *Prince*

Regent, giving him all the powers of a ruling monarch –
and that's when Prinny showed his true colours to the
Whigs – the damnable turncoat!

Instead of keeping all his promises, the Prince as
Regent decided to keep the Tory party in power – and
not because of any political principle on his part – but
because he had found a new group of *favourites* to
please – the new Tory darling who did not give a damn
about *reforming* anything!

All the Whigs had been *outraged* at such duplicity,
but it was in early 1812, when Byron was told of an
incident in St James's Palace, of Princess Charlotte, the
seventeen-year-old daughter of the Prince Regent,
breaking down in tears when she heard her father
speaking badly against the Whigs to Lord Lauderdale –
resulting in Byron dashing off a short piece of verse
about it, which he sent anonymously to the *Morning
Chronicle.*

The Tories had been in an uproar then, in 1812, when
the poem had been published to the nation, but it was
only now, it seemed, that their rage had been elevated
again due to discovering that the poem had, in fact,
been written by a "Lord of the Realm".

Fletcher arrived with his armful of newspapers, and
Byron saw immediately that he was front-page news –
the *villain* of the day – for daring to criticise HRH.

One paper called it "A *vicious attack on His Royal
Highness.*" Another called it "*A savage attack.*"

Byron had to smile as he read down the page, and
then looked from one front page to the next front page
and couldn't help laughing a little.

"Look at this, Fletcher? They are all so *outraged* by
my lines, and consider them so scurrilous – the idiots
have *republished* the poem in all their papers for those

who may have missed it the first time around."

Byron read the poem again, and thought it very *mild,* under the circumstances ...

Lines to a Lady Weeping

Weep, daughter of a royal line,
A Sire's disgrace, a realm's decay
Ah! happy if each tear of thine
Could wash a father's fault away!

Weep – for thy tears are Virtue's tears
Auspicious to these suffering Isles;
And be each drop in future years
Repaid thee by thy people's smiles.

John Murray called at Bennett Street a short time later, full of apologies for his mistake. "I have removed it, of course, so it will not be included in the final publication of *The Corsair."*

"No, leave it *in,*" Byron insisted. "Would you have them think I am ashamed of that poem? Or that I have taken it back to hide under my pillow? I'll be *damned* if I will allow you to take it out now."

"You'll be damned either way," said John Murray, his face troubled, "whether it stays in or not. I regret to say that this could greatly damage sales of *The Corsair."*

"So be it, but the poem stays in. My only regret now is that I did not write a harsher poem about the Prince Regent in 1812. I may as well be hanged for killing a lazy old swine, instead of consoling a tearful young lamb."

"Hanged?" John Murray looked shocked. "Oh, there is no risk of that, surely?"

"I was speaking metaphorically."

After a silence, John Murray asked, "Do you think I should postpone publication of *The Corsair?*"

"Why?"

"For the reason I have stated, the damage this will cause to sales."

Byron sighed, close to losing his patience. "If you postpone publication, or take even one step backwards now, you will give them the victory.

"Indeed?" John Murray looked thoughtful. "So, I take it then, Lord Byron, that you do *not* want me to postpone publication?"

"And when is that, exactly? Your scheduled publication day?"

"In six days. With a huge first print-run of ten thousand copies ... but that figure was based on the initial sales of your previous works. *The Bride of Abydos* sold six thousand copies in the first month ... However, it would be remiss of me not to warn you, that due to my own dreadful, *dreadful* mistake, we will be lucky if we sell a thousand copies of *The Corsair* in the next year. I am so terribly sorry for my negligence in shuffling the extra poems together so badly."

Byron smiled sympathetically. "If it does not sell, I can always write another for you that will."

John Murray did not reply, not having the heart nor the will to tell Lord Byron that it would be *his name* on *The Corsair* that would damage all sales now. Not many bookshops would want to stock anything written by a man who had used his pen to criticise the Prince Regent.

He left Byron's apartment in Bennett Street, heavy in heart and dreading the week to come. He had cherished such high hopes of *The Corsair* being the banker that would pay off his last mortgage on his establishment at 50 Albemarle Street.

~ ~ ~

After John Murray had left the apartment, Byron looked at Fletcher, a sardonic smile on his face. "Did you hear him, Fletcher, all his talk about the damage to sales?"

"No, my lord, I was not listening."

"Yes, you were. You were standing outside with your ear pressed against the door."

"No, I was polishing the mirror on the wall outside ... and the door was open a crack ... so I may have *overheard* a word or two."

"All his worries about the *money* that will be lost from lack of sales ... Murray must have forgotten that I don't take a penny from the profits on sales of my poetry, it all goes to himself and Robert Dallas."

Chapter Twenty-Five

~ ~ ~

Better than a month since I last journalised:– most of it out of London and at Notts. On my return I found all the newspapers in hysterics on the discovery and republication of two stanzas on Princess Charlotte's weeping at the Regent's speech to Lord Lauderdale in 1812. The Regent, on discovering the poem to be mine, has affected to be 'in sorrow rather than anger.'

The Morning Post, Sun, Herald, Courier, have all been in an uproar ever since. The abuse against me in all directions is vehement, unceasing, loud – some of the abuse is good, and all of it hearty. They are talking of a motion in our House of Lords upon it – be it so.

I have not answered Walter Scott's last letter (kind man) – but I will. I regret to hear from others, that he has lately been unfortunate in financial involvements...

Byron paused, wondering if his publisher, John Murray, was now also lamenting his misfortune in financial involvements? A full week had passed since his visit to Bennett Street, so *The Corsair* must have been published *yesterday*.

~ ~ ~

It was the winter *sunshine* beaming through his office window that John Murray remembered so clearly about that morning. Yet *yesterday* the rain had poured down, and he had commenced the day certain that the dark rain was a sign of bad fortune.

But now ... now, *this* morning, he and his editor William Gifford were absolutely dazed with disbelief and delighted shock.

The Corsair had sold out its first complete print-run of ten thousand copies on its first day of sale, making publishing history. It was unprecedented for any publication to make that amount of sales in *one day!*

Gifford was laughing. "The people have spoken. The newspapers may say what they like, but it's clear *the people* in this country all agree with Lord Byron. It has not stunted their appetite for his poetry at all, but *increased* it."

"Oh, they love him! They adore him!" John Murray exclaimed jubilantly. "Why did we ever doubt him and his magic? From that first day in 1812, Byron only had to come, and to be seen, and he conquered all before him. And then when they *read* his poetry..."

"And look at these," Gifford exclaimed. "Have you ever seen batches of new orders like *these* before?"

John Murray had to take out his handkerchief and wipe at his eyes, because *no* – he had never seen so many *new orders* before. His mortgage would be paid, and the premises at number 50, Albermarle Street, would at last belong to him, and *him* alone. No banks.

~ ~ ~

In Derbyshire, Thomas Moore was also pleased, if a slight jealous, of the instant success of *The Corsair.*

Of late, his own poetry was not doing as well as he had hoped, and nor were his earnings anywhere near the level of those of Byron or Wordsworth.

"To be sure," he said dismally to Bessie, "there are times when a man could be forgiven for thinking Byron and Worsdworth were the only two poets in the kingdom worth reading."

"And you, Tommy. I've heard so many people say how much they love *your* poetry."

"Then I wish they'd open their purses along with their mouths and *buy* it."

Tommy was fed up with it all, and took himself off to walk up and down behind his favourite tree at the end of the garden ... slowly meandering back and forth and thinking that writing poetry or anything else was a hard way to make a living.

Writing itself was hard, and no guarantee of success or payment at the end of it. That's why they had moved up to this cottage in Derbyshire – so much cheaper than living in London.

And yet there was Byron, ten years younger than himself, and already a huge success ... but then, as John Keats had said recently to Leigh Hunt ... "That's what you get for being six foot tall and a *lord*."

Tommy shrugged, knowing that was rather unfair to Byron, who was not six foot tall, but an inch or so shorter. And a nobleman of the aristocracy he may be, but he never deliberately flaunted it – and it was *not* Byron's fault that John Keats was only five foot tall.

Tommy sighed, looking up at the sky, asking God Himself what he should do about the invitation. He had not even told Bessy about it, because what was the point? She would not want to go, always so shy with strangers; and *he* certainly could *not* go. Although he would very much like to.

Returning to his study, he sat down drearily and read again Byron's letter asking why he had not received any replies to his letters, and why their correspondence had ceased and been *"put into quarantine."*

Yet how could he explain why he had not replied? If he had done so, truthfully, Byron would have immediately attempted to remedy the matter with his own money, and Tommy had too much Irish pride for that.

Finally, he picked up his pen and wrote a letter to his old friend Samuel Rogers about it all, explaining that along with Lord Byron, he had been invited by the Duke of Devonshire to spend a week at his country seat at the magnificent Chatsworth House.

I have no servant to take with me, and my hat is shabby, and the seams of my best coat are beginning to look white and – in short – if a man cannot step upon equal ground with these people, he had much better keep out of their way. I can meet them on pretty fair terms at a dinner or a ball; but a whole week in the same house as them detects the poverty of a man's ammunition deplorably. I think the obvious conclusion is that we ought to have nothing to do with each other.

Tommy's silent misery and gloom continued, and increased the following day, even when a packet with John Murray's business seal on it arrived. Tommy knew what it contained – Byron's promised copy of *The Corsair.*

For some time now, he had been working on his own epic tale, set in the East – *Lallah Rookh* – but what was the point of even continuing with it now?

People would say, in setting his tale in the *East*, he was following Byron, copying Byron, trying to *compete* with Byron – and who now could do that? Byron was the highest star in the sky, untouchable and unreachable, even by Wordsworth, because Byron wrote about passion, and love, and the *young,* but Wordsworth wrote mostly about Nature.

And he, Thomas Moore, what did he write? Nothing very worthy of late – not if his *income* was anything to judge by.

He opened the packet containing *The Corsair* in a half-hearted way, not even sure if he could bear to read it. In fallow times, the success of even our most favoured friends does not always uplift us.

He removed the book, looking at it ... almost with loathing ... and then opened it.

Some ten minutes later Bessy knocked and came into the study with a shirt in her hands. "Tommy ... I cannot mend this shirt any more. You see here, how it's come away at the shoulder seam ... " and then she stopped speaking, and stared ... Tommy had tears running down his face.

She immediately put the shirt down and went to him. "Dearest, what is it?"

Tommy looked at her with a face full of emotion, and said in a shaking voice. "He is so sincere ... and so genuinely fond of me ... and yet I ... I have been too wrapped up in *self."*

He handed her *The Corsair,* and she took it in her own hands, and saw that he had not read past the opening page ... and then Bessy's eyes welled up with emotion also as she looked at the opening page of the book by Lord Byron ... and there in the printer's ink for all to see was the proof of that young nobleman's sincerity.

> **MY DEAR MOORE,**
> *I dedicate to you this production ...*

Bessy looked at her husband. "Oh, Tommy, did I not always say —"

"Read on," said Tommy, "read on, dear."

And Bessie read on ... the most wonderful dedication and tribute that any friend could give to another.

> " ... *While Ireland ranks you the firmest of her patriots – while you stand alone the first of her bards in her estimation, and Britain repeats and ratifies the decree – permit one, whose only regret, since our first acquaintance, has been the years he had lost before it commenced, to add the humble but sincere suffrage of friendship, to the voice of more than one nation. It will at least prove to you, that I have neither forgotten the gratification derived from your society, nor abandoned the prospect of its renewal, whenever your leisure or inclination allows you to atone to your friends for too long an absence.*
>
> *It is said among those friends, I trust truly, that you are engaged in the composition of a poem whose scene will be laid in the East: none can do the scenes so much justice. The wrongs of your own country, the magnificent and fiery spirit of her sons, the beauty and feelings of her daughters, may there be found. Your imagination will provide a warmer sun, and less crowded sky: but*

wildness, tenderness, and originality, are part of your national claim, to which you have thus far proved your title more clearly than the most zealous of your country's antiquarians."

Tommy was so full of emotion he had to stand up and take himself off for another solitary walk behind his favourite tree, because now – this changed everything – his stock would rise – his reputation would soar amongst publishers and readers – and *all* would want to read the new tale set in the East written by "MOORE" the friend of Lord Byron.

It stirred him and stimulated him into a *blasting* new energy for writing and filled him with new hopes for his life. He would return immediately to continue his composition of *Lallah Rookh;* and then, with some more of that wonderful charm of his, Byron may even be able to persuade John Murray to publish it, and pay a high price for it!

~ ~ ~

In London, John Murray was in an absolute *fury,* and took himself off to the residence of Robert Dallas, demanding that *justice* be done!

"You have seen today's newspapers?" He threw down a copy of the *Morning Post.* "Another vicious attack on Lord Byron. You will have to refute them."

"I?" Still in his seat, Dallas stared up at him. "What can *I* do?"

"You can send a letter to *The Times,* and set the record straight. The Times, at least, *tries* to be impartial. The other newspapers are attacking the success of The Corsair as an excuse to accuse Lord Byron of writing poetry solely for the *money*, and due to his *greed* for money ... and you know that's not true."

Dallas was still staring. "I do."

"Lord Byron has never received as much as a farthing from the sales of his works because, due to his grace and favour and kindness, every penny of the money due to him has always gone to *you*."

Dallas was reluctant. For a start, he told John Murray, he did not want his friends and neighbours to know that he was quite wealthy now.

John Murray's eyes narrowed, the stern look of *business* back on his face. "Mr Dallas, if you do not write to *The Times* and tell them the truth, then *I* will do so. And as Lord Byron's publisher, I should know the truth of the matter, should I not?"

He sat down on a chair to wait. "It would be far more advantageous to your *honour*, Mr Dallas, if you were to write the letter yourself."

Dallas knew he had no choice. With John Murray sitting there watching him, he shakily wrote a letter to the Chief Editor of The Times newspaper, informing him as Lord Byron's literary agent, that Lord Byron had never taken a penny from the sales of his poetry, but instead, had kindly made – "*a gift of all such monies to myself, being also a distant relative of his Lordship.*"

And John Murray wasn't even sure about *that*. If anyone was a greedy money-grabber, it was Robert Dallas.

He had stood to take the letter, and now that he had read it, and all was in order, he asked Dallas to seal it.

Dallas did, muttering quietly, "I will post it later."

"Oh no, Mr Dallas, I intend to deliver it, by hand, myself."

~ ~ ~

Unaware of the dispute that had taken place between his literary agent and publisher, Byron was happily reading a letter from Princess Charlotte, who claimed she had read The Corsair, and had "*devoured it twice in the course of one day.*"

Byron smiled as he read on ... it was gushing, yes, but the girl was only eighteen or so ... "*there are passages in the Corsair that would admit of being written in gold.*"

He showed the letter to Fletcher, whose eyes popped when he saw the royal crest and the signature on the letter, and Byron grinned. "What more can a poet ask, than to have such a sweet admirer?"

"And me, having such a famous employer." Fletcher was almost shedding tears of pride. "Do you think she might come here? Princess Charlotte?"

"No, you fool, we are both *unmarried* so that would be scandalous, but I have been invited to a party she is giving at St James's Palace next week."

Byron later read the newspapers, pleased to see that Fletcher had complied with his instructions and torn away the first three pages from all of them.

Let the dogs growl, he would not listen to their barks. His only interest was in the literary pages, where he found that all the reviews for *The Corsair* were laden with praise, many claiming that Lord Byron brought the people of another place and time "to life" and made them "*live again*" for the pleasure of his readers.

His favourite of all, was the review by Francis Jeffreys of the *Edinburgh Review* who had once completely *demolished* his first attempt at writing poetry.

> "*Lord Byron, we think, is the only modern poet who has set before our eyes a visible picture of the present aspect of scenes so famous in history; but*

instead of feeding us with the unsubstantial food of historical associations, he has spread around us the blue seas and dazzling skies – the ruined temples and dusky olives – the desolate cities, and turbaned population, of modern Attica."

~ ~ ~

John Murray called again, and told him that a new print-run had been rushed through to meet all the demands for new orders from around the country.

"But as for London," Murray said, "you cannot meet a man in the street who has not read *The Corsair* and all have looks of satisfaction or speak with expressions of delight."

Fletcher handed Mr Murray his coffee, which he sipped, and then went on, "Of course, some were not so satisfactory and quite idiotic ... one young man told me that he and all his friends believe that *you* are the actual Conrad, the veritable Corsair, and that while you were abroad on your travels, they are certain that you spent part of your time as a pirate involved in piracy."

"Me, *a pirate!"* Once Byron started to laugh he could not stop. "Fletcher, you were there – were we pirates?"

For a moment, Fletcher looked as if he wished they had been, but then admitted, "No, not pirates, but we *did* nearly get drowned in a Turkish galliot that was *like* a pirate ship."

When the time came to leave, John Murray paused at the apartment door and looked at Byron with a soft smile on his face. "You do know, Lord Byron, that I feel very honoured to be your publisher."

Byron nodded. "Thank you."

"And whatever may happen in the future, storms or sunshine, you will always find in me a friend."

~ ~ ~

Byron found his *best* friend a few hours later, when Hobhouse arrived, back from his trip to Paris, more excited and jubilant than Byron had ever seen him.

"*I saw Napoleon!*"

"What?" Byron stared. "You *saw* him? My little pagod? What is he like?"

"Like your bust of him." Hobby looked across the room at Byron's treasured bronze bust of Napoleon. "No, not like your bust at all, much better."

"So what is he like?" Byron repeated.

"I was *that* close to him." Hobby used his hands to measure a gap. "And he looked *glorious!* An arrogant republican from head to toe."

Despite their Englishness, Byron and Hobhouse had always been private admirers of Napoleon, and it was not hard to understand why. Byron was born in the year of 1788, and so he had always claimed to be "*a child of the Revolution.*"

To both, their Whig liberalism was a revolt against the tyranny of kings and bishops and appointed placemen who ruled without election by the people.

"I was *that* close to him – to *Napoleon!*" Hobby said again, his hands in motion, while Byron admitted, "Hobby, I am *green* with envy. Tell me all."

Chapter Twenty-Six

~ ~ ~

The Corsair had now gone into its third edition and John Murray could not have been happier. His career as a publisher was proving to be very successful. And his authors? Oh, he now had a wonderful collection of authors ... Lord Byron, Walter Scott, Washington Irving and the list was growing by the months.

The new chapters for *Emma* were coming in quite regularly, and Miss Austen's book which had been sold to Egertons, *Pride and Prejudice,* was now selling very respectably, which was very commendable for a "*bonnet book*", as Gifford described them.

Although Miss Austen was very *definite* about not wanting her identity to be revealed to the reading public; and consequently all her books were "*Written by a Lady*"

An idea struck him; a good *business* idea. Now he had no particular desire to increase sales for Egertons, why should he? They were, after all, his competitors. Yet if this particular book was to continue selling respectably, and become a favourite with the ladies, then its success would reflect very well on *Emma,* help it get out of the starting gate more quickly, so to speak, especially if the advertisements for it carried the line "*By the Author of Pride and Prejudice*".

And, fortunately, he had a copy of that particular book here in his own home, belonging to his wife, Annie, who had not only enjoyed it, but had never stopped prattling about it – "*Mr Darcy this*", and "*Mr Darcy that* ... *"* and who was this *"lady"* who had written the book? Did he *know?* Could he *say?*

And the answer to both was "No." Although of course he *did* know, but a publisher's word and agreement with his author, or in this case – author*ess* – was as legally binding as that of a lawyer.

Later that evening, he called in on William Gifford, carrying his wife's copy of *Pride and Prejudice.* Gifford was not only a director, but also one of the main *critics* for the *Quarterly Review* – hence the reason he had been so eager to get *Childe Harold's Pilgrimage* into Gifford's hands, to see if he supported his opinion of it.

"William, I know this book is not one of mine, but the author soon will be; so I wonder if you would read it and give it an *honest* review in the *Quarterly.*"

"I never give anything less. If it's bad, I say so. What book is it?"

Murray handed him the book. "*Pride and Prejudice.*"

Gifford frowned, as if pensive with pain. He was smoking a cigar, and bit on it.

"This is all I need after a hard week. My sister, you know, a noisy girl at the best of times, but *this* week quite insufferable, capable of no other conversation but that of *Pride and Prejudice.* Don't ask me to read it, John, because I have already done so – under my sister's *duress.*"

"And?"

"Well, it's damned *good.* Much better than most of the overblown and preposterous dross our ladies write these days, especially those ridiculous *gothic* novels by Mrs Radcliffe."

"So will you write a review?"

Gifford sighed and said, "If I don't, then the next time my sister graces my home with her presence, I will be forced to suffer *pepper* in my tea instead of sugar."

He sat back and chewed on his cigar while looking at Murray.

"She does things like that, you know, my sister Evelyn, ever since we were children ... pepper in my tea, sugar on my poached eggs, vinegar in my wine ... all to make me give in to her mischievous force ... God knows how a dotty woman like Mrs Bennet would have coped with her."

John Murray smiled, his work had already been done for him; and sure enough, in the following edition of the *Quarterly*, a review of the book appeared, written in William Gifford's inimitable, straight-to-the-point, style:

I have for the first time looked into 'Pride and Prejudice'; and it is really a very pretty thing. No dark passages; no secret chambers; no wind howling in the long galleries; no drops of blood upon a rusty dagger – things that should now be left to ladies' maids and sentimental washerwomen."

Chapter Twenty-Seven

~ ~ ~

Tuesday 22nd

Last night, a 'party' at Lansdowne House. Tonight, a 'party' at Lady Charlotte Greville's – both a deplorable waste of time. Nothing imparted – nothing acquired – talking without ideas or much purpose – And in this way, half of London pass what is called life.

'Sdeath!

Albany, 28th

This night got into my new apartments at Albany in Piccadilly, rented from Viscount Althorp, on a lease of seven years. Very spacious, and room for all my books and sabres. Viscount Althorp – soon to be the 3rd Earl Spencer – has departed to be married, and kindly offered it to me.

Yesterday, dined tête-à-tête at the Cocoa Tree with Scrope Davies – from six till midnight – drank between us one bottle of champagne and six of claret, neither of which wines has ever affected me. Paid Scrope four thousand, eight hundred pounds, a debt of some standing, and which I wished to have paid him before. My mind is much relieved by the removal of that debt.

Lord Byron's mounting debts were a matter of great concern to his attorney, John Hanson.

For some time now, he had sent letter after letter to his lordship, warning him about his spending, but he now suspected that Lord Byron never read past the first paragraph.

The difficulty for Hanson, due to the busy life he led in his law chambers at Lincoln's Inn, was that he could rarely visit his lordship in the daytime, only at night; and to call on his lordship at night was to *always* be told that he was not at home.

Not that Fletcher ever *lied* about his lordship not being at home. Hanson read the social pages and had heard enough gossip to also know that Lord Byron was invited to attend at least three parties every night, and often attended *all* of them in one night – *an unapologetic playboy* – in Hanson's opinion. But he was young, and according to the gossip, his appearance anywhere was a competition in rivalry for all party hostesses.

All that, John Hanson could understand and forgive, but this latest news in the *Times* – that Lord Byron had never profited by a penny from the successful sales of his poetic works – was shocking, truly *shocking*.

Well, he would soon put a stop to that!

Hanson set off in his carriage immediately after his mid-day luncheon, only remembering at the last minute that Lord Byron had moved from his old address in Bennett Street, to that building of sumptuous gentlemen's apartments at Albany in Piccadilly.

Another extravagance!

Hanson sat back in his carriage, remembering what

Thomas Babbington Macaulay, who lived there, had once said to him about Albany – *"No son of a duke would be ashamed to put the Albany address on his card."*

And yes, right there next door was the grand residence of Lord Byron's new neighbour, the Duke of Devonshire.

Upon reaching Albany's front gate, and lowering the window to stretch out his arm to give the porter his card, Hanson could not miss the grand opulence of the porter's uniform ... a coat with scarlet cuffs and collar and white buttons, a scarlet waistcoat, and a round red hat on his head.

"Is it true," Hanson asked the porter curiously, "that the Albany apartments actually have cisterns that allow water to be pumped through to the bathrooms?"

"Oh, yes, sir, but the man who does that job, pumping the water through and keeping all the cisterns full, is the porter at the *back* gate."

And no doubt the porter at the *back* gate received a lesser wage, for it was known that the front porters of the Albany received a wage of £50 a year – a large wage for a mere porter.

"Which apartment, sir?" asked the porter.

"Apartment two. Lord Byron."

The porter nodded, and waved him on. It was not yet two o'clock and Hanson was certain he would find Lord Byron at home at this time of the day; and he did.

"Mr Hanson, what a pleasure to see you again!" Byron was all smiles, as if all the letters from Hanson had never been received.

Hanson was wryly amused. "Practising for a performance at the Drury Lane Theatre, my lord? If so, your acting skills need to improve."

Still smiling, Byron pretended innocence. "*Acting skills ...* whatever can you mean?"

Hanson stood for a moment in the huge drawing-room gazing at the large bow window which had a perfect view of the gardens ... and then he sat himself down on one of the sofas, and looked up shrewdly at his young charge.

"You forget, my lord, that I was your personal guardian from your childhood until you reached your majority of twenty-one. And I have also been looking after you and your business ever since."

"Indeed." Byron agreed.

"So I know you inside out and up and down in the same way I know my own sons, so can we pray stop this pretence of innocence and be serious?"

"If you insist," Byron agreed reluctantly, sitting down on the sofa opposite. "But can we not be *too* serious?"

"Impossible, under the circumstances ..." Hanson was opening his briefcase, taking out his copy of the *Times* and requesting an explanation.

Byron shrugged. "I can't take money for my scribblings. I prefer to hold on to my amateur status in all that."

"Because your true desire is to be a politician?"

"No, because I look at those who have gone before me. Voltaire *never* took any money for his writings, only books ... a few copies of his books now and again to give away to his friends."

"And no doubt he died in poverty."

"He died in Paris, a great writer and a great man, and no, I don't think he died in poverty, not with so many eminent friends who loved and supported him, such as Benjamin Franklin."

Hanson looked round as Fletcher carried in a tray of

coffee, and all conversation between the two men ceased, both well-trained in the old maxim of "Not in front of the servants."

While Fletcher poured the coffee and spoke to his lordship, John Hanson remained silent. His elegant features expressed nothing. He sat looking at Lord Byron, without illusion, and with great affection.

In the past, for so many years, Hanson reflected, he had been like a quasi-father to the boy-lord, bringing him to live in his own home with his other children in order to protect the boy from his horrendous mother. His schooling, his education at Harrow and Cambridge, everything had been of the highest concern to John Hanson, always endeavouring to ensure a good life for the boy; so he could not see the him *ruined* now.

As soon as Fletcher had left the room, he returned to business, taking out a wad of bank papers and querying a cheque here and a cheque there and – "For what reason did you give a cheque for the enormous amount of four thousand eight hundred pounds to Mr Scrope Berdmore Davies?"

"To go abroad in 1809."

"To go abroad? But I had already supplied you with the finances for that."

"Not enough. On the amount you gave me I would have had to live like a beggar, so Scrope came to my rescue."

"Is this the friend who makes most of his fortune from gambling?"

"Yes. Also, the amount that Hobhouse's father had given to him for his travels was so paltry, I decided to borrow enough from Scrope to secure us both."

"And yet, Hobhouse's father had not given him a penny for his travels, according to a letter to me at that time from your mother. He did not even know his son had gone abroad. Did Hobhouse ever pay that money back to you?"

"Yes, as soon he returned to England his father paid it into my bank immediately. You must have a record of it."

"I'm sure I do, but I will check when I get back to my office. Now, can you tell me why you paid two cheques for two more enormous sums – five hundred pounds each to James Webster and Lady F. Webster?"

"No, I cannot."

"Why not?"

"Because I choose not to, because that is *my* business."

Byron stood up, aggravated. "Mr Hanson, your job is to look after my estate and business overall, but you have no right, *no right,* to come here and question me about the personal details and the reason for every pound I spend. Do you think I am *still* a child?"

"Perhaps I do, but you are not any longer, are you? You are a grown man now – so now I will speak to you man to man."

~ ~ ~

Collecting Byron for dinner that evening, John Hobhouse was in a low and sullen mood; but he immediately forgot his own misery when he saw the same sullenness on Byron's face.

"What's wrong?"

"Nothing at all," replied Byron, swinging himself and his cloak out through the apartment door with all the haughtiness of a matador preparing to fight a bull.

Hobhouse followed him, knowing that now was not the time to tell Byron his own bad news.

"We will dine in the Albany Rooms," Byron said over his shoulder. "I've no wish to meet anyone else tonight."

As soon as they were seated, Hobhouse decided to start the evening by passing on some interesting gossip.

"Do you know what I was told today? James Webster, and his wife have spent the last few months residing in Scotland."

Byron turned his head and stared around the room, making it clear he was not interested in that particular subject ... although now that he *had* looked around, he could see a number of young gentlemen dining, leaning forward and whispering to each other and glancing back at him, while the ladies at their table were staring at him directly over the rim of their fans, murmuring to each other.

He abruptly turned his back on them and gave all his attention to Hobby. "I know that. The Websters are living quite close to Walter Scott, and he says that Webster has become a veritable pest of a neighbour. His actual words were – *a pest of the first water*. A Scottish expression."

Hobhouse frowned. "And who told *you* that?"

"The horse's mouth. Walter Scott himself. In a letter to me."

"Oh, good grief, Byron, why are we wasting our time with gossip? *You* are in a foul mood, and *I* am in a foul mood, so we should tell each other why."

Byron shrugged. "You first."

"No, you."

"Very well. But it's all my own fault." Byron filled his water glass. "My debts are so bad that Hanson now says I may have to sell Newstead."

A heavy shock seemed to run through Hobhouse as he stared. "Sell Newstead? You can't do that!"

"According to John Hanson I may have to. It's either that, sell Newstead – or find a Golden Dolly to marry, one rich enough to send all my debts flying away."

Hobby was horrified. "Marry a Golden Dolly? You can't do that either."

Byron sighed and shrugged. "No, but the end is nigh whichever option I choose, because both of those suggestions would result in me blowing my brains out anyway. I will *not* sell Newstead, and I will never marry unless I love."

"What about all the money from the Rochdale coal mines?" Hobby asked. "The money due to you from them is over sixty thousand pounds, at the very least, which would make you extremely rich. And how high are your debts?"

"Twelve thousand."

"So if the Rochdale business was settled and that money came to you, as well as what you receive yearly in rents from your estate, you could –"

"No. Hanson says the Rochdale lot have appealed again, and it could drag on through the Appellant Court for years. The High Court has already ruled that my great-uncle had no legal right to sell the mines, and the mines and all former profits should be returned to me, but still they keep on appealing the ruling, in order to stall for time."

Hobhouse sighed. "I have no wish to be an 'I-told-you-so', but you must admit that I *did* warn you in the past about your foolish generosity to others."

"And *you* must admit, Hobby, that I have in the past given you almost as much credit for all your good qualities as you do yourself."

Hobhouse ignored the sarcasm. "You have to learn that money is *not* for spending. Only poor people think money is for spending, whereas truly rich people know that money is to be used wisely and a part of it is to be used mainly for the making of *more* money."

"Truly rich people, like your father?"

"Indeed. He gives me the same lecture once a month. Assets, savings, interest, all that. But at least I am not foolish with money. You and Scrope Davies are as bad as each other."

"What the devil has *Scrope* got to do with it?"

Hobhouse waited until the waiter had taken their order before he continued, "Last night," he said in a low voice, "last night I was with Scrope at the Cocoa Tree club, in a back room, and what do think happened?"

Byron turned up his eyes with irritation. "I'm not a clairvoyant, Hobby. I can't *see* across London from behind my bed-curtains. I presume it *was* very late at night? The Cocoa being a night club."

"Oh yes, very late. Scrope had just had a considerable run of luck, and the two of us were about to leave the club, when a boisterous young gentleman, accompanied by his friends, entered looking for Beau Brummell, wanting to take him on in any game of cards, fair and square.

"So Scrope told him, '*Mister* Brummell is not here tonight'. Then says the young Heighho, 'So pray tell me where I may find *Mister* Scrope Davies?'

"'I am he,' says Scrope, and would you believe the impudent young brat then *challenged* Scrope to play him."

Even Byron had to laugh at that. "Was he drunk?"

"No, not at all, but very determined. I suspect he had made a second bet with his friends – probably a very high wager that he was good enough to take on the best two players in London."

Hobhouse paused when the waiter arrived to serve the food, very slowly, his eyes constantly darting excitedly to Byron ... which irritated Hobby who was itching to get on with his tale. But when the food was served, the waiter again took an endless time to pour the wine, until Byron finally lifted his napkin, and shaking it out, flicked it close to the waiter's face. "Oh, I'm sorry, I thought you had finished!"

Byron scowled as the waiter moved off. "Another of those idiots who think I am a pirate in disguise."

He lifted his glass. "So back to our young Heighho and his challenge. Did Scrope take him on?"

"Sadly, yes."

Byron stared. "No ... you're not going to tell me –"

"I'm going to tell you *exactly* what happened, and the reason why I say Scrope Davies is a fool with money."

"Not a word against him!" Byron knocked back a slug of wine. "I won't listen to one bad word against our friend Scrope, no matter what he has done or did – it's all *N'importe* to me."

"Scrope Davies," said Hobhouse, "was the perfect gentleman that he always is, and was calm and skilful throughout, as he always is – but the foolish fellow kept insisting on playing game after game and wagering more and more until he had nothing left to wager."

"Scrope?"

"No, the Heighho. Dawn it nearly was, when it was all over, and he looked a sickly sight at the end, as did his three friends who had for hours been pleading with him to stop, but, alas, his arrogance forbade it."

"So how much did Scrope win?"

"Everything that young man possessed. A *ruined* young man who had just reached his majority of twenty-one years and come into a sizable fortune. But by the end of play he had lost it all, his home, his estate, his yellow carriage parked outside, everything."

Byron was baffled. "Why did Scrope allow him to continue to play? And I'm surprised at Scrope taking up the challenge in the first place. You know he usually never plays against individuals – his game is always against the house. So why?"

Hobhouse shrugged. "I think he just wanted to teach the young upstart a lesson, and it was a lesson hard learned. Oh, if you had seen him, Byron, sitting there crying his eyes out, while Scrope had a long serious talk with him, listening to him sobbing that he was now reduced to being a beggar, and he about to get married in a few weeks time."

Byron slowly smiled, because he knew Scrope Davies. "Scrope gave him some of his losses back?"

"Scrope gave him *all* of his losses back! Every signed and witnessed IOU – but on *one* condition which he made the young loser promise – to *never* gamble again, which he readily promised to Scrope with genuine sincerity.

Byron was still smiling. "That's our Scrope."

Hobhouse nodded. "One of the best – a *Cambridge* man, you see?"

Byron laughed. "Scrope would be no different if he had gone to Oxford."

"Well, maybe not, but when I told him he was a fool to have given *all* of it back, he said, 'No, I'm glad I did, because I shall sleep better tonight because of it'."

Hobhouse chuckled. "So I had to remind Scrope that the night was long gone, and it was morning."

Byron suddenly noticed a young man accompanied by a lady entering the room, and immediately put his hand up to the side of his face, and turned away towards the wall, until the two new arrivals had passed on.

Hobhouse knew that habit of Byron's whenever he did not want someone to see him, and his eyes followed the young gent and lady, wondering who they were.

"Who?" he asked.

"John Claridge, a friend from my Harrow days. He kindly came to spend a few days with me at Newstead after my mother and Matthews died, and succeeded in making me feel even more despondent."

Hobhouse frowned. "That was indeed kind of him. So why did you not want him to see you tonight, if only to say hello?"

"Oh, I'm not in the mood to be sociable and friendly to anyone, not tonight, and when it comes to Claridge, the fault lies more with me than with him."

Byron glanced around to look down the long room and saw that Claridge was now seated with his back to him; and then relaxed.

"Now there," he said to Hobby, "is John Claridge, a good man, a handsome man, an honourable man, a most inoffensive man, a well-informed man, and a *dull* man – and the last undoes all the rest."

He sipped his wine. "And then there is our Yorick, Scrope Davies, with perhaps no better intellect, and certainly not half of Claridge's sterling qualities, and yet in *his* company, Scrope is the life and soul of me and everybody else."

"And 'alas, poor Yorick' is probably still asleep in his bed now after his long night of gambling," said Hobhouse, "which is where I should be too. I also had no sleep last night."

At the Albany porter's gate, where they stood to say farewell, Hobhouse did indeed look very tired. "One last thing, Byron ... now that you *know* your financial situation is precarious, you cannot go on accepting no money from the sales of your poetry. If nothing else it's stupid."

"Damned stupid." Byron nodded. "I see that now. Oh well ..." he turned towards the path, "no point in making presents of my work to my literary agent any longer, especially as I send all my work direct to John Murray."

Hobhouse could not stem his aggravation. "And yet *Reverend* Dallas is always there to collect his share of the profits."

"Oh," said Byron, remembering, and turning round to Hobby, "you said you were also in a foul mood, but you have not yet told me why."

"Oh good grief! ... I wish you had not reminded me of *that*," said Hobby, and then sadly told Byron *his* bad news; which, an hour later, Byron sadly recorded in his journal:

April 8th

My poor little pagod, Napoleon, has been pushed off his pedestal; – the thieves are in Paris. It is his own fault.

He put his pen down, and placed his elbow on the desk, resting the side of his face against his hand as he half-slumped over the desk in misery, utter misery, because what he had *not* told Hobby tonight, was that by the end of his long session with John Hanson, he had agreed to allow him to arrange for all the horses at Newstead, save two, to be sold in order to pay off some of the debts. His beloved horses!

But worse, oh, even worse than that, and still hurting his heart, was that he had also been forced to agree to sell off his cherished library of *books*.

It had to be done, if his honour was to be maintained,

pay off his creditors who deserved to be paid what they were due. Hanson intended to arrange the sale of the books by auction, certain they would raise a high price.

He sighed ... how could Hanson equate *books* with money? Books were the treasure-trove of life, full of ancient wisdom and philosophy and ... right down to the present day – Germaine de Staël, for instance – how much less would the world know about *Rousseau* if she had not written her brilliant biography about him? And Robert Southey? As much as he disliked Southey personally, his *Life of Nelson* was beautiful.

Well, it was either that, sacrifice his library of books, or sacrifice Newstead, or marry a golden dolly, and he would never do the last two ... although, sometimes he did think it might be nice to be married, if only to have someone to yawn with in winter.

Yet how would he ever cope with a wife in a house without a library of various *books* to read?

Sighing, he picked up his pen to write down the truth of his thoughts in his journal:

I think I am happiest when alone, in the company of only my lamp, and my utterly confused and tumbled-over library. If I always had books to read, I doubt I would ever feel the need to go out into society.

Chapter Twenty-Eight

~~~

The following morning, after reading the newspapers, Byron was furious and journalising again:

Saturday, April 9th, 1814

I mark this day!

Napoleon Bonaparte has abdicated the throne of the world.

What? Wait till they were in his capital, and then talk of his readiness to give up what is already gone!

The "Isle of Elba" to retire to? – Well – if it had been Capri, I should have marvelled less. But after all, a crown may not be worth dying for.

But to outlive Lodi for this! Alas, this imperial diamond hath a flaw in it, and is now hardly fit to stick in a glazier's pencil.

But I won't give him up even now; although all his admirers have fallen from him.

P.S: Hang up philosophy and political revolution – in Paris, those royal Bourbons are restored !!!

Closing the journal and removing the newspapers from his desk, Byron caught sight of an article about himself, which he stood reading with a wry and amused expression on his face.

He was still reading it when Fletcher rushed in. "My lord, pray do *not* read page three of the *Post* – I meant to tear it out, but Mrs Mule fussed me into one of her squabbles and distracted me."

Byron looked at him. "Have you read this?"

"No, my lord, I saw only your name at the top."

"Well, it seems, Fletcher, that a long *'Anti-Byron'* poem has been published, to prove to the public that I have formed a conspiracy to overthrow, by *rhyme,* all religion and government, and have already made great progress!"

"Overthrow the government?" Fletcher blinked. "Are they being serious?"

"Very serious." Byron could not help laughing. "I never thought myself so *important* before. To induce such an epic! It seems they believe I am becoming as dangerous as a new young *Voltaire!* Ooons! what a compliment to me!"

Fletcher did not think it a bit funny, knowing all the gossip it would cause, especially among other London *valets.* They would hear of it, and jibe him, and he would maybe have to punch a few of them.

"That will cause a lot of talk about you in town, my lord. Best to stay home for a few days, until all the gossip dies down."

"Stay at home? Why the devil should I do that? Am I not invited to a Masque Ball at Wattiers tonight?"

"Aye, my lord."

"And are Mr Hobhouse and Mr Davies invited also?"

"I dunno, my lord."

"Well they are, and so am I, and I shall go – as a *Highwayman!"* He chuckled again. "Do we still have that costume, and the black mask?"

~ ~ ~

The aspect that many of the aristocratic and wealthy

gentlemen of Regency London loved about the *masquerade* balls is that some of the high-class *courtesans* could attend in disguise, adding a flavour of sex and mystery to the night. Who was to know who was who, and therefore forbid entry?

The one and only main rule of absolute *forbiddance* at the balls, was to lift, or to try and lift, any person's mask, and reveal their identity.

However if any person decided to remove their own mask, that was their prerogative.

At the door, as one of the committee and organisers of the event, Beau Brummell was not wearing a mask, deeming it pointless, as everyone would know who he was due to his height – but Brummell instantly recognised Lord Byron in his black shirt and mask and grinned, "What ho! – the man in black! Now *who* could he be?"

And then Brummell's eyes moved past Byron to the stocky figure of Hobhouse wearing a huge turban on his head, and then moving down the body over the Turkish long dress that reached Hobhouse's shoes, making Brummell erupt with laughter.

"Hobhouse, dear fellow, have you come as a Turkish Sultan?"

Hobhouse lifted his mask to glare at Brummell. "My outfit is actually *Albanian,* which, I may add, I purchased myself, while I was *in* the province of Albania." He flipped his mask back down. "I have come as a Pasha."

"And my dear fellow, it *suits* you right down to the ground!" exclaimed Brummell, and then pulled Byron aside to tell him: "You are late, very late, which is fortunate in the circumstances."

"Why?"

"Madame de Staël is here, and she has spent a long time looking for you, constantly coming up to me and asking '"Ave you seen milord Byronn? Does 'e come? Why does 'e *not* come?"

Byron paused, knowing that Beau Brummell and Germaine de Staël disliked each other. *He* was not her kind of man – too English; and *she* was certainly not his kind of woman; a bluestocking with too much intellect who spent too much of her own and everyone else's time trying to discuss politics. And it was not only Brummell that Madame de Staël personally irritated, it was ... well, *everybody.*

"Why is it fortunate for me?" he asked curiously. "I'd rather enjoy speaking with her tonight, especially now that Napoleon –"

"Oh no, dear fellow, no!" Brummell's eyes stared in warning. "Not *tonight*! Keep as far away from her as you possibly can tonight!"

Byron looked at Hobhouse, then back to Brummell. "Why?"

"Because you are her chosen crown-prince, don't you know? She's hell-bent on making you her son-in-law. And tonight, she is accompanied by her daughter *Libertine.*"

Byron laughed. "Albertine."

Brummell shrugged. "Oh, well, she looks to me as if she wouldn't mind being a libertine if she was let. But don't worry, dear friend, you are quite safe now, because *we* have taken care of it for you."

"We?" asked Hobhouse. "Who is we?"

Smiling gleefully, Brummell went on to explain that he and two of his friends had quietly told Madame de Staël, "*in the strictest secrecy, of course*" that not only was Lord Alvanley filthy rich – worth over a hundred thousand pounds, he was here tonight —"*and looking for a wife.*"

"Lord Alvanley!" Hobhouse exclaimed. "Good grief, that man has to be the ugliest man in England."

"Ah, yes," Brummell grinned, "but a fortune of one hundred thousand pounds can give a man a lot of love appeal."

"And when she discovers the truth?" asked Hobhouse. "It's common knowledge that Alvanley has made some disastrous investments of late, and now has only his house still standing to support his name"

"Oh, stop fussing!" Brummell ordered. "I shall inform Libertine of the truth about Alvanley at the end of the night, of course I will."

"And here's our Yorick!" said Byron, delighted to see Scrope Davies walking in, dressed as a monk. "Did you get that robe from Newstead?"

Scrope nodded. "I've had it since your twenty-first birthday jamboree, packed by mistake. You don't mind, do you?"

"They *charged* me for that, the costumiers. They insisted Fletcher had returned one costume short."

"Blame my valet, Byron, blame my valet who must have packed it by mistake. *I* did not realise I had it until yesterday."

Scrope was taking in Byron and Hobhouse's costumes with smiling eyes; and then fixed on Brummell, dressed beautifully elegant in white cravat and waistcoat and a dark-blue tailed jacket. He was not wearing a fancy-dress costume, and surely the *only* man in the place not to be doing so.

"You are not wearing fancy-dress," Scrope said with some surprise.

"I certainly am," replied Brummell. "Why do you

think I am not?"

"Because ..." Scrope was puzzled. "So which famous personage have you come as? Who?"

"Who?" Brummell looked wide-eyed at Scrope as if the answer was obvious. "I have come as Beau Brummell!"

~ ~ ~

After more jests and laughter with Brummell, the three friends moved through the wide hall and past the immense suite of rooms towards the ballroom, pausing every few minutes to scoop up a glass of champagne from a footman's tray and knocking them back like thirsty camels.

"As a matter of fact," said Hobhouse, "camels can go for a very long time before feeling thirsty ..." to which Byron and Scrope looked at each other and laughed.

"For goodness sake, Hobby, stop being so *correct* about everything!"

All the footmen at Wattiers were dressed alike in light blue dominoes and wore no masks; and now another footman rushed up with his silver tray, and the three helped themselves to champagne again; until Hobhouse, at least, was slightly tipsy by the time they reached the ballroom ... Although even by then, and everywhere he moved through the crowds, a certain *shepherdess* in a mask kept following Byron, and he knew *who* it was, so she must have recognised him even in his mask – Lady Caroline Lamb.

He pretended not to recognise her, ignoring her at all costs, more interested in a delightful Greek nymph, whom he suspected to be a courtesan in disguise, and the two became flirtatiously close, until a dancer on the floor bumped into them and broke them apart – Lady

Caroline Lamb.

"That infernal woman!" said Byron, watching her dance away, and then turned back to his nymph who pulled him into a corner behind the crowd, moving close and lightly touching his neck above his open black collar with gentle fingers. "You once told me, Lord Byron –"

"You know who I am? Even behind my mask?"

"Of course. You are as distinguishable as Beau Brummell, even behind your mask."

Byron shrugged, and smiled. "Oh well, let's continue, so that I may get a clue as to who *you* are. I once told you what?"

"That I was not beautiful."

"*Not* beautiful? *I* said that? Oh, surely not? Even with a mask over your eyes you look very pretty, from what I can see."

"Yes, you said I was pretty, but no, *not* beautiful."

So, she *was* a courtesan in disguise. She had to be, because he knew he would never have said anything that truthful to a lady of *finesse.*

Minutes later, when he rejoined Scrope Davies and Hobhouse further down the room, both standing on the sidelines scrutinising the dancers and trying to guess who was who in their masks and costumes, until they turned to look at him, surprised that he had left his Greek nymph.

"But ... a minute ago," said Hobhouse, "the last time I looked –"

"I know, I know," Byron shrugged. "She informed me that I had once told her that she was *not* beautiful, and what woman would ever forgive a man that?"

"Very few," Scrope agreed.

"Then she must know you from some other occasion," Hobhouse said. "One of your *evening squeezes*, perhaps?"

"No, I'm damned certain she is a courtesan, and if I had ended up with her, she would probably have spent the night *biting* me in *revenge* until I was black and blue."

His eyes were on the dance floor, just as a certain *shepherdess*, Caroline Lamb, danced along the floor near to him, and seeing him looking at her, she suddenly lifted up the back of her dress to show him her frilly green pantaloons – which caused some gasps around the room.

"Anyhow, I wish women were more modest," Byron said, ignoring the green pantaloons and deciding that Caroline Lamb was as mad as King George. "I'm off for a stroll in the garden to get some air."

He did not get very far, for along one of the corridors *another* woman, sitting on one of the settees, caught his attention and his smile ... Colonel Armstrong fancily dressed as an old, stiff, maiden-lady of high rank in the reign of Queen Anne. He wore no mask; but his face, patched and painted, was easily known. He was sat on the settee in his hooped skirt and ruffles and brown curly wig, fanning himself in the heat, and then looking around –"What ho! Lord Byron! Ha! Ha! Ha! Like your disguise! Capital!"

"It's not a good disguise if you instantly *recognised* me."

"It's that light limp of yours," Armstrong said. "Who would not recognise it? One or two others do walk with a limp, but they are *old* and so plod it, but you have a way of walking with that very *light* limp which is very recognisable, what?"

Byron's limp had been a part of him for so long, he had forgotten that others would notice it.

"Then I may as well take this off," he said, removing his mask and sitting down beside Armstrong to chat awhile.

Occasionally Byron glanced at the passing footmen who could hardly keep their faces straight at the sight of the colonel in his wig and skirts and hoops.

Others passing by also stopped to look and laugh at the colonel, but Armstrong answered all their questions with the most dignified politeness in the voice of his lady character; while the roars of laughter which were bestowed on his efforts to make himself look so very ridiculous, never once tempted him to change a single muscle of his face or the high tone of his voice as he answered all. "Immense crowd! Charming evening! Charming"

Byron was unable to sit straight from laughing. Armstrong's had to be the best costume and best character of the night.

And then the Duke of Devonshire arrived without even a hint of a smile on his face and – as a member of Wattier's committee – presented Armstrong with some tickets for a raffle.

"These," said His Grace bowing low, "will entitle your Ladyship to one chance each in the lottery, which will commence drawing at midnight."

"Capital!" exclaimed Armstrong in a high plummy voice. "So kind of you! And perhaps one mayt even *win*, mayt one?"

Only then did the Duke's face crack slightly as he presented a few more tickets, trying to hold back his laugh. "And for you, Lord Byron ... the lottery ... twelve o'clock ... good luck."

A few moments later a short and stocky middle-aged woman, accompanied by six younger short and stocky females, came down the hall and stood to stare at Armstrong, who obviously knew the woman, yet spoke to her in the high voice of a Queen Anne dowager:

"I say, Madam, those poor girls, your daughters, you have been hawking those poor girls around for the last five years or more. Maybe they'd be more successful if you offered them all in a lump, eh? Or if you were to tie them up in bunches, you see, like they do with cherries?"

The woman and her entourage rushed on towards the ballroom as quickly as possible, and Armstrong turned to Byron and said quietly in his own voice, "That's told her, eh what? Though I'd never have *dared* to say it to her as a gentleman."

Byron smiled. "Yes, I suppose there is something *free-ing* when wearing a disguise. Although I'm certain she recognised you."

Armstrong's eyes popped. "No! You don't say ... oh, good Lord! Now there will be salt on her tongue whenever she meets me in the future ... hell to pay ... oh, damn!"

Chapter Twenty-Nine

~ ~ ~

Inside the ballroom and throughout the spacious and luxurious rooms of Wattiers club, there were a number of high-class courtesans in fancy-dress with their faces and identities hidden behind masks, but none were as high class as Harriette Wilson.

Only the very privileged were allowed her favours, and then rarely so, unless they gifted her with many *favours* in return; and certainly no person below the aristocracy, except, of course, her dear friend Beau Brummell.

But then Beau Brummell was so *un*predictable; sometimes he loved her, and at other times he ignored her, depending on his mood. And he was never willing to *own* the friendship, always ignoring her blankly in public as if he did not know her any better than a stranger.

Yet he was such *fun* to be with, in secret, and he always agreed to help her when she asked for advice, even though his advice was usually quite useless and too *flippant* to be tolerable.

Only last week, as he was heading towards the bedroom door, she had asked him, with some sadness: "Beau, how does a woman make a man stay with her after sex?"

He had turned and stared at her. "Stay?"

"Yes, when a woman is wide awake and blissful after their lovemaking, but the man is ready to leave her all alone, what should she do?"

"Do?" Brummell had stared at her in that way of his,

as if the answer was obvious. "She should read a book!"

And then he was gone, and in truth she knew he did not care a fig for her; but she was beautiful and dainty and her fine manners and delicate behaviour would surpass those of a Duchess or any member of royalty, and so, *so* many men had fallen in love with her, although *never* the men *she* loved.

Harriette looked around her; the crowd was quite huge, and she had lost her dear friend Julia Johnstone, and Amy, and her sister Fanny, all lost in the crowd.

The four had excitedly set off today in high spirits, and had been advised to get into their carriage at five in the afternoon, if they were to stand a chance of getting into the Ball at nine or ten o'clock. Others, it seemed, had been given the same advice, and so they had been obliged to sit in their carriage on the road for hours, behind the long queue of other carriages, until they were finally admitted into Wattiers around nine o'clock.

The newspapers, every year, had always described this event in glowing colours as the most *marvellous masquerade,* but only the *elite* and their friends were invited to attend. So how Harriette had obtained her four tickets was a matter she refused to discuss, not even with her sister Fanny. They were here, and that was that – *Victory!*

And what did they find here? So many men to choose from; so many men to tease. Yet as the night wore on Harriette realised she had only met *boring* men so far, because most were accompanied by their wives. And those that were single were not as inspiring as she had hoped, and she had run away from them as soon as she had discovered their stupidity. A *stupid* man could never be inspiring, no matter how handsome or rich.

But she loved a masquerade, because a female can

never enjoy the same liberty anywhere else. So delightful to be able to wander about in a crowd wearing a mask, speaking to whomever she pleased, without being stared at or remarked upon.

Yet there was *one man* Harriette had long wanted to have, not only in her bed, but also in admiration of her, and what a notch that would be on her bedpost! To be able to say she had been loved by *Lord Byron* himself. And that famous young poet was said to be *here* tonight.

Harriette paused to inspect herself in one of the long wall mirrors. She was dressed as a flower-girl, wearing a bright red, thick silk petticoat, with a black satin bodice, the form of which was very enhancing to her shape. And it was not too *high* on the breast. Her shoes were black satin and her stockings were fine blue silk with red clocks on them.

She turned her head from left to right and to the front again ... on her head she wore a small black hat, almost flat in shape, which she wore at one side of her head. Her dark hair fell over her mask and neck in a profusion of careless ringlets. *Perfect!*

The grand supper-rooms had been thrown open earlier to accommodate everyone, and now Harriette rushed to find her seat, confused at finding no place-setting for "Miss Harriette Wilson" – forgetting that the name on her official invitation carried the fake name of an Italian countess. Finally, seeing Fanny and Amy, she arrived at her table and sat down panting from the efforts of her search.

Supper consisted of every rare delicacy and one course after another was sublime to the taste. The wines were delicious and the members of Wattier's club were as attentive as though they had all been trained valets; all the members, that is, except for Mister George 'Beau'

Brummell, who was the only exception. Instead of parading behind their chairs to inquire if anyone needed anything, he sat teasing a lady wearing a wax mask, declaring that he would not leave her until he had seen her face.

Such an insult to herself!

Harriette chose that moment to stand up and let Brummell know that she was furious with him, by walking out of the supper room. Although she was *not* furious with him at all, simply full to the gills, and the thought of having to remain sitting at the table ... when she could be *investigating* the less-crowded rooms of the exclusive Wattiers club.

One of the immense suite of rooms formed a delicious, refreshing contrast to the dazzling brilliancy of all the others. It was dimly lit, and contained a profusion of almost every rare exotic plant and flower. The room was lighted by large ground glass, with French globe-lamps suspended from the ceiling at equal distances. The rich draperies were of pale green satin and white silver muslin. The Turkish ottomans, which were uniformly placed, were covered in green satin to match the drapery, and fringed with silver.

Harriette stood at the door, her eyes wide in awe, for the room was like the rooms of the luxurious palaces of the fairies described in her childhood storybooks.

At first she thought the room was deserted, and was about to step inside, until she saw the dark figure of one solitary individual. His head was uncovered, and presented a fine model for the painter's art. He was unmasked, and his bright eyes seemed earnestly fixed, she could not discover on what ... for when she looked in the same direction, she saw only exotic plants – not enough to hold a man's interest so earnestly. He seemed to be looking into another world, and not into the room at all.

He must have foregone the eating of supper, and come in here instead.

Harriette watched his unchanged attitude for some minutes, and slowly began to realise who he must be. His age might be six or seven and twenty, or less. His complexion clear olive. His stance was graceful in the extreme, and his face so beautiful, Harriette realised that no, she would be too afraid to love him. There was a strange remoteness about him that was ... forbidding.

"Still, while I have this chance, I will speak to him," Harriette decided, and moved forward daintily and quietly on the tips of her feet.

He seemed not to have heard her, for he did not change his position, nor did his eyes move from their fixed gaze on what seemed to be just space and air, until she went up close, and spoke softly to him.

"Lord Byron?"

He started violently, as if her voice had shocked him, and when he turned his head and looked at her, she saw his mouth was beautifully formed, and the brightness of his blue eyes and their questioning expression, fixed her attention on him like a staring child.

He looked back at her, but did not say a word.

"I do not know you," she said breathily, "and it has only this moment struck me that you *must* be Lord Byron, whom I have heard so much about."

"And you are Harriette Wilson."

She was shocked. "How do you know?"

"Beau Brummell pointed you out to me."

"Oh ... so now ... do you *hate* me?"

He sighed, as if thinking the question silly. "How can I hate you, when I don't even know you? And it would be a high flight on my part if I hated you for who you are, and what you do, which I'm sure is quite delightful."

"Well then, take out your watch," she said smiling back at him. "And in one quarter of an hour you shall be free from my persecution; but pray – give me that short time just to talk with you, Lord Byron – pray do!"

He shook his head impatiently. "Miss Wilson, you would be wiser to bestow your attention on someone more worthy of you, because not only am I a bad masquerade-companion, I also have to leave."

And then he was gone, leaving her standing alone in the beautiful exotic room, heavy with the scent of fresh flowers.

~ ~ ~

It was the room, the room, the *room* – something about *that room* with its exotic shrubs and the scent of its flowers, which had lit his imagination and sent his mind drifting back to the East.

Without saying farewell to anyone he left the masquerade and was soon back at home, sitting at his desk accompanied by only his lamp, writing – *Lara* – a new poetic tale.

He wrote on and on through the night, and when Fletcher entered his bedroom in the morning to wake him, he found the bed untouched and unslept in, which made Fletcher smile; certain that his lordship must have slept somewhere else last night, as he sometimes did.

Still yawning while walking into the drawing room, Fletcher took a quick step back, startled to see his lordship seated at his main desk, his lamp still burning, although it was daylight. He was placing a batch of pages into a cover, which he then held out to Fletcher.

"I know it is Sunday, but as soon as you have had

your breakfast, Fletcher, I want you to take this up to Albemarle Street and deliver it to John Murray. And tell him, Fletcher, that if he likes it, and wants to publish it, he must give me one thousand guineas for it immediately, in return for which he can own the copyright."

Fletcher was agape –"*One thousand* guineas*?"*

"And not a penny less."

"And not a penny *less?"*

Byron looked around searchingly. "Is there an *echo* in this room? Why do I keep hearing my words repeated to me?"

He looked at Fletcher. "Albermarle Street, will you go?"

Fletcher pulled himself together and nodded. "Aye, my lord, up to Albermarle Street ... that will be just a short walk for me."

Byron looked at him critically. "And if this was to go somewhere else, that required a *long* walk?"

"Then ... then that would be a *long* walk for me," Fletcher shrugged. "Are you in bad humour today, my lord?"

"No, just a slight tired."

"Was the masquerade last night no good?"

"On the contrary, it was very enjoyable; but now my bed and sleep beckons dreamily to me, so pray ask Mrs Mule to make me some tea, and then *you* call me at three."

~ ~ ~

In his drawing room, John Murray sat reading page after page of *Lara* while Fletcher remained in the waiting room downstairs.

Murray was more than surprised, shocked even,

because only two days ago, at luncheon, Lord Byron had shaken his head and confessed he had no ideas whatsoever for any more poetry in the near future ... and yet here was a *new* manuscript, a *new* piece of poetry, and every word of it wonderful!

Rising from his seat, he ventured down the stairs to speak to Fletcher. "When did Lord Byron write this? Do you know?"

"Aye, sir, those pages in the package what I gave you, his lordship wrote them sometime between coming home from the masquerade ball last night, and going to bed this morning."

"All in *one* night?"

"Aye, sir."

John Murray smiled. "Such is the fire of genius."

"Indeed, sir. His lordship's lamp was still burning on his desk this morning."

"So, Mr Fletcher, will you pray tell his lordship that I agree to his proposal and price, and that I shall send the contract for the purchase of the copyright by the end of business tomorrow."

"I will indeed, sir."

When Fletcher had gone, John Murray returned to his drawing-room where he stood for some time by the window, reflecting on the surprise of it all.

Of course, he was absolutely delighted to be offered the copyright of *Lara,* but the biggest surprise and joy of all, was that Lord Byron was now taking care of business himself, without consulting Robert Dallas.

John Murray was glad, very glad – Dallas had been unfairly getting rich through his lordship for the past three years. No *decent* literary agent would allow himself to keep *all* the profits from an author's royalties and put them into his own bank account, no matter how foolishly generous that noble author may be.

Yet now that travesty appeared to be over and done with, and Murray could not help wondering why? What had brought about this change in Lord Byron? And what a surprise to learn that he was quite capable of doing business in such a firm and concise way? No endless haggling, as was the usual routine of Reverend Dallas. No, his lordship came straight to the point – this is what I want, and this is what you shall receive in return. Fair play.

And so very *reminiscent* of how Miss Jane Austen also conducted her business with him, so *direct*. Well, not exactly so *direct* in Miss Austen's case, because her brother Henry always conducted the negotiations on her behalf, but John Murray had no doubt – no *doubts* whatsoever – that every word Henry Austen spoke to him, was an exact parroting of the words given to him by his sister.

Murray smiled, gazing up through the window at the blue sky and the bright sunshine on this Sunday Sabbath Day, giving thanks for all his blessings, and considering himself to be a very lucky man.

Chapter Thirty

~ ~ ~

Monday morning brought it's usual delivery of mail. Byron read through the letters, pausing to reply to one here and there with quick, short notes, rapidly written.

The next letter he opened was from Miss Annabella Milbanke, which was quite long. He read through the first paragraph, wondering if he was really in the mood for such a serious tome.

... Nothing can be more satisfactory or more agreeable to my wishes than your open & explicit manner of answering my enquiries. You are very liberal in not estimating Christian morality by the Professors who disgrace it. I am not desirous that you should study the arguments of popular advocates for Religion. I have not a very high opinion of most Orthodox vindications.

I believe you assert that the maxims of the Gospel may be found unconnectedly in heathen writings, but were they ever united in a system so wonderfully and so wisely adapted for the good of mankind? In my –

He put the letter aside, deciding to read it some other time when he was in a better mood for it.

The next letter he opened made him sit back and stare at the page ... from Miss Harriette Wilson ... who the devil was she?

She reminded him quickly and bluntly enough – "*The masquerade ball on Saturday night, when you refused to make my acquaintance because you held me too cheap...*"

Oh, *now* he remembered her – the *incognito courtesan* who had disturbed him in the silence of the empty room, before he had dashed home to write *Lara*.

He read on:

For my part, I never aspired to being your companion, and should be quite enough puffed up with pride, were I permitted to be your housekeeper, attend to your morning cup of chocolate, darn your nightcap, comb your dog, and see that your linen and beds are well aired, and, supposing all these things were dutifully and properly attended to, perhaps you might, one day or other in the course of a season, desire me to put on my clean bib and apron and seat myself by your side, while you condescend to read to me in your beautiful voice your last new poem!

God bless you, you beautiful ill-tempered, delightful creature, and make you as happy as I wish you to be.

Harriette

P.S. Can I forward you a bundle of pens, or anything?

He had to smile at her humour. No wonder Brummell liked her. And he himself loved nothing more than a woman with a sense of humour who could make him laugh.

However, she was one of Brummell's pieces, and as

much as he liked sharing Brummell's coat designs, he had no intention of sharing his women.

Hobhouse arrived then; asking for coffee, complaining about the rain, and sitting down to read Byron's letters.

"Hobby, do you *never* receive any letters of your own?"

"Not often, no."

Byron quickly made sure there were no *private* letters for Hobby to see, and then left him to carry on.

Letters being the only form of communication with anyone who was not actually in one's *sight*, the sharing of letters was common, and a way of letting someone know how another person was faring, without having to actually *tell* them.

"None are personal, are they?" Hobby asked.

"Well they *are* addressed to me, not you, but go ahead."

So Hobby did; unable to prevent himself from smiling at the letter from Harriette Wilson; and then frowning at the letter from Annabella Milbanke.

"You have been receiving quite a few letters from Miss Milbanke of late."

Byron looked up from his newspaper. "Yes ... and the longer ones are all full of religion and metaphysics

"That does not answer why she keeps writing to *you.*"

"I think she is wishing for me to reform."

"Reform? From what?

"From whatever she thinks I am now."

Hobby sat thinking about it. "Byron, you can be very obtuse in some ways. Can you not see what this woman is about?"

Byron looked at him again. He kept his face still, and waited.

"These letters of hers," said Hobby, "I've read quite a few of them now, and all I can say is that if a woman kept writing letters to me, I would start to believe she had special interest in me."

Byron shrugged. "Nonsense. I proposed to her once, remember, and she rejected me. I think her letters are just her way of keeping in touch with people in London."

"Yet you and Miss Milbanke were never 'in touch' in London."

"No, but I write regularly to her aunt, Lady Melbourne."

"So? What's that got to do with her? Or more importantly, Byron, what do *you* think of her?"

Byron mocked a face of profound surprise. "And what does that have to do with *you*, Hobby? Surely that is *my* business? But I'll tell you anyway ..."

"Thank you."

"She writes long letters to me endeavouring to discuss all the highs and lows of the spirit – so she's a metaphysician as well as a mathematician. Which makes me think her a very *superior* woman."

"So, nothing at all like Harriette Wilson then?"

Byron grinned in a rakish way. "Oh, no, *she* is a different dish entirely ... and to quote John Ford in his famous play – 'tis a pittee shee's a whore'."

Yet he heard from Harriette Wilson again a week later, informing him that he had hurt her by not responding to her letter. He read on and on to the last paragraph –
"*I know my acquaintance with your Lordship is very slight, since we have met but once in our lives, so Que faire, Lord Byron, Que faire?*"

What's to be done, indeed? He would have to reply.

Albany, April 18th, 1814

<u>*To Miss Harriette Wilson*</u>

If my silence has hurt "your pride or your feelings", to use your own expressions, I am very sorry for it; be assured that such an effect was far from my intention. Business prevented me from thanking you for your letter as soon as I ought to have done. If my thanks do not displease you, now pray accept them. I could not feel otherwise than obliged by the desire of a stranger to make my acquaintance.

I am not unacquainted with your name or your beauty, and I have heard much of your talents; but I am not the person whom you would like, either as a lover or a friend. I did not, and do not suspect you – to use your own words once more – of any design of making love to me. I know myself well enough to acquit anyone who does not know me, and still more those who do, from any such intention. I am not of a nature to be loved, and so far, luckily for myself, I have no wish to be so.

In saying this, I do not mean to affect any particular stoicism, and may possibly, at one time or other, have been liable to those follies, for which you sarcastically tell me, I now have "no time": but these, and everything else are to me, at present, objects of indifference; and this is a good deal to say, at six and twenty.

You tell me that you wished to know me better, because you liked my writing. I think you must be aware that a writer is in general very different from his productions, and always disappoints those who expect to find in him qualities more agreeable than those of others.

I shall certainly not be lessened in my vanity, as a scribbler, by the reflection that a work of mine has given you pleasure; and to preserve the impression in its favour, I will not risk your good opinion, by inflicting my acquaintance on you.

BYRON

Chapter Thirty-One

~ ~ ~

In Newmarket, on April 15th, Augusta had given birth to her fourth child. Another girl, whom George Leigh insisted upon naming *Medora*, after a horse he had once yearned to own.

Augusta approved and agreed to the name, because it was also the name of the beautiful young wife whom Conrad had so loved, in her brother's Turkish tale, *The Corsair*.

Although Augusta had originally argued that the name was too foreign, "*too Eastern*" for an English girl; and so the child was eventually christened on May 20th as Elizabeth Medora Leigh.

"So *that* is where I got the name from!" Byron said to George Leigh on day of the Christening. "I thought it had come to me out of the blue, but no, I remember now, *you* were talking about a horse named Medora at Christmas."

It was a small affair, the Christening celebration in the house at Six Mile Bottom. The child had two sponsors; her uncle, Lord Byron, and the Duke of Rutland, the proud possessor of George Leigh's once-coveted horse, named Medora.

In order to avoid much of George Leigh's boring conversations, Byron spent some time talking to the Duke of Rutland, only to discover that the Duke was even more horse-mad in his talk than was his brother-in-law. It would be far easier all round if the two men just *neighed* instead of talking, and then one would not be required to answer them.

It was not until later, when everyone had left, and George was sozzled with too much wine and fast asleep in his chair in the drawing-room, that Byron and Augusta were able to sit together on the piano-stool and have a quiet conversation about all things important.

"And Mary Chaworth?" Augusta asked. "How do you feel now?"

"Oh, much the same ..." Byron sighed heavily. "But it's a lost cause, so I am trying to forget all that was, and concentrate on all that is."

"Have you received any more letters from her?"

"Yes, quite a few ... no *love* though, just friendship ... He lowered his head and tinkled out a note or two on the piano ... "I'm not interested in *just* friendship.

"Is she still at Miss Radford's?"

"No, thank God. Her lawyers have now settled the separation agreement, and she is to have the house at Annesley, in addition to three thousand pounds a year from the estate, while Musters gets all the rest. At least *he* has moved out now, to allow her and the children to move back in. She tells me that he is in the throes of setting up his own establishment at Wiverton Hall in the valley of Belvoir, and has taken half the furniture and plate and linen from Annesley with him."

"Three thousand pounds *a year* to live on?" Augusta could not help feeling envious. "That's a great deal of money."

"But you have to remember, it is all Mary's money. She is not being *given* anything by Jack Musters. No, *he* is receiving a fortune from her. And Wiverton Hall? That also belongs to the Chaworth estate, so it is *his* now to claim and live in."

Augusta sat thoughtful. "It is the law, we know, that upon marriage a man inherits everything his wife once owned..." she bit her lip ... "but I'm afraid my poor George inherited very little when he married me."

"Which proves he loved you," Byron smiled. "And so do I."

Augusta smiled back shyly at such encouragement of her own worth, until she saw a kind of mute despair come into Byron's eyes.

"I do wonder, though," he said, "what Mary is playing at? What's in her mind? All my answers to her letters must be written – not to 'My Love' as before – or even 'Dear Mary,' but to *'Dear Friend'* and all my answers must not have a signature, as she knows my handwriting so well."

Augusta frowned, not liking the sound of this at all.

"And if she wants us to be no more than friends," Byron continued, "then surely the only thing that can make it look *more* than friendship, is *mystery*. I wrote to her and franked the letter with my seal, thinking there was no need of concealment ... but she desires me not to frank, and so I obey."

On a practical level, Augusta thought it silly that Mary Chaworth did not allow Byron to *frank* his letters. The cost of posting a letter was based on the weight and number of pages marked as enclosed; and the cost was paid by the person who *received* the letter, not the sender. But all members of the Peerage were excluded from paying postal charges and had their own frank, so the *receiver* did not have to pay any charges at all.

And on an emotional level, Augusta thought Byron should forge on with his own life, and forget all about Mary Chaworth, and she told him so.

"Mary cannot be seen with you openly, as that would make *her* the infidel, and give Jack Musters the legal right to take the children away from her and secure custody."

Byron lifted his eyes from the piano keys and looked at her; he had never thought of it in that way.

"And also," Augusta said, "from everything you have told me, I believe Mary would *never* be willing to leave Annesley Hall, not even for you. Annesley has been her home from the day she was born, she has never lived anywhere else. It is her only sure security now, and not only for her, but also for her children."

When Byron made no answer, Augusta said softly, "I say all this, because I am a mother too, so I know how mothers think and feel and what their priorities are."

Byron nodded, and without saying another word, left Augusta to retire to his room where he stood at the window looking at the night sky for a long time.

He remembered once being asked a question by somebody – and answering that, in his opinion, to be a *poet* a man had to be either, in love, or in misery, and now he was in both.

~ ~ ~

Upon his return to London, the weeks that followed were weeks of non-stop celebrations by the general population of the metropolis.

This summer of 1814 is "*the summer of sovereigns*" Byron wrote to Thomas Moore in Derbyshire.

Napoleon had been defeated. The Russians and Austrians were now united with the English against France. The allies were in Paris supporting the Bourbon "Louis the Lunatic" as Byron politely referred to him.

Napoleon had been defeated by the armies of *four* nations against *one* nation. Four *sovereignties*: Russia, Prussia, Austria and Britain – against the Republic of France.

Byron wrote to Lady Melbourne: – *"I can't help suspecting that my little Pagod will play them some trick still – if Wellington or one hero had beaten another hero – it would be nothing – but to be handled by brutes and conquered by recruiting sergeants – –"*

In celebration of the victory, the Prince Regent hosted a *Garden Party* at Carlton House, to which two thousand of the *best* people in the kingdom were invited – (half of them were actually *dead* but they were sent invitations anyway). Even Lord Byron was sent an invitation, but he declined to attend; although many of his associates *did* attend.

Everything that day was obscene in its extravagance. The long tables in the green gardens and parklands for the less important guests were decorated in luscious flowers and fruits. But inside the great Gothic conservatory of Carlton House, a two-hundred-foot long banqueting table was laid with silver and crystal for the *créme de la créme* of the guest list.

At the top of the table, in front of the Prince Regent's seat, a fountain fed a stream that flowed the length of the centre of the table, with tiny plants and miniature bridges, and small gold and silver fish swimming past the guests as they dined.

The only unwelcome disturbance on that day, was to the guests as they sat in their carriages on the road outside waiting impatiently for the gates to swing open – when a young poet named Percy Bysshe Shelley ran recklessly down the ever-increasing long line – throwing through the windows of the carriages copies of a satire he had written on these "*disgusting splendours*" in a nation where half the people were on the verge of starvation:

It is said that this entertainment will cost the Nation and its Parliament £120,000. Nor will it be the last bauble which the nation must buy to amuse the overgrown bantling of the Regency...

And Shelley was right, because at a similar cost to the nation, there had been the same obscene extravagance in the same theatrical setting at His Royal Highness's inauguration from Prince of Wales to *Prince Regent* in 1811.

Byron was smiling with delight when he heard about Shelley's actions; and yet it was all still very depressing.

England was celebrating the Allies' possession of Paris, but he could not think of a single cheerful thing to write in his journal about this eighteen-year-war.

Until, finally, he *did* think of something cheerful, and no one could say it was not true.

Great news – the Dutch are in possession of Holland!

Chapter Thirty-Two

~ ~ ~

In mid-June, Byron received a distressed letter from Mary – *"Is it true? The gossip I hear from Nottingham? That due to pecuniary problems, our dear Newstead may have to be sold?"*

As always, the letter to him was signed, *"A Friend."*

He wrote back and assured her that Newstead was still his property, and would remain so.

And then – aware of the absurdity of it, because anyone reading the letter would know from the contents that the owner of Newstead had written it – he complied with her wishes and also signed his letter: *"A Friend."*

Why she insisted upon this *charade*, Byron did not know, nor did he know how she felt about him now? At least now she was free of the poisonous influence of Ann Radford.

Even so, he would not go near Annesley again – not unless Mary *invited* him to do so. He would not risk her rejection again, leaving him to wear his hurt in the best way he could, the *only* way he could – by covering it up with *distractions*.

And one of those distractions now – was yet another letter from Harriette Wilson. Accepting that all hope of an acquaintance with him had been denied, she took off her mask and came straight to the *main reason* behind her trade ... although he suspected she also got great pleasure from it too; clever and funny little whore that she was.

My Dear Lord Byron,
I hate to ask you for money, because you ought not

to pay anybody; not even turnpike men, postmen, or tax-gathering men: for we are all paid tenfold by your delicious verses, even if we had claims on you, and I have none. I only require a little present aid, and that I am sure you will not refuse me, as you refused to make my acquaintance. At the same time, pray write me word that you are tolerably happy. I hope you believe in the very strong interest I take, and shall always take, in your welfare, so I need not prose about it. God bless you, my dear Lord Byron.

Harriette Wilson.

PS: I have never affected a friendship with Mr George Brummell. I don't even know him.

He couldn't help smiling. So, a pretty little liar too! Should he respond to her? Should he not? Was she lying again or was she truly short of money? Even a whore had to eat, even if it was only a few *bon-bon* sweets now and again to keep her figure. *Que faire,* indeed?

And yet, before he had time to decide his response, who should "drop by" to see him but Mr George Brummell himself.

"Byron, my dear friend, I hope I have not come at an inconvenient time?"

"No, not at all," Byron quickly shoved the letter from Harriette under a pile of papers, "but it is a surprise."

"Why so?"

"Aren't you usually *socialising* at this hour? All your many invites to luncheons?"

"Oh, one gets so bored with all that. And how else is

one to have a private little *tête-à-tête* with a recluse like you?"

Byron laughed. "I'm not a *recluse.* I just don't have the inclination to flit around socialising all day, as you do."

"Because you prefer to write?"

"No, because I'm lazy."

Brummell sat down on one of the sofas, crossed his legs elegantly, and then took from his inner coat-pocket a silver snuffbox.

"It is in fact your *poetry* that I have come to speak to you about."

Byron sat down on the sofa opposite, a sardonic smile on his face. "You've decided to *read* it?"

"No, I have already read it all, of course I have. And bought from a common bookstore, just like everyone else, which is not the *same,* is it?"

"The same as what?"

"Having one's own *personal* copy, signed by the author?"

"Well I can rectify that straight away," Byron said, standing up to move over to his bookcase and taking out a copy of *Child Harold's Pilgrimage,* and then pausing as he opened it ... "No, this copy would be no good for you ... every page has my pencil notes written down the margins."

"Then *that* is the one I want," Brummell said, standing to join him. "Would you?"

Byron shrugged. "It is yours if you wish. Although as it *does* contain my notes, do keep this copy personal to yourself and show it to no one else."

"Why worry," said Brummell, flicking through the pages, "your notes are disgracefully *indecipherable,* so who on earth would understand them? And you'll sign it for me?"

"Of course." Byron moved to his desk and Brummell followed him; but when Byron lifted his pen, Brummell said in a quiet voice ... "Byron, my *dear* friend, may I ask of you a great favour of kindness?"

Byron looked at him.

"Could you pray sign the book in the same pencil you used for the notes?"

"The *same* pencil?" Byron smirked. "Do you think I am a miser? That pencil was used up or thrown away two years ago." He opened a drawer. "But I do have a numerous amount of *other* pencils I can use. Will one of them do?"

"Perfectly. Pray excuse my *fastidiousness,* it's such a damnable curse; but you know, *pencil* here, *ink* there ... you do understand?"

Byron did not, but signed the book, handed it to Brummell, and then called for Fletcher to bring in refreshments, which were followed by an hour or so of good conversation and quite a few laughs. How could one *not* laugh when in the company of Beau Brummell, especially when he told Byron about a scrape he had recently extricated himself from ...

"No names, of course, but I fell for her quite badly, and the damned thing is, I was truly a good friend of her husband, and was in the habit of calling on him quite frequently when he was in town. Yet during an invitation to his country house ... there was this situation with his *wife.*

Byron understood, all too well, and listened as Brummell related the scene.

"In the library, one morning, I went in and told him sincerely that I was sorry, very sorry, but I must leave.

'Why? You were to stay a month?'

"Yes, but I must be off."

'Why? What for?'

"The fact is ... I'm in love with your wife."

'Oh, my dear fellow, never mind that, so was I twenty years ago. Is she in love with you?'

"I'm so sorry, but, yes, I believe she is."

'Oh! Well that changes matters. I shall send for your horse for you immediately.'

Byron was laughing, and Brummell stood to leave "And now I must be off again. Thank you for the book, Byron, good man."

At the door of the drawing room, Brummell suddenly hesitated. "Oh, by the way, I hear that you keep fair copies of all your letters and all your poems ... written in a *fair* hand and not your rushed scrawl?"

"And you could only have heard *that* from our mutual friend, Scrope Davies."

"Is it true?"

"Yes."

"I don't suppose you have the odd poem or two that you no longer esteem, do you?"

Byron frowned. "Why?"

"Oh, well, you know ... " Brummell appeared slightly embarrassed, "it's simply that if *you* no longer esteem them, I most certainly would ... every word."

"You?" Byron simulated a face of amazement. "I did not realise you were *so* interested in my poetry."

Brummell smiled. "I'm so pleased I amaze you, but seriously, do you?"

"As a matter of fact ..." Byron walked back across the room to his desk, "there are one or two poems here that I *should* have destroyed a long time ago, but you may have them if you wish."

He sifted down to the bottom of his poetry file and

finally found the two poems. "They are neither good nor sincere, because they were written during my early friendship with Lady Caroline Lamb."

Brummell took the two short poems, quickly read them, and then looked at Byron with a grin. "They are good enough for me."

Which left Byron wondering, after Brummell had left, if the cad was going to send the poems to some lady under the pretence that *he*, Beau Brummell, had written them.

~ ~ ~

George Brummell had no intention of doing anything with the two poems, other than keeping them safely for himself.

His luck at gaming had not been so good of late, and the fortune he had made from gambling was beginning to dwindle. It was merely a chance conversation with Scrope Davies, who was laughing at the way Byron would sit for a long time writing a poem or a sonnet, and then after reading it, would scrunch it up into a ball and throw it across the room into the fire.

"And never misses hitting the fire," said Scrope, "so it shows you how many times he has done it through the years."

Byron's accurate aim was of no interest to Brummell, more interested in the work that was thrown away. And what was rubbish to one man, could be another man's gold.

On arriving home at his own apartment, and entering the drawing-room, Brummell's long-time valet, Captain William Jesse, was pleased to see that the frowns and worry had gone from his master's face.

"Has something good happened to make you look so

pleased, sir?"

Brummell grinned, and held up the book of *Childe Harold's Pilgrimage,* and then from within the pages he took out the two short poems.

"See these three things, Jesse? These will be gaining compound interest for me every day from now on. And one day, if necessary, will prove to be worth more than enough to pay off my debts."

Jesse could not comprehend it. "A small book, sir, and just two pages."

"Not *just* two pages, Jesse, not *just* anything. These, you see, were written by the man who has replaced me in the firmament of everything this metropolis holds dear."

"Who, sir, the Prince Regent?"

Brummell sighed. "Jesse, I despair of you, I really do. You must stop sniffing the linen and ironing the cotton and get out into town more often."

"I believe I should, sir. Would it be Walter Scott? Or Mr Wordsworth?"

"Here's a clue," said Brummell, "Who has great political talent; is courted by all of society; admired for his genius and beauty; has tastes and habits almost as luxurious as my own; writes epic poetry that sells as fast as hot pies – and is also *a dear friend* of mine to boot?

"Oh," Jesse nodded, "I believe you are referring to Lord Byron?"

"Yes, Lord Byron, Jesse, these were all written and pencil-noted and whatever by *Byron* himself! Now lock them away in the safe straight away, and once that's done, you have my permission to *shoot* anyone who goes near the safe in future."

PART SEVEN

She Walks in Beauty

'Many women were welcome to love him if they liked; but only one woman had the power to make him suffer, and that woman was Mary Chaworth.'

Francis Gribble

Chapter Thirty-Three

~ ~ ~

Mary was visiting the town of Nottingham where she had known many friends since her childhood; and she was visiting one of those friends today ... but in a wave of blankness, she could not remember which one?

Her mind was suffering so many distractions these days, so many thoughts she did not want to think.

"Where to, Mistress?" John asked her; but all she could do was to stare at him blankly.

A moment later, recovering herself, she said, "Just drive me into Nottingham town, John, I need to buy a few things."

Inside the carriage, her eyes were on the window, staring at the passing fields outside, so brightly green and beautiful in the sunshine, so why was her mind so dark?

Whatever the cause, she knew she only had herself to blame. It was a weakness in her nature, a sensitivity and meekness in her attitude that had led her to allow so many people of a *dominant* nature to control her for so long. First her mother, and then her stepfather, Reverend Clarke; and then her husband, Jack Musters; and then her cousin Ann Radford. So much control, and what had she gained from it all? Certainly no happiness.

Reaching the edge of the town, John parked the carriage inside the yard of the inn, and then came to open her door, looking at her strangely. He had been anxious with worry from the moment they had left Annesley, and now he dared to say why.

"Surely, Mistress, you don't intend to walk about the

town on your own?"

"Why not?"

"It's not safe these days for a lady on her own. You could be robbed."

She half smiled. "Then will *you* be my knight in shining armour, John, and escort me?"

"Oh, my pleasure, Mistress, but whereabouts in town do wish to go?"

"Nowhere in particular, I would just like to walk and see the town again. It seems so long since I did."

John dutifully took her arm and led her out of the inn's yard; and then fell into step, just one pace behind her slim figure ... until she forgot he was there, and strolled through the streets in a world of her own, seeing Nottingham as if she was seeing it with the eyes of a stranger.

Never before had she realised that Nottingham had such contrasts. She had always thought that Nottingham was full of rich people, but now she realised that the reason for that was because she had always been driven past these very streets where she was now walking ... driven past to some grand house on the outskirts. This was the centre of the stocking and lace-making industry in England, but of course, now there were so many unemployed and in poverty, not only due to the new machines, but also the long war with France. Thank goodness that was all over now.

Why, even from the terraces of Annesley she had seen the mail coach flying past with all flags flying and its horn blaring, celebrating the fall of Napoleon. And she had known Byron would not like that. Although why he had such admiration for Napoleon was still strange to her.

Her hand went to her throat, her breath quickened;

how badly she had treated him, and how much she loved him. Even now her letters had the appearance of being distant and cold, but his letters in return were always light and warm ... he had forgiven her, and she did not deserve to be forgiven ...

When the news reached her that Newstead Abbey and its estate may have to be put up for sale, and she knew her last link with Byron would be gone, she had fallen into such a fit of despair and misery, she had wanted to die to escape the grief of it ... She took a deep breath and blinked rapidly to clear her mind of all disturbing thoughts.

She had now reached the centre of the town and the market place surrounded by houses and shops. John took her arm and pointed to a shop she usually browsed through during her visits to town. "Is that where you wish to go, Mistress?"

Mary did not answer; she was standing dead still, staring at a young couple walking along in front of her, hand in hand. He looked like a young farmer, and she possibly a milkmaid, and they looked so *happy*, smiling at each other as they walked. She watched them as if she was in a dream. Love was a beautiful thing. And Love was only appreciated by the young ... for the short time they had it ...

Her face had gone very pale, and John caught her arm again. "Mistress, is something wrong?"

"No, John ... I am just feeling old, so very old."

John stared at her in confusion. On her birthday this year she had become twenty-eight ... still only twenty-eight, and beautiful, even more beautiful than she had been as a girl with her wide eyes and gentle-like smile ... like a pretty flower she been then, and now the years had aged her into beauty. He himself was forty-one now, so for the life of him he could not understand why she thought she was so very old at twenty-eight?

Her face was turned away from the direction of the shop he had pointed to, and she herself was now moving towards one of the market stalls selling bales of cloth. He stood beside her silently as she asked the trader for one yard of black velvet.

"One yard only?" asked the trader, and when she nodded her head in agreement, the trader made a big palaver of lifting down his bale of cloth and cutting off only one yard.

Mary held the folded square of velvet to her breast all the way home in the carriage ... if she could have one last chance ... just *one* last chance to make life right again ... *happy* again ... she would grasp it with both hands and never let go.

At Annesley, stepping down from the carriage, Mary suddenly remembered where she was supposed to have gone – not into Nottingham at all, but to West Bridgford Hall on the outskirts, to see Sarah Ann Vaughan. So why had she forgotten it? Why had her mind gone blank?

Or was it simply that she had *not* really wanted to go to Bridgford Hall to engage in small talk over tea and scones and play cards. All the ladies in Nottinghamshire spent most of their leisure time playing cards, something Mary no longer had any patience for.

"Ah! I did not expect you back so soon!" exclaimed Nanny Marsden, shooting a look at John. "Not from Bridgford Hall! Did something go wrong with the carriage or one of the horses?"

Without making a reply, Mary ran lightly up the stairs, and Nanny Marsden stared at John. "Well! Are you going to tell me?"

"The mistress told me she wanted to go into

Nottingham town and do some shopping."

"Did she not tell you to go to Bridgford Hall?"

"No, so she must have changed her mind at the last minute, because all she told me was Nottingham."

"And what did she buy there?"

"Some black velvet. Just a yard of it, is all."

"A yard?" Nanny said, perplexed. "And what in God's name is she going to be able to make out of a piece as small as that?"

John shrugged. "Don't ask me."

Chapter Thirty-Four

~ ~ ~

Three days later Byron got the surprise of his life when a gift arrived in the post from Mary ... a small black velvet purse for his coins, which she had made for him.

And with the purse, a small and pretty notebook, its pages containing a number of dried flowers ... all *violets,* which – according to the first page of the notebook – she had "*collected in the spring from Annesley Wood.*"

Violets from *Annesley Wood*? Was there a message in that? An *intimate* message?

He lifted the purse again and slowly turned it over in his hands ... his mind imagining her sitting in her chair by the window of her sitting-room, her head bent as she sewed ... sewing something for *him.*

And with the gifts a short letter, telling him she intended to visit London the following week and hoped he would be free to see her.

He kept staring at the letter, because unlike her other letters to him, she had not written "My dear Lord" – which could be a letter to anybody, as there were numerous noblemen residing in London – but had openly written "*My dearest Lord Byron* ... and signed – '*Mary*' ... instead of the usual signature from "A Friend'.

Coming to London? Of course, now he remembered, Mary had been schooled for a time in London, and the Chaworths still had a house here. Although, according to Mary, it was used only now and again by the socialite, Sophie Musters, Jack's mother, and so the staff had a very easy life.

His immediate impulse was to write to his friend

Lady Melbourne and tell her the good news, and then he realised he could *not* do that.

Some months previously, Lady Melbourne had written to him making inquiries about Mary Chaworth, due to Lady Harrowby, – after returning from a visit to Nottingham – inquiring of Lady Melbourne what she knew about Lord Byron and Mary Chaworth.

"There has been some gossip about you two, and Lady Harrowby is very suspicious. Now, sweet boy, what are you not telling me?"

Her letter had alarmed him; not on his own behalf, but Mary's. And he would hate Mary to think that *he* had broken his pledge and said anything to anyone.

He had immediately written back to Lady Melbourne in a disparaging tone, saying it was all news to him: *"I have not seen Mary Chaworth for years."*

And Lady Melbourne believed him, not due to her taking his word on it; but because Sophie Musters, the mother of Mary's departed husband, was outraged at the very suggestion.

"She tells me," wrote Lady Melbourne, *"that you do not know Mary Chaworth at all, and if you say you do know her, then it all must be a dream in your head."*

He had laughed at that, because now he had been supplied with the title for the poem he had been writing about himself and Mary throughout the years, writing a stanza here and there – which he would now call *"The Dream."*

He wrote back to Mary, thanking her for the gift, and telling her warmly how much he was looking forward to seeing her again, and *"You will find and make many friends here in London."*

Just the *thought* of seeing his angel again put him

into such a good mood, he even relented and finally replied to the letter from Harriette Wilson, asking him for money.

To Miss Harriette Wilson

I will send you fifty pounds, if you will inform me how I can remit the sum to you, or perhaps you can get someone to cash this cheque for fifty pounds from me.

With regard to a refusal of mine to comply with a very different request of yours, you mistook, or chose to mistake the motive: it was not that "I held you too cheap" as you say, but that my compliance would have been a great wrong to another person: and whatever you have heard, or may believe, I have ever acted in good faith with things, even where it is rarely observed, as long as good faith is kept with me. I told you that I had no wish to hurt your self-love, and I tell you again now, when you may be more disposed to believe me.

Yours etc.,
BYRON

"So, he wants to act in good faith to his friendship with George Brummell! Oh, well, *la la la,* the sheer *delight* of my devotion shall be *his* loss!"

Hopeless spendthrift on luxuries as she was, and being in need of money, a requirement that was not unusual for Harriette, she was absolutely delighted with her fifty pounds, and managed to get the cheque cashed quite quickly.

Yet she was still not fully appeased by Lord Byron, complaining to her sister, Fanny:

"I agree, Lord Byron *does* write such nice and polite letters to me, but why must they always contain a *sting* at the end?"

Fanny smiled. "Well, that's what they all say about him in town – he's a mixture of salt and sparkle."

Harriette's eyes widened. "A mixture of salt and sparkle? Why, that's a *perfect* description of him! And I shall now write to him again and tell him so."

Chapter Thirty-Five

~ ~ ~

He had cleared his diary, declined all invitations, and waited through every day of the following week for a messenger to bring a note from Mary, informing him she was now in London, and asking him to call.

The only time he went out, was at night, after a respectable hour for a lady to send a messenger to a gentleman; and once that hour had passed, he joined his friends in Brooks's or the Cocoa Tree.

During the day he wrote, for now he was inspired, and also a soft melodious tune was playing in his mind.

> *She walks in Beauty, like the Night*
> *Of cloudless climes and starry skies;*
> *And all that's best of dark and bright*
> *Meet in her aspect, and her eyes*
> *Thus mellowed to the tender light*
> *Which Heaven to gaudy day denies –*
>
> *One shade the more – one shade less*
> *Had half impaired the nameless grace*
> *Which waves in every raven tress*
> *Or softly lightens o'er her face*
> *Where thoughts serenely sweet express*
> *How pure - how dear their dwelling place!*
>
> *And on that cheek, and o'er that brow,*

So soft – so calm – so eloquent,

The smiles that win, the tint that glow,

But tell of days in goodness spent –

A mind at peace with all below –

A Heart – whose love is innocent!

Even as he read it over, he knew he had been writing about an angel.

Perhaps it was Providence, or merely a coincidence, that less than an hour after he had finished the poem, a stranger called at Albany: a gentleman named Isaac Nathan, carrying a card of introduction from Douglas Kinnaird.

"Mr Kinnaird, as you know, is one of the executive directors of the Drury Lane Theatre."

Byron smiled. "His family also own my bank! Are you also indebted to him?"

Nathan smiled. "Thankfully, not yet. He tells me you are a friend."

"Indeed."

Instinctively Byron knew that he liked Isaac Nathan, although he was not sure why. He was a dark-haired, genial-faced man, no more than a few years older than himself.

He instructed Fletcher to bring refreshments, but Mr Nathan begged, "Not for me, thank you."

"Are you sure?" Fletcher looked offended. "Nothing at all, sir?"

"Well, perhaps ... a glass of water?"

"Water?" Fletcher looked at his lordship as if the man had just blasphemed. "Water?"

Byron nodded. "If you please, Fletcher, and quickly."

He then sat down opposite Nathan and said, "I know

Kinnaird would not have sent you here on some trivial whim, but I am expecting a messenger to call me away at any time, so to what purpose have you made this visit, Mr Nathan?"

Faced with such directness, Isaac Nathan became a little unsure of himself.

"I know ... that you are not Jewish, Lord Byron, yet Douglas Kinnaird tells me that you have shown to him some Hebrew poetry you have written."

"Oh, yes ..." Byron smiled, "two Hebrew poems I wrote some time ago."

"May I see them?"

"May I ask why?"

"I am a composer, Lord Byron, a Jewish composer of music. So that will explain why I am so interested in your Jewish poetry."

Byron stared at him, and Nathan stared back, until the two men slowly began to smile.

And then they talked, and talked, and both became excited at the ideas coming into their heads; but then Byron always became stirred and emotional when he thought or spoke of Israel's sad history; as he also did about Ireland's history, and Greece's sad plight. Byron always placed himself on the side of the outcasts.

"This one I could think of no title for," he said, drawing Nathan over to his desk and showing him the two Hebrew poems, "so I have simply called it, '*On the Day of the Destruction of Jerusalem by Titus*'."

Nathan was almost in tears as he read it, and then tears did fall down his face when he read '*By The Rivers of Babylon We Sat Down and Wept*'.

Nathan gave his idea of the kind of traditional Jewish music he would like to compose, singing notes here and there, and Byron with his own love of music, picked up the notes immediately and sang the first words that came into his mind to match the music ... "*On Jordan's Banks the Arabs' camels stray ...*"

Time disappeared, vanished, lost in the enjoyment of it all.

Finally the time came for Isaac Nathan to leave. He took a deep breath and asked, "So, Lord Byron, do we agree to collaborate? You to write the words, and I to compose the music?"

Byron also took a deep breath, for he knew that to collaborate with a Jew on anything would be frowned upon by most of his class. Jews were disbarred from so many privileges and professions, forbidden to take oaths in court or become Members of Parliament, or deal in trade; and were presently allowed even fewer rights than the Catholics.

So to collaborate on a collection of Hebrew poetry and music with a Jew? His reputation would be smeared and his name scandalized, but he was beyond caring about such trivialities.

"Mr Nathan, it will be my very great pleasure to collaborate with you on the Hebrew Melodies."

Amidst smiles and promises to meet again, the two men shook hands vigorously.

Only when Isaac Nathan had left, did Byron shoot a glance at the clock, and saw with dismay that it was past the respectable hour, and still no messenger had come with a note from Mary.

What was she doing? Why was it taking her so long? Was she *walking* it all the way from Annesley down to London?

~ ~ ~

After ten days of waiting, Byron was half demented from

the endless waiting and disappointment; and then he received a letter through the post from Mary, from *Annesley* – telling him she had been ill, and was still unwell, due to an infection in her eye, for which the doctor had administered blister patches every few hours.

She described herself as looking "thin, pale, and gloomy" and she really did not wish Byron to see her looking that way, not after so long a parting, so she had postponed her journey to London for another few weeks.

Byron erupted with rage, not believing a word of it, certain she was playing games with him again. All of Fletcher's efforts to calm him down were useless.

"She is a woman, Fletcher, that has *never* been able to make up her own mind!"

"No," Fletcher agreed.

"Not when she was sixteen or eighteen or twenty-seven or even now at twenty-eight!"

Fletcher stayed silent.

"And *who* has she always hurt in the process? Perhaps in retaliation for others always hurting her? Why, who else but her idiot friend and neighbour from Newstead! Well, no more! *No damned more!"*

His fury took him out of London and straight down to Augusta in Six Mile Bottom, only to find her also looking – "thin, pale, and gloomy."

Yet for her, his dear sister, he felt only concern.

Augusta was pushing her hair back off her brow again in her distracted way. "It's the baby," she said tiredly. "All the nights feeding her with no sleep. You know we can't afford to hire a wet-nurse, not that there are any around here, and even if there was, I would not want to use one."

He listened silently as she told him that George was away, it being the summer racing season, and the children were all rather cranky with jealously of the new baby and all the loving attention she was receiving, even from the servants.

"And we're *bored*," sulked Georgiana, who had been listening at the open door.

"Ah! it's *my Georgiana,"* Byron exclaimed, and she came running to him and he sat her on his knee.

"I think, what you need is a rest," Byron said to Augusta. "A rest from running the household and all the small demands that go with it."

Augusta looked at him curiously. "And how can I do that?"

"A change of pace and scenery ... you have never been abroad, have you?"

"No."

"Then I can tell you, going somewhere else changes everything. After Cambridge, as soon I left England, all my tensions with my mother and others fell away."

"I would never leave England," said Augusta. "I would be too frightened of all those strange foreign places."

"No, but it might do you good to have a holiday. And from what you say, it sounds like the children could do with a holiday too, away from these same old green fields. Somewhere by the sea, perhaps?"

Augusta was smiling at the very thought; and Georgiana, her head back, staring up at him as if wondering what he was saying ... there was something *new* here, but her little mind could not quite grasp it.

"Harrogate," Byron suggested. "Scrope Davies is there. If I sent him a note, he could find a place for us."

"For us?" asked Augusta.

Byron smiled. "I need a holiday too. London has been driving me mad, and Nottingham ... well, no matter."

A minute later, he changed his mind.

"No, not Harrogate ... simply because I'm not sure if I could *trust* Scrope Davies to find the right place for a family with children ... How about Hastings? That's by the sea, and Francis Hodgson is summering in Hastings this year – now *he* is the man to do things right."

Georgiana finally spoke. "Are we going away somewhere, Uncle By?"

"If your mother agrees, yes."

Augusta was smiling, but with embarrassment. "You know George could not afford the expense of it."

Byron shrugged: if he could send fifty pounds to a whore, cheeky as she was, he could stretch to a little more to provide a holiday for his sister and nieces.

Later in his room, he took out his writing case and dashed off a letter to Francis Hodgson.

July 8th, 1814

My dear Hodgson,

I send this in the chance of your still being at Hastings – if so – pray answer by return of post. Will you take a house for me at Hastings – it must be good and tolerably large – as Mrs Leigh, her 4 children – and three maids will be there also – besides my own valet, and my Coachman (& his horses).

I shall also want a housemaid and a pro tempore cook of the place, and wish all this to be settled as soon as you are disposed to take the trouble – It is very tiresome to bore you in this manner, but I have no other acquaintances in Hastings, and prefer the place for that reason & quiet – for this last – let my bedroom be some way from the Nursery or children's apartments – and let the women be near together – and as far away from me as possible – but I wish this soon, & I hope you will excuse the trouble.

If I don't hear from you directly, I will conclude you are not at Hastings. There will be room needed for two carriages – I suppose and hope there is good bathing and swimming, as that will be my principal activity.

Will you favour me with an early response to this, and believe me,

Ever yrs truly & affectly
BYRON

Byron was proved correct in his estimation of Francis Hodgson who had acted swiftly to secure all that his friend had requested; especially as he was looking forward to enjoying his company again.

July 11th 1814

My dear Hodgson – Hastings House by all means – and the month will do very well – Next week is fine, but I am not sure what day I will arrive after the family.

This goes with a thousand thanks to you for taking so much trouble. Do whatever is expedient – and make me responsible for any expense.

Ever yrs truly
BYRON.

P.S: You will like Augusta much. She is as shy as an

Antelope – but the best hearted, gentle, inoffensive being in the <u>world</u>.

PART EIGHT

A Cherished Madness

My hope on high – my all below,
Earth holds no other like to thee,
Or, if it doth, in vain for me;
For worlds I dare not view the dame
Resembling thee, yet not the same.
The very crimes that mar my youth,
This bed of death – attest my truth!
'Tis all too late – thou wert, thou art
The cherish'd madness of my heart!

– The Giaour

Chapter Thirty-Six

~ ~ ~

Mary truly had been ill, but now she was recovered, and her decision had been made, irrevocably. She had thought about it long and hard, and the fact that Byron had not yet answered her letter, was a sign to her that he was disappointed and sulking ... or in a rage ... she knew him so well.

So the time had come ... there would and *could* be no other time to show him that she was sincere in her love, because he would not wait for her forever, and why should he? He had already waited long enough ... ever since their youth ... and yet, in those early days, how carelessly she had always laughed off his adoration.

Nanny Marsden was very pleased to be told she was being taken down to London town with her mistress. *At long last*, she would be able see that great and glamorous city; and she was chuckling with delight.

Although, when she had calmed herself, she realised that it was very *unusual* for a housekeeper to be removed from the house she kept, and taken off and away to London or anywhere else – but Mary had *insisted* upon it.

"I want you with me, Nanny. I want you to finally see London. And it's such a long time since *I* last saw it."

"And how long will we be down there?" asked Nanny Marsden.

Mary hesitated in her reply. If things happened as she hoped, she was quite prepared to leave Annesley behind her forever and never return. To apply for a divorce, and then go abroad with Byron and live somewhere private and warm; that was her dream now, and it had been *his* dream once. Was it still?

She was sure it was, because he had written to her so warmly of late, as if all his hopes had been restored to him.

"And are you bringing the children too?" Nanny Marsden was very surprised about this – to see Mary overseeing the packing of so many of her children's clothes. "All the way to London?"

Mary smiled, and nodded that it was so. "Yes, Nanny, I am bringing *all* my personal belongings with me."

"She won't go," William Caunt said later to Nanny Marsden in a cynical tone. "She'll wait until the last minute and change her mind again."

"Aye, happen so; but I'm packing for it anyway. The hope will be nice to enjoy for a while, until it's gone."

Not even when they had all packed themselves into the carriage, could Nanny Marsden truly believe it.

Not until they had reached and passed through the Nottingham turnpike did she realise her hopes were not to be dashed – letting out a laugh of delight as she beamed at the children – "We're going all the way down to London, me ducks! All the way! Down to where King George and the Prince Regent live!"

And then she pulled out her handkerchief and dabbed at her eyes. "Oh my! I thought I'd never see this day..."

~ ~ ~

Hastings House was rather grand and spacious and perched on top of a cliff; quite remote and desolate in its way, yet Francis Hodgson had believed it would be *perfect* for Byron; away from all the other houses dotted over the hills and separate from the crowd, a place of peace and tranquillity high above the world.

Yet when Byron stood looking down at the beach and sea below, he was shaking his head with incredulity, wondering why Hodgson had selected such a ridiculous house for him?

"If I wish to swim, how the devil am I supposed to get down there – and worse – climb back up again?"

"Oh, dear ..." Hodgson had forgotten all about Byron's damaged foot, and the strain those hills would put on his right leg. "I completely forgot about your limp."

"I wish *I* could forget it too," Byron said tersely, and then leaned over farther to get a better view of down below.

"I see now ... there's a narrow sand-path running down the side there, so at least Augusta and the children and their maids will be able to get down to the beach."

"But not you?"

Byron turned his head to look sulkily at Hodgson. "Hardly. At least, I doubt it."

He leaned over again and looked down. "Mind, if the children's squalling drives me demented I could always *jump down* and break my neck, and that would solve at least *a few* of my problems."

Hodgson was beginning to feel quite bad about his mistake, and sought to help and advise. "Apart from the height of the cliff, do you have other worries, more *personal* worries?"

"No, no *personal* worries, apart from the wish to pick up my pistol and blow my brains out." Byron shrugged, "But I have always been too squeamish for that kind of thing."

Something was wrong, very wrong, and Francis Hodgson became extremely concerned. He knew Byron suffered from very dark moods of depression at various times, and this seemed to be one more of those times. Something bad had happened in London, something personal, but what?

"You may exchange houses with me, if you wish. Mine is lower down."

"No, no, the house is fine. Pay no heed to me and my grumbling. Augusta and the children seem to love their house in the clouds, and if there *is* a way down there to the sea for me, I'm sure I'll find it."

~ ~ ~

After the sameness and flat fields of their home at Six Mile Bottom, Augusta and the children loved Hastings House, so high up in the air; and they displayed no real inclination to go down to the beach.

"There is a large sandpit at the back of the garden for the girls to play and build sand-castles, and I find great peace in just looking at the ocean," Augusta told Byron. "Simply gazing out to sea can be *very* relaxing, don't you think?"

Byron wondered if that was how she truly felt? One thing he *did* know, was that no matter how unsuitable a situation, Augusta would always smile and make the best of it without any complaint.

"And anyway," said Augusta, "what would be the point of going all the way down there? Men can venture out in the water to swim, but it would cause a terrible scandal if a *woman* did that."

Byron looked at her; he had forgotten that.

Augusta giggled at the naughtiness of it. "My goodness! If a woman was to even *remove* her *shoes* in public, she would be branded a trollop."

Byron smiled, thinking of the girls he had seen in Portugal and Spain and Greece who had felt no shame in walking along the sea's edge in their swirling skirts and bare feet.

"I do love the children of the sun," he said. "The ladies of Hastings will be a poor substitute."

So he kept away from them, away from everybody, making his way down to the deserted beach and walking for hours along the sea's edge in his boots, staring out to sea in long thoughtful gazes, wondering what he was going to do with his life now?

The long dream of Mary was over for him, finished. Too long he had held onto that hope, but now he knew that Augusta had been right – Mary would never be brave enough to break from convention and defy the world to be with him; and Mary would *never* leave Annesley.

~ ~ ~

Settled into the house in London, Mary's exhilaration was growing by the day – even her mirror showed her just how *well* she was looking now. Her eyes were sparkling, her cheeks were pink, and her heart was beating with excitement. How soon? One hour, two hours, three hours maybe; and then she would see her dear and devoted Lord Byron again. See him walking through the door, hear his voice, enjoy his playfulness and admire his grace ... and when she looked into his eyes she knew she would see only his love for her. *Why* had she waited so long?

A short time later, much shorter than she had expected, she heard John's voice in the hall and rose quickly from her seat in the drawing-room, almost tripping over in her excitement to rush towards the door and see her beloved again.

Yet only John appeared. "He's not there, Mistress.

not at home and not in town. The porter at the gate said Lord Byron had left London to go away somewhere, and he didn't know when he would be back."

Mary's hands went to her throat in shock. "But ... but he *knew* I was coming to London. I wrote and told him so. In a few weeks I said ..." she stared at Nanny Marsden who had appeared at the open door. "In a few weeks I said ... and those few weeks are here now."

"Oh, he'll probably be back tomorrow then, or in a day or two after, rushing round here and apologising for his delay." Nanny frowned. "But did you not say exactly what *day* you would be coming?"

"No ... no ... because I did not know myself."

"Ah! Well there you have it! His lordship is a busy man with all his fame and all. So if *you* didn't know what day you would be coming to London, how was he expected to know it?"

Mary realised that Nanny was right, and calmed a little. "But, John," she said anxiously, "will you go again tomorrow to find out if Lord Byron has returned so you may speak to him?

John nodded. "I will, Mistress."

~ ~ ~

Even in Hastings, down on the beach, as alone as he thought he was, Byron had more than one unseen admirer spying on him through binoculars from those houses dotted over the hills.

One young lady almost bit her lip to bleeding as she worried so terribly for him, watching him climbing up the hills in a limping way and over rocks and – on several occasions – almost falling down again.

She finally wrote a letter to him, her idol, at Hastings House, telling him that she was praying day and night to ask God to awaken him to the sense of his own danger.

He did not reply to her letter. It seemed fated that he was not to be left quiet or alone even when he was disposed to be so.

Instead he wrote a letter to his friend Thomas Moore.

Hastings

I am here renewing my acquaintance with my old friend Ocean; and I find his bosom as pleasant a pillow for an hour in the morning, as his daughters of Paphos could be in the twilight.

I have been swimming, and walking on cliffs, and tumbling down hills, and making the most of "dolce far-niente" for the last fortnight.

I met a son of Lord Erskine's who says he has been married a year, and is "the happiest of men". And Hodgson, who is hoping to marry, is also "the happiest of men" so it is worthwhile my being here, if only to witness the superlative felicity of these foxes who have cut off their tails, and would persuade the rest to part with their brushes so as to keep themselves comforted and in countenance.

Oh! I have had the most amusing letter from Hogg. He wants me to recommend him to Murray –

Byron paused, because he knew that John Murray had now offered Thomas Moore a good sum of money for the copyright of his Eastern epic *Lallah Rookh* without yet seeing even a word of it – all based on his own dedication to Moore in *The Corsair* – and now every damned scribbler in the country was writing to him begging for his recommendation to Murray.

Hodgson dropped in and interrupted his letter and Byron greeted him warmly. He was more relaxed now in Hastings, especially learning the history of the place, which was connected with his own ancestors, being the coast known for its first connection with the Norman Conquest.

"Oh, and I also found out," Hodgson said, "that *this* is the very house in which General Wellington set up as his headquarters and residence, when he commanded the garrison here at Hastings."

Byron looked at Augusta to see her reaction to this news, but she was more interested in knowing whether the men had enough *turbot* to eat, and was it good, and the taste to their liking?

"It should be, seeing as this is a *fisheries* town," Byron replied, and then started an enjoyable disagreement with Hodgson about the difference between Wellington and Nelson.

"Nelson *was* a hero, but Wellington is a mere sergeant in comparison."

Hodgson snapped at the bait – launching into a soliloquy on Wellington and demanding to know why Byron could have such an opinion?

"Because Nelson was always *in* the action, right there with his men. Even at Trafalgar, his ship was right alongside the enemy's ship, so close alongside that Nelson got shot by a sniper and lost his life. And before that, in another battle he got shot in the eye – how close to the enemy is that? And after that he lost an arm, *before* he later lost his life at Cape Trafalgar. But *General Wellington* – what does he do in battles? He sits on his horse at the back of the field along with all the other generals and doesn't go anywhere *near* the fighting."

"That's because he is a great *commander,* and also a genius in tactics!"

"And Nelson was not?"

Before retiring to her bed, tired after a long and happy day, and seeing dear Mr Hodgson so heated, Augusta interrupted to *remind* Mr Hodgson that her brother had once given a wonderful speech about the Duke of Wellington to all his peers in the House of Lords.

"Did you *have* to spoil it?" Byron asked her with a slight grin; and Hodgson stared – and then sighed and smiled and shook his head at the realisation that Byron had been ribbing him again.

~ ~ ~

The following morning Byron was up before dawn, due to having slept badly, and took himself off for another scramble down to the sea, strolling along the sand in a blue light that was barely dawn, when he saw a small boat with its sails lowered, being rowed by four men towards a cove in the rock's face further down.

Curious, he walked down in that direction, his steps silent on the sand, approaching the boat as the men pulled her ashore and then turned to look at the lone dark figure of a man standing and watching them.

"'Oly Christ! " exclaimed one. "Ooo are you?"

"Lord Byron."

"Ah! So you ain't one of them customs and exersise men then?"

Byron walked closer and looked into the boat and its cargo, seeing at least a hundred bottles of cognac, a few kegs of some other liqueur, and bags of other stuff wrapped in netting.

"Well," he said, "that don't look like a haul of fish to me." He looked at each of the four men and said in an exaggerated stage-whisper, "So you men must be *smugglers.*"

A short time later, having been allowed to peek through their haul, he had bought from them six bottles of cognac, six gentlemen's' silk handkerchiefs, and two exquisite female scarves made of French silk."

"An' tha's a fair price yu got 'em as too," said the oldest man of the four, "cheapest yu'll find our side of t'channel."

Byron nodded, although he was now realising his dilemma as he looked at his sack full of illegal booty.

"Yes, but my problem now, gentlemen, is how am I going to carry this heavy load all the way up to the top again."

"Abe!" ordered the oldest smuggler to the youngest one. "Lift 'is lord-hip's sack an' yu do carry her up top fer 'im!"

The house was still silent when Byron returned to it. He placed four of the bottles of cognac in the dining room, ready to be enjoyed by himself and Hodgson.

The two scarves he placed on Augusta's chair, and then carried the remaining two bottles of cognac to his room; one for Hobby, and one for Scrope Davies – knowing both men would enjoy the bottles even more than usual, once they knew they were French *contraband.*

~ ~ ~

Mary was in a state of great distress, certain now that Byron no longer loved her, had never loved her – why else would he stay away from London for so long when he knew she was due to arrive?

More than three weeks had passed now, and poor John was worn weary from his trips to Albany, three times a day, and still no sign of his lordship.

Feeling a fool, and in a rage of tears, Mary took from her trunk all of Byron's letters, every light and warm letter he had sent to her in the past year, and tore them into pieces and flung them up in the air – and just as quickly she relented and got down on her knees to pick all the pieces up again, where Nanny Marsden later found her ... crawling over the paper-strewn carpet picking up pieces of paper and trying to match them together again like doing a jigsaw.

She finally got Mary into bed and calmed her, stroking her hand until she had stopped crying and eventually fell into a troubled sleep.

John sat alert when Nanny Marsden finally returned below stairs, shaking her head woefully as she said to him, "We should never have come down to London. She's not fit for anything now."

Yet, to Nanny Marsden's surprise, only an hour later, while walking through the hall, she turned as Mary came running lightly down the stairs, fully dressed in a burgundy velvet outfit and hat, a smile on her face.

"I've been so foolish, Nanny. Of course Byron did not believe me when I wrote and said I was coming to London, especially as I did not come the first time. Perhaps he did not even believe I was unwell. So *I* will now go to *him*."

Nanny Marsden was flabbergasted. "How can you go to him? You don't know where's he's gone!"

"No, but his attorney, Mr Hanson will know." Mary adjusted her hat in the mirror. "John Hanson knows everything about Byron, and always has done."

~ ~ ~

Facing Mary in his office at Lincoln's Inn, John Hanson's expression was full of consternation and amazement. He had not been aware of the fact that Lord Byron and Mrs Chaworth had become such close friends of late.

"Do you know where he has gone, Mr Hanson?"

Such information was something that John Hanson would not normally disclose to anyone. But Mary ... Mary Chaworth ... of course, it had to happen sometime, he supposed ... Byron and Mary Chaworth ... yet how strange that it should be *her* now looking for him, and not the other way around.

"And you say his lordship was expecting you?"

"Yes, but my arrival was delayed, by a few weeks, and so I believe he thought I was not coming at all."

"But surely you do not intend to travel all the way to Hastings, Mrs Chaworth?"

"Hastings? Is that where he has gone?"

"He has taken his sister and her children for a holiday down there. He should be back in town ... well, I'm not quite sure when."

"Do you know where in Hastings?"

Hanson could not help noticing that Mary's hands holding her purse were very agitated, twisting the small burgundy velvet bag this way and that way and then squeezing it up as if trying to form it into a ball ...

He picked up his pen and quickly wrote down the address. "Here is the address if you wish to send a letter to his lordship. *'Hasting House. Hastings'*, that will suffice enough for your letter to reach him."

"Thank you, Mr Hanson. How far is it to Hastings from London?"

"Oh, a little under seventy miles." Hanson suddenly

stared at her and asked again – "Surely you have no intention of travelling down there, Mrs Chaworth?"

"No intention at all," Mary replied, and turned and fled from the office out to her carriage where she called up to John – "Straight on to Hastings, John."

"Mistress?" John was all of a fluster. "You want me to drive you there now? Down to Hastings? Like, right this minute?"

"Yes, *immediately.*"

"But the housekeeper, Mrs Marsden – "

Mary furiously bashed her bag against the step up to his bench. "Are you deaf, man! I said *immediately!*"

Chapter Thirty-Seven

~ ~ ~

Byron arrived back in London the following afternoon, in order to keep his appointment with John Murray. *Lara* was about to be published, and Murray needed some last-minute corrections.

"And your sister, Mrs Leigh?" asked John Murray. "Does she remain in Hastings?"

"Yes. She needs more time to pack than I do, but I believe she and her entourage will be vacating the house this morning."

"May I ask, is *Lara* a male name in the East?"

"No, it is a male name in *Spanish*. I chose it because I liked the liquidity of its sound."

Byron sat down at the desk in the room John Murray had provided for him, and began to read through *Lara*, noting the required corrections. It was really a sequel to *The Corsair*. Conrad was not dead, but had returned, using his new covert name of *Lara*, ready to lead the peasants in a revolt.

Life had made Conrad an even harder man than he had once been, and so returned in disguise as *Lara*, a less sympathetic character; proud, scornful, brooding ... and yet Byron knew that many people would believe that *Lara's* inner self and thoughts were autobiographical. He would have to front it with a similar note to that in *The Corsair*.

He asked Murray for a copy of *The Corsair* and read the front note, skimming over his dedication to Tom Moore, and reading on to his words to the readers –

May I add a few words on a subject on which all men

are supposed to be fluent, and none agreeable? – Self.

With regard to my story, and stories in general, I should have been glad to have rendered my personages more perfect and amiable, if possible, inasmuch as I have been sometimes criticised, and considered no less responsible for their deeds and qualities than if all had been personal. Be it so – if I have deviated into the gloomy vanity of "drawing from self" the pictures are probably like, since they are unfavourable; and if not, those who know me are undeceived, and those who do not, I have little interest in undeceiving.

I have no particular desire that any but my acquaintances should think the author better than the beings of his imagining; but I cannot help a little surprise, and perhaps amusement, at some odd critical exceptions in the present instance, when I see several bards (far more deserving I allow) in very reputable plight, and quite exempted from all participation in the faults of their heroes, who, nevertheless, might be found with only a little more morality than "The Giaour" and perhaps – but no, I must admit Childe Harold to be a very repulsive personage; and as to his identity, those who like may give to him whatever "alias" they please.

Nevertheless, despite the front note in *The Corsair*, it had made no difference, because so many readers had now convinced themselves that the author himself had once been a pirate involved in piracy and dark deeds; and who could fight public opinion? So it was a waste of time writing anything. People will always believe what they *want* to believe, and if that keeps them warm at night and helps them to sleep with a righteous conscience, then be it so.

~ ~ ~

Hastings House was empty: all of its previous occupants gone. Only the household servants remained.

"Lord Byron *was* here in residence with his family –"

"His *family?*" Mary said in puzzlement. "He has *no* family."

The butler nodded. "I was referring to his sister and her daughters."

Mary's hand moved vaguely over her eyes. "Oh, yes, his sister, Mrs Leigh."

She had not slept in the carriage throughout the very long journey, convincing herself that she had been right to travel down to Hastings herself. She had to let Byron know the truth, and to get a written message to him through the post would have taken too long, *too long*.

John stood beside her, looking as worn and weary as she felt. And now that she had arrived too late, *too late,* both of them must now rest.

"Could I ..." she mumbled to the butler, "could I trouble you for a ..." her mind went blank, and she could not remember what it was she wanted to trouble him for.

"Could I ..." she said once more, and then sank to the floor in a dead faint.

"Smelling salts!" the butler called to a maid. "Bring the *Sal Volatile* "

When the butler and John, aided by the bottle of

smelling salts, had brought Mary back to consciousness, John said to the butler, "I think we must get her to bed. Is there a room, a spare bedroom, a maid to assist her?"

"Of course," the butler replied, as if this kind of thing happened every day of the week. "I will get a maid *de chambre* to assist the lady immediately."

"Byron ..." Mary said in a voice so weak that the butler could hardly hear it. "Pray, will you tell Lord Byron ..." she looked vaguely at John, "that I cannot see him today."

Mary closed her eyes in complete confusion and despair, knowing something had gone terribly wrong, but she could not remember what it was.

Chapter Thirty-Eight

~ ~ ~

Some days later, Byron received a letter from Francis Hodgson, who was still residing in Hastings, and would be remaining there until the commencement of Cambridge's autumn term in September.

My dear Byron,

I regret to inform you that Mary Chaworth has been in Hastings for some days now, residing at Hastings House, and she is very ill indeed.

As she had come down to Hastings in order to see you, the household staff contacted me, knowing I was your friend. At first I believed the poor girl was merely exhausted from her journey, but alas, I regret to say that the doctor's diagnosis is far more severe.

I regret the delay in informing you of this, but my time has been devoted solely to her care and assistance.

I shall be accompanying her with a nurse back to London this very day, and when she is settled in her Town house, I will call on you and we will talk then.

Yours, as always,
Francis Hodgson.

Byron was stunned; the shock took his breath away; so much so that he almost fainted himself and had to quickly sit down.

Mary in Hastings ... looking for *him* – he snatched up the cover of the letter again and looked at the black post marking and circular datestamp – two days ago – so they should be back here in London by now.

He called for Fletcher, throwing on his cloak in the hall. "If anyone drops by, tell them I have been called away."

At the door, he halted, and turned his head to stare at Fletcher. "*Damn!* he exclaimed. "Why did Mary not remember to tell me the *address* of her house in town? How can I go there if I don't know *where* to go!"

Fletcher didn't know ... nor did he know what this was all about – and seeing the expression on his lordship's face, he did not dare to ask.

The tension was unbearable, his lordship in the drawing-room pacing up and down like a caged wild animal, unable to do anything at all but wait for Mr Hodgson to call.

When the knock came, Byron beat Fletcher to the door to answer it, relieved at last to see Francis Hodgson standing there, looking tired, but also very grim.

"What news? Is Mary any better now?"

"Byron, I think we should both sit down, because I believe you will find my report very upsetting."

Hodgson turned to Fletcher. "And pray bring some brandy, if only for me. The journey here has been a long one."

When they were seated, Byron listened intently, his eyes on Hodgson, as if transfixed, not really taking it all in, because surely *he*, of all people, would have seen the signs ... but then, no, she had always been *happy* with him ... very happy ... on that last day in the cottage in Annesley Wood, she had put her arms around him and they had made love and it had been every bit as good as the first time, every bit as loving ... and yes ... most days she had been happy and full of smiles ... that is, until the day Ann Radford visited Annesley ... and then it had all changed.

"According to the housekeeper, Mrs Marsden," said Hodgson, "it has been coming on in fits and starts for some time, and especially when she was living with her husband. The staff were all worried it might lead to something like this. And now it has ... a complete mental breakdown."

Byron's eyes flickered and widened and after a silence he said, "Explain that to me ... what does it actually mean?"

Hodgson took a large slug of his brandy. It was his duty to be honest; Byron had to know the truth.

"It has nothing to do with you, Byron, you must understand that. It started long ago, before you and her ever ... you gave her some contented respite for a time, that is all. But now ... now I'm afraid Mary has descended into a total mental darkness all of her own. She cannot deal with her life any more, so she has found her own way of escaping from it ... two physicians attended upon her in Hastings, and I'm afraid both have doubts about her recovery."

"No. I will not believe that!" Byron stood up and lifted his cloak from the chair. "I must go to her. You have the address, Hodgson?"

"Byron, no, pray don't go – the doctor has sent for her husband."

"The address, Hodgson? The *damned address* of the house where she is now?"

There was no stopping him, and Hodgson knew that, so he gave him the address.

When the door had slammed, Fletcher went in to the drawing-room and Mr Hodgson, who merely sighed and said, "Does his lordship have a spare room here, Fletcher?"

"Yes, sir, but it's up on the top floor. It's a maid's room, and Mrs Mule lives out, so I've never given her the key, so the room has never been used."

"Is the bed made up?"

"Yes, sir, and never been slept in since I made it up when we first moved in here."

"Then lead me up there, will you? I am very tired and desperately need some sleep."

~ ~ ~

Mrs Marsden was not sure if she should let him in. The house was in darkness and silence and even she was in her dressing-gown and wearing her nightcap.

"Nanny, please," he begged quietly, "I have to *see* her, even for only a moment."

Nanny Marsden opened the door wider to let him inside, whispering – "Very well, but don't you let anyone know that I let you in."

She led him quickly and quietly down the hall and whispered again. "I have her down here in my own bedroom on the ground floor, to make it easier for me to keep an eye on her."

"Is the nurse not with her?"

"No, she's been with her all day, so I made her go and get some sleep. I've taken over that duty now, resting myself on the chaise-longue in there."

Nanny opened the door quietly and peeked in. "She's asleep, so do you not wake her, promise me that?"

Byron nodded.

"Five minutes, while I get myself a cup of tea. Five

minutes only, m'lord, and then you must leave again."

The room was in dimness, lit only by a solitary candle in the far corner. He moved quietly across the room, and sat down in the chair by the bed and looked at Mary propped on the pillows. Her long hair was down and over her shoulders, her face was pale, and her hands lay on top of the cover, but her eyes were not closed ... her eyes were fixed in a dreamy gaze on the candle in the corner. She did not seem aware of his presence.

"My love ..."

She did not respond.

"My very precious love ..."

Her eyes remained in whatever dream she saw in the light of the candle.

"If it was me who broke your heart and your mind ... I'm sorry."

Her eyes blinked then, and her head slowly moved to the side until she was looking at him. He saw her eyebrows twitch slightly, as if wondering who he was.

He gently lifted one of her hands into his own and spoke to her softly, and she listened to him in bewildered silence, like a child listening to a stranger speaking in a foreign tongue.

His heart was breaking, his tears seeping down his face, and still she lay gazing at him with her brown eyes devoid of all recognition.

He had to go. He could not bear it any longer, to see her like this.

He gently laid her hand back down on the coverlet, stood up and slowly began to walk away. He had walked no more than a few steps before he heard her moan – swiftly turned to look at her – and saw that she was staring in the direction of his legs ... "Byron?"

"Mary ..."

And then it dawned on him – she had recognised his limping walk. Nothing else but that – his damned *limp*.

"Byron?"

She was sitting up when he moved back to her, saw the quiver on her pale lips, the tears gathering full in her eyes, and he bent over her and held her while they silently cried together.

Later, he looked into her dazed, dark eyes, and said, "Sleep now, my angel, I will come again tomorrow."

Chapter Thirty-Nine

~~~

He had promised Nanny Marsden that he would not attempt to visit Mary in daylight. "That would cause a terrible *scandal*," she had said. "Aye, and ruining *both* your reputations too."

Before going to bed, he had written a letter to Augusta, telling her all. He knew Augusta would write back giving him good feminine advice.

The day passed slowly, very slowly, until at last the sun had set over the roofs of all the townhouses in London, and he prepared himself to go out.

Minutes before he was about to leave, John arrived with a message from Nanny Marsden, begging him not to come, as Mary had been seized with a violent fever and the onset of a delirium.

"It's the same sort of delirium she suffered in Hastings," said John, "but this one is very violent."

"Violent? Mary? In what way?"

"Crying ... keeps on saying she is *evil,* and in her delirium, my lord ... I'm afraid to say she has mentioned you."

"So?"

"Well ..." John looked greatly embarrassed. "Mr Musters has just arrived ... her husband."

"From whom she is now separated."

"Happen so, but he seems concerned and says he is willing to take charge of her."

"Take *charge* of her?"

"I mean ... care ... take *care* of her. He says he is removing her immediately to his mother's Townhouse in Grosvenor Place, and the mistress's own mother is on her way down to London also. The whole household is in chaos and distress, my lord, and Mrs Marsden says your presence could only serve to do more harm than good."

So, he had been dismissed from her life yet again. He stood looking around him, hardly able to take it all in ... now what was he to do?

"What am I to do?" he asked John.

"If you please, my lord, Mrs Marsden asks and begs you to do nothing. She says her mistress needs no more disturbance, and will probably now need months or even years of rest and peace to recover her mind back to what it was."

"And do the doctors agree?"

Again John hesitated, fumbling with his hands and tears coming into his eyes.

"No, my lord, the doctors say things that even Mrs Marsden don't understand. They keep telling Mr Musters that his wife is in her own world now and has sunk into madness."

"And a great deal of the blame for that must fall on *him*, Jack Musters!" Byron snapped. "After years of being married to *him*, here she is at eight and twenty, still in the prime of her life, beautiful, and now out of her mind and senses due to years of his neglect and abuse and also, I fear – injuries still more serious. And yet this woman made his fortune – and brought him love and beauty besides. *These* be your Christian husbands?"

Byron walked into the hall and threw on his cloak.

"My lord?"

"A walk," he said to John. "I am merely going for a walk in the night air."

~ ~ ~

He walked, and walked, heartbroken and tearful, wracked with grief and guilt, knowing he could not put *all* the blame on Jack Musters. Some of it must fall on him.

She had been neglected and separated and so was highly *vulnerable*, and he had taken advantage of that, her vulnerability ... even though ... even though he had known she was a good girl who had had always kept true to her strong Christian values and, in the past, just the thought of not adhering to them would have been appalling to her. That was the reason, he knew, that she was now referring to herself as *evil;* a sinner. She had broken the Seventh Commandment and had committed adultery; something which must have inwardly plagued her, and which that she-cat Ann Radford must have reminded her of many times.

And then to have been deserted again, finding him gone from London when she had arrived, and then gone from Hastings when she had arrived there also ... no wonder the poor girl was now in pieces. In her mind he had treated her almost as bad as Jack Musters had.

And now he had been ordered to stay away from her; their secret love must remain a secret, if only for the sake of her reputation, yet bedamned to his own, he did not care a fig for that.

He kept on walking, his gaze occasionally turning upwards to the dark sky, and there as always were the lucid stars.

He came out of a narrow dark street into brightness, pausing to gaze down the long stretch of Pall Mall, now illuminated by the warm glow of the Mall's new gas lamps.

These new gaslights on the streets were slowly

changing London, making it a brighter place for all, because the gas kept on burning; unlike the oil-lamps that usually fizzled out after a time, leaving the streets in an uncertain darkness.

He walked along Westminster Bridge, pausing halfway to lean over the iron balustrade and gaze down at the calm flow of the Thames below.

The reflected lights from the row of gas-lamps along the bridge flickered down over the dark waters as he stood there thinking.

Of course, it must end. This long lingering love for Mary Chaworth. His feelings for her now were no different than they had been in adolescence, and as determinedly as he had tried, his response to the slightest endearing word from her showed him that his heart could never be hardened to her, never.

And now ... even now that she had taken herself away from him, and was back in the care of her husband, she would always be the one he truly loved. The only one. It had been so from the beginning – no matter how hard he had tried, he could only *love* but one, and that one was his Mary.

The flowing dark waters of the Thames transfixed his tear-filled eyes.

But now, what of the future? How was he to manage that?

He would handle it like a man – and not, as in the past, like an adolescent, impassioned boy.

Chapter Forty

~ ~ ~

Instead of returning to Albany, he took a cab to Brooks's club where he met up with his friends and assumed a brave and smiling face.

"Here he is!" said Scrope Davies to Beau Brummell. "You may ask him yourself."

"And I shall indeed ask him," said Brummell, scooping up a glass of champagne from a footman's tray and handing it to Byron.

"Now, Lord Byron, my dear fellow, Scrope and I have a wager about something you are supposed to have said. Do tell me it is not true?"

Byron took a sip of the champagne. "I would need to know what it is first."

"Scrope insists that you recently said to him that you – *'would rather be Beau Brummell than Napoleon.'* Is that true or false?"

Byron smiled. "Well, since poor Napoleon is now imprisoned on the Isle of Elba with very few comforts, then of course I would prefer to be you instead of him."

"But did you say it on a *general* level, in the normal view of things, that you would prefer to be me than Napoleon?"

Byron nodded. "Yes, I believe I did."

"Damn!" said Brummell. "That has now *lost* me a neat fifty guineas!"

Yet Scrope could see that Brummell's eyes were smiling, very pleased with the compliment.

"So now," said Brummell, "what is your news? Tell me all. What have you been up to?"

"Oh, nothing." Byron shrugged. "I actually live a very simple and dreary life."

Brummell and Scrope looked at each other and laughed.

"Ah, you must be feeling depressed about something," said Brummell. "So we must rectify that immediately and bring you back to cheerfulness."

"I'm not depressed about anything. I'm as cheerful as a gypsy's violin."

"Then you must cheer us," said Brummell, "well, me, because I have just *lost* fifty guineas"

"After winning a hundred guineas from myself at the card table," said Scrope. "So thank you, Byron, you have *halved* my losses."

As the night moved on, and he sat and calmly joined in the cheerful conversation of his friends, any onlooker standing nearby and watching Lord Byron would not have detected anything wrong in his manner or mood. Like all rich and very famous persons, as few as they were, Byron had the world at his feet, the waiters dancing attendance upon him at every opportunity ... a very fortunate young man, indeed.

The Boy ... The Man ... The Legend

A RUNAWAY STAR

Book 4 of The Byron Series

With the instant success of his brilliant new works, *The Corsair* and *Lara,* Lord Byron's literary fame as a poet of stature has spread to all parts of America and throughout Continental Europe.

Mary Chaworth still invades Byron's thoughts, but two other women now seek to move her completely out of his way — Miss Annabella Milbanke, who has now turned into a persistent letter-writer in the hope of renewing Byron's interest in her; and his half-sister, Augusta Leigh, who wishes only the best for him.

Byron draws down more disrepute upon his name in the anti-Semitic Press, for the calumny of collaborating his poetry with the music of a Jewish composer; something considered to be base and revolutionary and not to be expected from an aristocrat.

Lady Caroline Lamb finally sees a way to wreak her obsessed revenge on Byron, so damning and so unproven, it infuriates all his friends who rush to his defence, but the catastrophic aftermath rings down through history, destroying Byron's reputation, and almost destroying the man.

Thank You

Thank you for taking the time to read *'Mad Bad and Delightful to Know'* the third book in the *BYRON* series. Please be nice and leave a review

If you would like to follow me on **BookBub** go to:- **www.bookbub.com/profile/gretta-curran-browne** and click on the "*Follow*" button.

I occasionally send out newsletters with details of new releases, or discount offers, or any other news I may have, although not so regularly to be intrusive, so if you wish to sign up to for my newsletters – go to my Website and click on the "**Subscribe**" Tab.

Many thanks,

Gretta

www.grettacurranbrowne.com

mail@grettacurranbrowne.com

Also by Gretta Curran Browne

LORD BYRON SERIES

A STRANGE BEGINNING

A STRANGE WORLD

MAD, BAD, AND DELIGHTFUL TO KNOW

A RUNAWAY STAR

A MAN OF NO COUNTRY

ANOTHER KIND OF LIGHT

NO MOON AT MIDNIGHT

***

LIBERTY TRILOGY

TREAD SOFTLY ON MY DREAMS

FIRE ON THE HILL

A WORLD APART

***

MACQUARIE SERIES

BY EASTERN WINDOWS

THE FAR HORIZON

JARVISFIELD

THE WAYWARD SON

***

ALL BECAUSE OF HER
A Novel
(Originally published as GHOSTS IN SUNLIGHT)

RELATIVE STRANGERS
(Tie-in Novel to TV series)

ORDINARY DECENT CRIMINAL
(Novel of Film starring Oscar-winner, Kevin Spacey)

Printed in Great Britain
by Amazon